The Ogallala Trail

***Also by Dusty Richards
in Large Print:***

Ralph Compton: The Abilene Trail

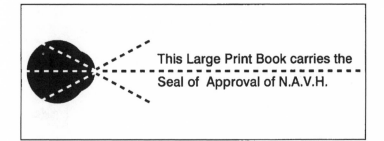

This Large Print Book carries the
Seal of Approval of N.A.V.H.

Ralph Compton

The Ogallala Trail

A Ralph Compton Novel

Dusty Richards

Thorndike Press • Waterville, Maine

Published in 2005 by arrangement with NAL Signet, a division of Penguin Group (USA) Inc.

Thorndike Press® Large Print Western.

The tree indicium is a trademark of Thorndike Press.

The text of this Large Print edition is unabridged. Other aspects of the book may vary from the original edition.

Set in 16 pt. Plantin by Al Chase.

Printed in the United States on permanent paper.

Library of Congress Cataloging-in-Publication Data

Richards, Dusty.
    The Ogallala Trail : a Ralph Compton novel / by Dusty Richards.
        p. cm. — (Thorndike Press large print westerns)
    At head of title: Ralph Compton.
    Originally published: New York : Signet, 2005, in series : Trail drive series.
    ISBN 0-7862-8065-4 (lg. print : hc : alk. paper)
    1. Cattle drives — Fiction. 2. Cattle stealing — Fiction.
3. Nebraska — Fiction. 4. Texas — Fiction. 5. Large type books. I. Title. II. Thorndike Press large print Western series.
PS3568.I31523O35 2005
  813'.54—dc22   2005018470

The Ogallala Trail

As the Founder/CEO of NAVH, the only national health agency solely devoted to those who, although not totally blind, have an eye disease which could lead to serious visual impairment, I am pleased to recognize Thorndike Press* as one of the leading publishers in the large print field.

Founded in 1954 in San Francisco to prepare large print textbooks for partially seeing children, NAVH became the pioneer and standard setting agency in the preparation of large type.

Today, those publishers who meet our standards carry the prestigious "Seal of Approval" indicating high quality large print. We are delighted that Thorndike Press is one of the publishers whose titles meet these standards. We are also pleased to recognize the significant contribution Thorndike Press is making in this important and growing field.

Lorraine H. Marchi, L.H.D.
Founder/CEO
NAVH

* Thorndike Press encompasses the following imprints: Thorndike, Wheeler, Walker and Large Print Press.

THE IMMORTAL COWBOY

This is respectfully dedicated to the "American Cowboy." His was the saga sparked by the turmoil that followed the Civil War, and the passing of more than a century has by no means diminished the flame.

True, the old days and the old ways are but treasured memories, and the old trails have grown dim with the ravages of time, but the spirit of the cowboy lives on.

In my travels — to Texas, Oklahoma, Kansas, Nebraska, Colorado, Wyoming, New Mexico, and Arizona — I always find something that reminds me of the Old West. While I am walking these plains and mountains for the first time, there is this feeling that a part of me is eternal, that I have known these old trails before. I believe it is the undying spirit of the frontier calling, allowing me, through the mind's eye, to step back into time. What is the appeal of the Old West of the American frontier?

It has been epitomized by some as the dark and bloody period in American history. Its heroes — Crockett, Bowie, Hickok, Earp — have been reviled and criticized. Yet the Old West lives on, larger than life.

It has become a symbol of freedom, when there was always another mountain to climb and another river to cross; when a dispute between two men was settled not with expensive lawyers, but with fists, knives, or guns. Barbaric? Maybe. But some things never change. When the cowboy rode into the pages of American history, he left behind a legacy that lives within the hearts of us all.

— Ralph Compton

Chapter 1

In a cloud of dust, slapping the road flour off his clothing with his goatskin gloves, he headed for the bat-wing doors of the Tiger Hole Saloon. One more cold beer before all the ice melted. Marty O'Brien usually ran out of the cold stuff by midsummer. From then on, his customers drank warm brew. On Sam Ketchem's last trip to Frio Springs, the supply of cold had still not all evaporated.

After a wave to some familiar faces sitting around at tables in midmorning, Sam stepped up to the long bar and ordered a cool one. The burly red-faced owner, Marty, nodded and put a large glass mug under the tap to draw him one. Sam tucked his gloves in his gun belt and hitched his .44 around on his hip to be more comfortable. Mouth watering, he wet his sun-cracked lips in anticipation of the delivery coming toward him.

"There you are, Ketchem! You no-good sum bitch!" someone shouted from behind him.

Sam turned, looked mildly toward the doors and blocking the bright glare from outside stood Harry Wagner. Broad-shouldered as a bear and dispositioned like a sore-pawed one, he waded inside the Tiger Hole.

"I don't know what's got your tail over the dash, Wagner, but you better spill it out." If that bully thought for one minute Sam was backing down from him, he had another think coming.

"I'm talking about you cutting my bull, Ketchem." The big man came like a bulldog down beside the bar, with his elbows at his side and his fists clenched.

"I don't recall cutting any bull that didn't need it recent like. Which one was yours?"

"A red pinto longhorn."

Sam shook his head, deep in recall. "Don't remember doing that one, but last spring at roundup, everyone agreed the longhorns had to go. Any bull on the range wasn't at least half white face or Durham was to be cut."

"Well, by Gawd, I never agreed to that."

"Your brothers were there representing you. They agreed to it."

Wagner was standing so close, Sam could smell his sour body odor and see the curly black hair on his chest between the lacing on his faded blue shirt.

"Boys, I ain't having any trouble in here," Marty said.

"You ain't having any trouble in here. I'm going to kick his ass for cutting my bull." Wagner flashed his tobacco-stained teeth and roared.

Sam threw up his right arm in time and blocked the first blow, but Wagner's second one knocked the wind out of him. Staggered backward, he tried to recover his breath and defend himself. No time. Wagner closed in on him with hard blows. Lefts and rights were coming at him like a battering ram.

A surge of knuckles hit the side of Sam's face, and his head bounced off the rim of the bar. The last thing he could recall seeing was Marty O'Brien in his white apron coming over the top of the bar, billy club in hand, to end the fight.

"You coming around?" Marty asked, looking him in the eye.

A shake of his head didn't clear the fuzzy vision, so Sam closed his eye lids and wished his body didn't hurt so bad. Sprawled in a chair, he knew he was surrounded by concerned faces.

"Where did he go?" he managed to ask.

"I put him out the door with me club. Guess he's long gone, the worthless piece of shit."

Good. Sam rubbed the back of his neck and tried to piece things together in his mind. He'd come to Frio Springs for a few supplies and a cold draft beer or two. Whatever had come over the eldest of the Wagner boys to set in on him, he wasn't certain about. But castrating some cull bull, even if he had done it, wasn't the real cause. Harry Wagner had something else on his mind. Sam couldn't recall doing anything to any of the Wagners to make the man that mad at him, but somewhere out there something festered. From here on, he'd have to keep an eye open for all of them.

This incident might be the start of a Texas feud. Didn't take much to start one, but they never ended nice. Folks got shot in the back and innocent ones, too. He'd have to speak to his brothers, Tom and Earl, and warn them about it.

"Here's chunk of ice," Marty said, handing Sam the piece wrapped in a bar cloth. "Put it on the right side of your face. He really worked you over. Sorry I didn't move fast enough to stop him."

"Hey, you sprung over that bar like a kid."

"Well, I was a wee bit angry at him for causing trouble in a respectable place like mine."

The half dozen friends standing around in the half circle laughed and clapped the bartender on the back.

"You going to be all right? Might ought to have Doc Sharp look at you," Oscar Mott, a silver haired rancher, said, looking Sam over.

"Aw, I'll be fine."

"Next time, you better watch out for that bully. Someone sure needs to teach him a lesson," Oscar said, and the others agreed.

The cold compress held tight to his sore cheek, Sam nodded. There wouldn't ever be any next time. He'd put a couple of bullet holes in Wagner's worthless carcass before the other man got in close enough to even swing a fist.

Marty went to the bar and brought back a bottle of bonded whiskey and a glass for him. "Drink some. It's the best medicine I've got in the place."

"What the hell was the ruckus about?" Everyone looked around to see who'd come in. Dressed in a boiled white shirt and a shoestring tie, and with galluses holding up his high-waisted pin-striped pants, the law in Frio came striding across the bar room. Whit Stuart served as the town marshal and deputy sheriff. With his wavy black hair and trimmed mustache, he cut a fancy figure

13

with the womenfolk in the county — those on both sides of the street.

"Fine time for you to finally get here," Mott grumbled. "Fight's all ready over, and one man was near beat to death."

"Who did this to you?" Stuart asked.

"Harry Wagner, out of the blue," Sam said.

The lawman took a seat. "Want to swear out a warrant?"

Sam shook his head. "Wouldn't be worth it."

The lawman slapped his palms on the table, ready to get up. "All right, if you won't swear out a warrant, there is nothing I can do here."

"You could keep riffraff like that run out of town," Mott said.

"Mr. Mott, if Sam Ketchem won't swear out a warrant against the man, there ain't a blessed thing I can do about it."

"Do you have to wait till a stray dog bites someone to shoot him?"

"No, the city council gave me the power to do that beforehand. But not on the rest."

"Wouldn't hurt anyone one damn bit to shoot him and a few more like him."

"Good day, gentlemen. You require my services, call me." Stuart straightened his tie and strode out of the Tiger Hole.

14

"Now that fancy Dan is some lawman. Bet he's going off on a picnic with Etta Faye Ralston," Bobby Barstow said and went to the front window to see. "Sure enough, boys, she's sitting out there in the buckboard under her little umbrella all set to go on a picnic. Why, that old maid must be thirty years old."

"And she ain't getting hitched to no one. Not even to our well-dressed, supposed legal protection," Mott put in.

"No, she might get some sweat dropped on her," Marty said. "Try some of that whiskey, son. It'll make you forget the pain anyway."

Sam still couldn't clear all of his vision. In the end, he downed the glass Marty had poured for him; then he settled down in the chair, trying for a comfortable place. "I'll be fine, boys. But I would like that cold beer I came in here for in the first place."

"Coming up." Marty threw the bar rag over his shoulder.

"You shipping your cattle next spring with the colonel?" Mott asked, scraping a chair up close to him.

"I hope to," Sam said. "I sure can't afford these railroad-car charges. They wanted twenty-two dollars a head to ship mine from San Anton to the Kansas City Stock Yards."

"And you pay the same whether they die or get there."

"And they might not even be worth that when I get them there."

"Right. These railroads springing up all over ain't been all that big a deal for ranchers. High-priced bandits is what I call them."

Sam agreed. " 'Course with the Dodge City market closed, the colonel's going to have to take them around through Colorado and up."

"They say there's a good market for heifers and cows up north there, too," Mott said.

"Yeah, they've opened lots of that grass north of there for grazing. But the colonel ain't said yet if he's taking the stock, has he? Mixing steers and cows coming in heat can sure be a headache on the trail."

"Yeah, and you generally lose several from being rode to death by them steers."

"Right, it's a pain. What were you thinking of sending?" Sam winced at a new pain in his side.

"I've got over three hundred Durham-cross heifers coming twos that are open. If they'd bring thirty bucks up there, I could be out of debt," Mott said.

"Be nice to say that. Out of debt, I mean."

"I'm not getting any younger. Be sixty-seven this fall. Maude and I only got one daughter. Silva's up at Fort Worth with her man. So we ain't got anyone to look after us. If I was out of debt, that old place of ours ought to bring in enough to get us by."

"I savvy that," Sam said.

"I plan on sending my steers up there with him," Carl Brunner said, joining them. "What've you got, Sam?" Brunner was a man in his forties. A saddle-tanned face with a white forehead when he pushed the felt hat on the back of his head. His blue eyes were crinkled in the corners from squinting against too much sun.

"Two fifty or so two-year-old steers."

"How many could he drive up there?" Carl asked.

"Fifteen hundred would be a big herd for that far. It can get awful dry out there and finding enough water for even that large a herd could be the kicker."

"Why don't you make a drive?" Mott asked. "You been up and down the trail a dozen times."

"Let the colonel do it." Sam shook his pain-filled head to dismiss their asking. "I'm simply burned-out on trail drives. I went to Abilene when I was fifteen with Gus Price. Then later with Mark Stinger and

17

Hall Brett to Wichita, Dodge and then Nebraska with the Carp brothers. It's a long, dusty road up there and even a drier one coming back. I grew up on the deck of a mustang chousing steer tails, trying to sleep in a wet bedroll, plus eating gritty frijoles and fighting flies over the title to the rest of my grub."

"Well, you'd sure have my cattle to drive if you wanted them," Mott said.

"Thanks, but besides that, I'm too sore to drive anything anywhere," Sam said.

"What did you come to town for anyway?" Carl asked.

"This mug of cold beer. In another thirty days, all that ice he's got out back there in his shed'll be gone."

"Hmm." Mott snuffed out his nose. "Folks up north cut that stuff out of rivers and sell it to us rebs. No wonder we lost the damn war."

Carl frowned in disbelief at the older man's comment. "What else did you come after?"

"I needed some baking powder. Ten pounds of shingle nails. Raul and his sons are coming to roof the newly completed horse shed next week. What else? Guess that and this beer's all I needed." The beating from Wagner had been thrown in no doubt for good measure.

The longer Sam thought about what he still considered an unprovoked attack, the madder he became. He had no recollection of ever cutting a pinto in recent months. Harry had his facts twisted. He'd have more than that if he ever came at Sam again.

"I'll go get that stuff for you," Carl said. "Have to go get some new nippers. Mine broke and I need to shoe some horses. Just rest awhile. No trouble. See you boys later." The rancher went out to a chorus of good-byes.

"I need to get home too," Mott said. "Got all my business done."

Sam thanked him. The longer he sat there, the stiffer he would get. Maybe he should climb on Sorely and head back for his own pea patch. He'd declined Marty's offer of another cold beer. He was ready to get up and go when Carl returned with his things.

In a few minutes, Carl stuck his head in the doors. "It's all tied on your saddle. You take care now."

"Thanks." The effort to get up hinted that his ride home would be one from hell.

"You sure you can make it?" Marty asked.

"I'll be fine once I get in the saddle." Sam waved away any offer of help.

Outside in the sun, he checked the cinch. Then he grimaced from the effort to tighten it and redid the latigos.

Reins in his hand, left boot in the stirrup, he swung his leg over the pony's back. A cold chill ran down his jaw and he closed his eyes as arrows shot into his body when he settled in the seat. Trying to ignore the sharpness, he reined Sorely around.

There is a short moment when nine hundred pounds of cowpony feels like a boiling volcano. That's in those last few seconds before he bucks. Why a seven-year-old gelding, broke to death, ever decides that he's had enough, no one will ever know — 'cause horses ain't telling.

"Whoa — Sorr — lee!" Too late.

Cranking and kicking over Sam's back, the show was on. The two were scattering the town's dog population, who retaliated by falling in on his high-flying heels to bite and bark at this belligerent invader of their siesta.

Instead of slowing down, the red horse began to buck higher and wider. He crashed into a row of horses at the Silver Moon Café hitch rail, and the impact about shook Sam out of the saddle. He recovered in time to see that the other horses had all stampeded, snapping their reins before they left in a cloud of dust.

For a short while, Sorely danced his frog hop on the boardwalk; then he cut back across the street in high-flying fashion and sent two ladies screaming for cover inside a saddlery. But when the winged gelding side-swiped a buckboard team, Sam took flight and landed in the dust.

With pained eyes, seated on his butt, he could make out Sorely standing hip shot clear down by the pens. *Damn that horse. He would have to act up on a day like this one.*

Chapter 2

The last glimpse of twilight bathed the Texas hill country, when Sam sent Sorely off the ridge. The summer-night bugs sizzled and the first evening star shone in the western sky. Every step the gelding took descending the ridge shook Sam's too sore body. Sam wanted to climb off, lie down beside the wagon tracks and sleep for a month. Maybe he would wake up feeling well again. He owed that Harry Wagner for the beating. Maybe he'd work Wagner over with a double tree.

Somewhere down on Lost Horse Creek, a coyote yipped and another answered. Then a third, more mournful voiced one answered them. When Sorely reached the small stream, Sam allowed him to drink his fill, then booted the horse on to his outfit. The night was light enough to make out the figures and forms of his place when he rode up to the corral. A moon was coming up when he dropped heavily from the saddle.

One hand on the horse to steady himself, he fought the wet leather latigos loose and eventually dropped the saddle, pads and all, on the ground. No strength left, he pulled the bridle off Sorely's head and let him go. Shaking his own weary head, Sam headed for the small frame house. Walking was no better than riding. He paused at the porch post, using it for support. In the morning, he'd feel better. Lots of things needed to get done — shinglers would be there in a few days to put a roof on his new horse shed.

Supper? He dismissed the notion as too much trouble and fell across the bed. In minutes, exhaustion swept him away into troubled sleep. In the middle of the night, he awoke, sat up in bed and remembered every blow Wagner had hit him with. Suddenly he realized something was out there in the night. His hand felt for the Colt still in his holster. Sore swollen fingers closed around the walnut stocks. He hefted the Colt in his fist.

A horse snorted. Pained, he stood and then made his way across the smooth wood floor to the open door. His ears strained for any sound. Then he heard someone mounting a horse.

"Get out of here," someone said. Then riders fled in the night.

Sam tried to see them as they raced away, but they were a blur in the starlight. What the hell had they been up to? He walked on tender soles to the corral and saw a piece of white paper. Looking all around to be certain there was no one there, he lit a match and checked the note.

Get out of kounty! Last warning!

They'd get a *warning* all right: buckshot in their backsides, if they ever came back. Better find him a watchdog. Those Mexicans down on the Lee ranch had lots of dogs. One or two of theirs should be enough. Get him one mean enough that he'd bite someone. What was going on? He and his brothers, and their father before that, had been running cattle in that section of the hill country for years.

He stepped on a stick that made his foot sore and he hobbled on to the house. Next thing, he had better learn all he could about the Wagners. Never had had a cross word with any of them until the day before. He yawned and moved his sore body back inside after brushing off his soles with his hand. What were they up to anyway?

He drew himself bathwater the next morning. Couldn't carry two full buckets from the tank to the house, so he half filled them. Heating water on the stove to raise the temperature of the rest, he was on his knees, stoking wood to the range.

"You be home, Mr. Ketchem?" a familiar voice shouted. It was Abraham, the black who worked for the colonel.

"Yeah, Abe, what can I do for you?"

"My Gawd, Mr. Ketchem, what's done got ahold of you?" His brown eyes turned to saucers. Dressed in loose fitting pants and an oftenmended shirt, the thirty-some-year-old man held his battered straw hat in his hand.

"Harry Wagner and I had an altercation yesterday."

"How bad him look?"

"I think he looks lots better than I do. What do you need?"

"Well, sah, the colonel, he ain't been feeling so good lately and he asked if you'd drop by and see him."

"Right away?"

"If'n you ain't got lots to do."

"I could come over in a couple of hours. What's wrong? I saw him two weeks ago, and he looked fine."

"He had him a spell or two after that. They done had Doc Sharp look at him. You know how the colonel hates doctors."

"What did he say?"

"Never told me nothing. But I's worried

about him." The look on his walnut-shaded face was one of deep concern.

"I'll ride over in a few hours. Hope I don't scare him."

Abe shook his head. "You do look pretty bad. Bet you hurt a lot."

Sam nodded. "You tell the colonel I'm coming."

"I's sure he be mighty pleased, sah."

From the doorway, Sam watched the former slave ride off. He could hardly believe anything serious was wrong with the man. Colonel Ishaid T. Brant served as the leader of the ranchers up and down the Frio. His cattle drives over the years had helped make most folks landowners. A ten-dollar steer in Kansas bought ten acres of land back home in the Lone Star State. The ex-Confederate officer also had rebuilt his own fortune and holdings, but not at the sake of others. Sought after for his sound advice and strong counsel, Brant was the patriarch of the land.

What was wrong? Sam stripped off his clothes and poured the heated water. It would not be the warmest bath he ever managed to take, but haste sounded like his obligation. He soon learned the truth about the water temperature and shivers ran down the back of his arms, but he disregarded them

26

and set to lathering.

After bathing, he found that one-eyed shaving proved to be a difficult task, but he looked at his swollen left eye and laughed. One more thing he owed that Harry Wagner for. He sloshed soap off the razor in a pan of hot water.

He brushed down his brown hair. As he put on his best collarless white shirt and canvas pants, all movements reminded him how much he still hurt. Galluses up and vest buttoned, he slapped on his weather-beaten felt hat, then sat in a chair and pulled on his boots.

Spurs strapped on, he wondered more about the colonel's request. The man had never summoned him to his house except in times of an emergency, like when a band of Comanche had stolen some horses. Sam, along with five others, ran them down in a running gunfight and recovered all but two head. The other incident was when he and some others caught the Cripes brothers blotching brands — justice was swift in that case.

Disregarding his pain, he went to the pen and caught the big dun horse. He decided Sorely might want to buck again and his body was in no condition to contest with him. He slipped the bridle on Rob and led him out to saddle him. The chore was not done without his wincing. Even throwing his leg over the cantle wasn't easy. At last seated, he let the arrows in his jaw subside before he put on his thin roping gloves.

Reins in his hand, he nudged Rob out into a trot and headed for the colonel's. On the way, he swung by his brother Tom's. Karen, Tom's wife, came out, drying her hands on a sack towel and blinked in shock at him.

"Who — what?"

"I guess Tom's. Oh, don't fuss. Harry Wagner had his tail over his shoulder yesterday about someone cutting a pinto bull of his. I wanted Tom to know and have him tell Earl. I got a gut feeling them Wagners are stirred up about something."

"None of you have done anything." The willowy-figured woman in her early thirties had always been the beauty of the county — the one whom boys saved every dime they could get their hands on for months to buy her box supper at a charity auction.

The night Tom bought her basket, it took all the money the three brothers could scrape up. But sitting his horse and looking at the blue-eyed woman with their two fine children on her skirt in the doorway, he felt Tom'd sure not wasted their money that night.

"I don't know. It may be isolated, but tell him to keep his eyes open. They're bullies and like to jump you alone."

"They want a feud?"

He chewed on his lower lip, then shook his head. "Dumber things have happened. Christy and Mark, you help your mother today. I forgot to get any candy yesterday, but I will next time."

"We will. Thanks anyway, Uncle Sam."

"I need to ride over and see what the colonel's got on his mind. Abe rode over this morning and said he wanted to see me."

"Hmm, about the drive next spring?"

"Maybe. I'll let you know when I get back. Tell Tom to watch out."

"He'll get word to Earl. You get well. You look a mess."

"I'll be fine." He touched his hat and rode on.

Two hours later, Sam rode up the bottoms toward the Brant place. The colonel's herd of seed stock was behind the rail fences in the grassy field. The big Hereford herd sire, King Arthur, raised his head and bawled at the whole world. He had been imported from England by ship, and they'd brought him and four heifers by cart from the Gulf Coast. Other female herd additions had come down the Mississippi from Illinois and Ohio and up the Red River to Shreveport.

Sam always enjoyed seeing the white-and-red calves bucking and playing. The cattle business was in his blood. King Arthur's progeny and the other breeders' Durham/Shorthorn infusion of seed stock was fast changing the scene of hill country cattle from the black-brown marked longhorns to cattle with lots of meat under their hides. Getting them by the tick fever had been the hardest part to establishing any other breeds besides Coronado's strays in south central Texas. The colonel managed — but not without losses.

Sam dismounted at the rack, removed his spurs and hung them on his saddle horn. Then he decided to do the same with his gun belt. He sure didn't want to appear impolite to Thelma Brant. She'd have him stuffed with lemon cookies in no time. Gloves off, he started up the walk to the two-story house. Freshly whitewashed, it shone in the midday sun.

"Abe told me you'd be here before lunch," Thelma said, coming out on the porch. The white-haired lady stood erect and proper as always with a mild look on her still smooth face — the picture of a colonel's wife in a fine dress despite the time of day.

She'd gotten herself ready for company, and hat in hand, he hugged her.

"You do look as bad as Abraham said you would." She shook her head, guiding him toward the door. "Whatever came over that boy to do that to you?"

"I have no idea."

She stopped and paused; then, her brown eyes looking troubled, she spoke. "Doc Sharp says it's his heart. Of course, he'll act like it's nothing."

"Anything they can do for him?"

"Give him a new one, but that's impossible."

"I see."

"Ishaid trusts you. That's why he asked you over on such short notice."

How long did he have to live with this condition? A million questions flew through Sam's brain, until he saw the colonel seated in his high-backed leather chair, wrapped in a light quilt despite the day's heat.

"Morning, Sam."

Absently, Sam handed Thelma his hat and started across the polished floor toward the man.

"By jove, he did pound you to a pulp. How is one-eyed vision?" A cough cut the colonel off short and he shook his head in disgust. "We both are in bad shape. Have a chair."

31

"Sure. How are you feeling?" Sam pulled up the high-backed kitchen chair sitting by him.

"Let's not be like two old maids and talk about our aches and pains. I need some help."

"Fine. That suits me. What do you need?"

"You know I've carried lots of debt through the years to establish this place. Well, I'd have it all cleared out next year if cattle prices will hold. But I didn't need Doc to tell me, I'll never make the drive."

"That sounds serious."

"That's why I sent for you. I want you to take all our cattle to Nebraska next spring. Everyone up and down the river needs to sell."

"Aw, surely you'll be up and around and over this spell by then."

The colonel shook his head with a serious stare in his eyes. They weren't the usual sparkling blue — the fiery-deep denim color like the day when they had hanged the cattle rustlers or the times he was shouting orders to the crew when Red River crossings went from bad to worse. There was a dullness in them that stabbed Sam in the heart. Colonel Brant would never swim his horse over at Doane's Store again.

"I know you still blame yourself for the death of those three Langham boys. A storm stampeded those cattle — you didn't. Could have been you or I on any other drive."

"I would have taken their place." Sam clasped his fingers together in his lap and squeezed them.

"I would have taken the place of my soldiers killed in Mississippi, too. But I couldn't. You are the best man for the job." Then Brant threw his fist up to his mouth to cut off a debilitating coughing fit.

"I've swore off ever going up there again."

Brant nodded and cleared his throat. "I've sworn off lots of things, but this one is sure important to everyone."

"If you knew how many nights I stared at the ceiling, you won't ask me to do this."

"We've all got our own hell. But we have to put them behind us."

Thelma arrived with two tall glasses of yellow lemonade and a platter of her famous cookies. She set the tray on the stand. "Be good for that cough," she said softly to her husband and then nodded to Sam. "Cookies are for you."

"Well?" Brant asked when she left the room.

"Colonel, I've never turned you down

before, but I couldn't stomach asking young boys to ride off to their deaths. To face mothers who know about the incident and say that I'd look after their sons for the next six months."

"Rivers got Pete and who else?"

"Howard Pike."

"But that shootout could have happened in Frio Springs."

"Nelson and Biars weren't gunfighters. Hell, they weren't even dry behind the ears." Sam felt trapped by his own conscience being divided in half by the request: on one side, what he owed the colonel and his deep-rooted regrets; on the other, his own feelings of inadequacy. "I left San Anton that spring with over a dozen boys and came back with half of them." Sam didn't ever want to recall the clothes whipping on the line like runaway horses in the wind and him telling Ty Nelson's fifteen-year-old wife, with his baby son in her arms, that their child's daddy wouldn't be coming home.

"Sam, you can find the strength inside yourself to go on after that. That's why I'm asking this favor of you."

"Colonel, there're demons out there on that trail that I can't whip."

Brant's reply was broken up by his cough

again. Sam waited and noticed how the once robust man had overnight shrunken away.

"We've got some time to think on it. Think hard on it. What this drive means to folks around us. Your leadership is a lot greater than you give yourself credit for. Now watch out for those dumb Wagners."

"There won't be a next time."

"Think on my request and drop back by. I'm kinda tired now. I might take a nap."

"What about your lemonade?"

Brant wrinkled his nose. "Whiskey would be a lot better. Get some of those cookies or she'll be hurt."

"I'll think on this drive business. Maybe I can find you a good man."

"The man good enough for me is right here drinking her pee juice." The colonel chuckled until his coughing cut him off. "Dang stuff will have you up all night. Runs right through me."

After a short chat with Thelma, Sam tightened up the girth and rode Rob back toward the house. His mind and conscience held a tug of war over what he should do next. Neither side winning, he remained in confusion.

Donner's Branch was a spring-fed course that except in dry seasons maintained a stream of water from the big springs at its source under Hales' Bluffs. When Sam dropped off on the Lone Deer Schoolhouse Road above where it crossed the creek, he could see a buggy and someone under an umbrella on the spring seat stopped in the ford.

What was Etta Faye Ralston doing out there? All his life, Etta Faye had been the beauty no one could touch. Growing up, she kept boys at a distance and she always wore the finest dresses to school. With her chin stuck out and her head high, she must have — Sam always figured — been coached by her mother every day that she was a lady, despite those nasty farm boys who put toads in her apron pocket and lizards in her lunch pail. Why she could honest to God shiver and make disgusting noise like no other female he'd ever known about things she found repulsive.

He reined up Rob short of her and the big horse lowered his head and snorted in the road dust. He removed his hat and wiped his sweaty face on his sleeve.

"Howdy, ma'am."

"Good day, Samuel." She acted preoccupied with her driving horse, who had finished getting a drink.

"Nice day," Sam said, looking at the

cloudless sky. "What brings you out here?"

"The school board asked me if I would be the teacher out here at the school for the next session. There are several students out here that apparently cannot get into Frio Springs to attend classes."

"Etta Faye, have you ever taught school?"

"I am fully accredited as a qualified teacher by the Texas State Teachers' Board."

So there. He'd done it again, gone and affronted that woman. Why, she fluffed up on that seat like a setting hen guarding a nest full of eggs. And she would've pecked him if he'd got close enough. He dropped his gaze to the saddle horn. Looking at that fine, ripe figure wasting away was a bitter disappointment to him, but he sure didn't know how to break through the guard she kept up.

"As I recall you never liked toads, lizards and snotty-nosed kids. How in the Sam Hill are you going to tolerate a roomful of them?"

"Well, you know I consider a good education as important for each individual child and I have been taught the skills for that purpose."

"But Etta Faye where will you board?"

"Mrs. Fancher has agreed to board me for the session."

He nodded in approval. The widow woman on Stony Creek over the hill — that might work. But still —

"I shall drive Chelsea out of the branch now," she said and clucked to the dish-faced mare who came on the road next to him. "You may not know, but I taught school last year for two weeks while Miss Chester was ill."

He shook his head amazed at the notion. "No, I didn't know that."

"I'm sorry that you of all people obviously have such a low opinion of my professional skills."

"Did I say that?"

"No. But I can certainly tell by the tone of your voice and the demeanor of our conversation that you do not feel like I would be adequate for this position."

"Lord, Lord, Etta Faye. Hold on. Why I think you'd be overqualified for every thing, but handling the real things."

"Real things?"

"A dead mouse in your desk drawer."

Unfazed by his words, she smiled in her condescending way. "Samuel Ketchem, I might surprise you."

He nodded. *You will if you last.* Maybe she would. He hated to underestimate her. Besides, having her in the community for three months to look at wasn't so bad either. There would be social events, pie suppers and dances. He could hope against hope that under her icy exterior was a real woman to go with the body.

"When it gets cooler, they usually have a dance up here." He nodded toward the schoolhouse on the knoll. "I'd be pleased if you'd save me one."

"Why, Samuel Ketchem, I would be honored to dance with you."

Really? "Thanks and, Etta Faye, my friends call me Sam."

She looked at him with her sharp blue eyes and pursed her lips before she spoke. "Samuel, someday you will be a man of great respect in this county. And I find Sam too ordinary for the lofty place you will hold with your peers."

He couldn't hold back his amusement and snickered out his nose. "Well, I sure hope that lofty part ain't when they hang me."

She gathered the reins to her mare in her white-gloved hands. "You will see, Samuel. You will see. Oh, there are some repairs that need to be completed on the schoolhouse."

"If you have a list made up, I'd get some of the folks up here to pitch in and get them done."

"I don't have it with me, but if you would be so kind as to drop by my father's house next time you are in town, I shall have one ready."

"Fine. I'll drop by."

"Very good. You look to be healing from the altercation you had."

He rubbed the sore side of his face. "I'll live."

She reined up the mare, who acted anxious to go on. "I am sure you will. In fact, I think you should consider getting into politics."

"For now I have enough to do."

Her head rose, with that superior look on her handsome face, and she smiled like she knew a lot more than he did. "We shall see. Oh, and thank you so much for your help on the schoolhouse repairs. Get up, Chelsea."

He removed his hat and beat it on his leg as he watched her drive away. Even thinking about her might be a waste of his time. With dandies like the town law and others courting her, what chance did a two-bit rancher have with her? Besides she'd had enough marriage proposals from lovesick men to fill a big steamer trunk, and she'd turned them all down. Etta Faye might make an old maid schoolteacher, but — he stuck the hat back on his head and booted Rob across the ford — she sure would never make a rancher's wife.

Chapter 3

Sam recognized the roan horse hitched at his rack when he came in sight of the house. His youngest brother, Earl, was waiting for him. Seated on the front porch in his bullhide chaps, hat cocked on the back of his head exposing his curly hair, he whittled on some cedar with a jackknife.

"Hey, what brings my youngest brother over here?" Sam dismounted and undid the girth to remove the saddle.

"Well, for one thing" — Earl strained to cut a large notch in the red stick — "how are you doing?"

"Fine." Sam lifted the saddle and pads off the gelding and carried them to the porch to stow on the horn end.

"You look like hell." A frown crossed his tanned face, and he gave a head shake of disapproval before he turned his attention back to the wood.

"I'm alive."

"That cussed Harry do that to you?"

"Claimed I cut his favorite pinto-colored bull."

"What's wrong with that bunch?"

"You had trouble with them?"

"Byron, the youngest, came by the other day and told my wife to tell me we'd better watch whose beef we were eating."

"Told Lupe that?"

"If I'd found him, I would've tied into him."

"Don't let them get you into a fight. My first mistake yesterday. That won't happen again. How did us Ketchems get so crossways with that Wagner bunch anyway?" Sam shook his head trying to think of a reason. "I don't recall us even having words with them before."

"Won't be words I have with them."

"Well, ease down a notch, little brother. There's a time for everything, and I really want to know their reasons for all this."

"Ignorance. They're all stupid."

"I can't disagree with that. But what provoked them?"

Earl shook his head with no answer, folded the jackknife blade and dropped it in his vest pocket. "I came over to see if you needed anything done, and hell, you're up riding around."

"The colonel sent word he wanted to talk to me."

"What about?"

Sam rubbed his upper lip with his index finger and looked off at the live oak on the far hillside. "About taking the herd north next spring."

"He ain't going?"

"Earl, he may not live that long."

"The colonel?"

"His heart's gone, the doc said."

"What're you going to do?"

"Told him I had to think on it."

"I savvy that. But you know this one's liable to be a smooth one."

"No, Earl. No cattle drive is ever smooth. This one won't be either. That western trail out to Colorado and up that line could be as tough as any."

"It was just bad luck that all those boys got killed."

"Well, I don't have any lucky horseshoe today. Let's make some coffee."

"Thought you'd never ask."

"You'll never guess who I met on the road."

"Who?"

"Etta Faye Ralston."

"You always were soft on her. What's Miss Social Lady doing out here?"

Sam poured water in the enamel pot and then he opened the range burner to stoke the fire back to life. "She's going to teach school out here."

"Fancy that."

"You sound sarcastic about her deal."

"Has she set her bonnet to marry you or what?"

"Earl, that girl has no intention of marrying anyone."

"I ain't so all-fired damn sure."

"You don't know her like I do." Sam began to turn the crank on the coffee grinder after filling it with some roasted beans. "She don't want a husband or she'd have one by now."

Slouched down in a high-backed kitchen chair, Earl grinned big. "The right one just ain't asked her."

"Don't hold your breath."

"I won't, big brother. But I'd sure dance at your wedding." Then he threw his head back and laughed out loud. "I can't wait to tell Tom."

"Well, for my part, you can save the whole thing."

"Oh, you're touchy now?"

Sam didn't answer him. He went after the lemon cookies Thelma had sent home with him. He'd almost forgotten them. No matter what Earl said, Etta Faye Ralston was not serious about any man in her life, nor did she intend to be so. She enjoyed her role as a spinster and having all the dandies with plastered-down hair courting her prim and proper. Maybe the cookies would take the edge off Earl's tongue. Sam could count the times that boy's smart mouth caught a backhand from their pa or a hair jerking from their mother. Didn't do much to dull it, Sam decided, going back inside.

"Before you turn down that drive, you better think about all us small cattlemen. Them buyers will come pick us off. We won't get nothing for our work." Earl picked up a cookie, looked at it and nodded in approval. "Thelma's, ain't they?"

Sam nodded. "I'll think on it."

"Think damn hard. I've got a baby coming. He'll need some diapers, and I don't know what all that woman says we've got to have."

"Congratulations. Tell Lupe I'll be glad to be an uncle again."

"Yeah, and you think about the drive." Earl stood. "I've got to run along."

"Earl, watch your backside. Them Wagners got a problem the way I figure."

"I will. You, too. And get healed up. You look bad." Earl waved from the door and left Sam with a mouthful of sweet cookie to wash down with his coffee. He'd think about it — and then wonder what he should do.

Chapter 4

Nothing healed fast enough, least of all Sam's cuts and bruises. Raul and his boys, Hector and Manford, arrived to roof the horse barn in a wagon pulled by two scruffy mules. Sam had hired an old Mexican named Chico to split the shingles out of cedar blocks and make stacks of them. Raul inspected them and agreed the old man was the best. Sam gave him his nails and then asked Raul if he'd go look at the school-house roof and see what it needed.

"When I get the first run started for them, the boys can do the shingles. Then I will go look at the schoolhouse with you."

"Sure, I'll saddle you a horse." Since they had come in a wagon pulled by a team of mules, he figured riding would be quicker.

"In a little bit," the thin-faced man said and went to where the boys had stuck the ladder on the west side of the new structure, with its lathing all in place for them. Sam went after the mare Dutch, the gentlest one in his herd, and left them to put up a string on the edge.

Sam saddled Dutch. With her ready, he tied her at the rack beside Rob. When the barn was done, the saddle horses would have an open dry shed on one side to get into during bad weather. With stalls and a tack room, it would be a nice addition, and it would be paid for as well when he completed it. The big loft above was for hay storage.

In an hour, they rode over to the schoolhouse. The roofer examined all he could on the rickety ladder they found out back. "I think we can replace a few shingles and stop most of the leaks."

"Good. They never mentioned having any money. I'll pay you to do this when you get the barn roofed."

"*Sí.*"

Sam took the time to look at the rest of the structure and the grounds. Etta Faye would need the stovepipe replaced. It was pretty rusty. Two windowpanes needed to be reglazed and someone had broken the lamp globes. The bell needed a new rope. Raul's boys could reattach it in the belfry when they did the roof. The one outhouse needed some carpenter work and the other its door rehung — maybe new pits dug, too, since the old ones were smelly and close to full, but he didn't tarry long with the flies to examine them too close.

"Can you ride back all right? I need to check on some things in town," Sam said to the craftsman.

"I'll be fine. Good horse, plenty gentle."

"See you tonight?"

"We camp at your house while we work there?"

"Good idea. You and the boys be careful working up there."

"*Sí,* senor. See you later."

The ride to Frio Springs went uneventfully, and he rode up in front of the white picket fence that surrounded Judge Ralston's spacious, two-story house. Rob hitched at the rail, he went up the walk and was barked at by a small black dog.

"McGregor! Come here," Etta Faye commanded. With a short, jerky stride, the dog made a wide circle around him and ran for the porch and his mistress. With the dog safely in her arms, she smiled at Sam.

"You look much better today."

He quickly agreed. "I dropped by for the list you promised me."

"Oh, yes. Have you looked at the schoolhouse?"

"Yes. My roofer thinks he can fix the small leaks. I think a workday and dance would do the rest."

"When would you do that?"

"Two weeks from this Saturday should give me a chance to gather forces and have the women get ready to feed them."

"I shall be prepared to join you up there."

"Good. It should be a show of community spirit. And everyone likes to dance."

"I shall be in your debt, Samuel."

"You'll work it off teaching those kids their ABCs."

"It'll be a challenge, won't it?"

"I hope you know how much."

"I do."

Rather than get in an argument, he took the list and then smiled at her. He skimmed over it and nodded. "We should get lots of this done."

"Oh, Samuel, how will I ever repay you?"

"We'll work that out. See you at the workday."

She made a disappointed face. "You obviously don't have time for tea today?"

"No, ma'am, not today," he said and hurried for his horse, waving goodbye.

He left word at Sutter's General Store about the workday at the schoolhouse. Elmer Sutter promised to make a note about the planned project and dance and post it.

Then, with his order of coffee beans,

sugar, flour and lard, Sam headed back to the ranch. He'd considered getting a cold beer at the Tiger Hole, but instead turned Rob west. Too many things to get done.

Near sundown, he dropped off the ridge in the bloody light. The rolling hill country was bleeding away the day. He would be grateful for sundown. In a short while, the day's heat would dissipate some; he felt tired after all his running around. The healing process must be sapping his usual energy, he decided.

Raul was cooking over a campfire when Sam rode in.

"You could have used my stove," Sam said reining up Rob.

"Oh, we cook outside all the time."

"Whatever."

"Come and join us. We will have beans and some chili I brought from home. We have plenty."

"I may do that. Beats anything I'd cook."

The boys, seated on the bench they had set up, smiled at him.

"I'll put Rob up and then wash."

"It will be ready by then," Raul promised.

Sam turned at the sound of a rider coming in at a hard run. Someone was sure pounding ground to get there. He squinted against the fading light. Who was it?

50

"Sam, you better come quick," Jason Burns said, sliding his hard-breathing horse to a halt. "Somebody's shot Earl!"

"When?" Sam asked, catching Burns' horse by the bridle.

"An hour or so I guess."

"How is he?"

"Not good." The grave look on the man's face in the twilight told him enough.

"Tom know about it?"

"Yeah, he sent me after you."

"Who did it?"

"Don't know. He was shot in the back."

"Damn. I'll get a horse saddled and be ready in a minute." Sam took off in lope. Someone had shot his brother in the back. Why? Damn, if those Wagners were behind this, he'd get every one of them. He caught Sorely, led him out and tossed on the saddle. When the horse was cinched and ready to go, Sam noticed Raul standing there.

"Here are some beans in a tortilla. You will only be weak without some food."

"*Gracias,*" he said and took the wrap from him. "Go ahead, Jason. I'm coming." He reined up his horse and spoke again to Raul. "You and your boys keep an eye out. I don't expect any trouble here, but there might be some."

"We will. God be with you," Raul said.

Sam nodded. Then he hurried to catch Jason in the gray twilight. The burrito was still hot when he finally took a bite. He hoped it would fill some of the emptiness in his belly. Trotting his horse, he ate between bumps. His thoughts were on his youngest brother's condition and how, only hours earlier, they had visited and argued over him and Etta Faye — but Sam had sworn off ever again getting that involved with her again. She was not the marrying kind — period. Besides she was always acting like his mother — *You'd be good in politics.* He wouldn't be good at anything but raising cattle, and he was only half good at that.

He could see the lights at Earl's house from where he and Jason rode through the bottoms. Running his horse wouldn't save that boy's life, so they made steady progress up the flats at a trot. Several horses and rigs were in the yard and Doc's buggy was there. Good, Earl at least had some medical help. Sam dropped to his feet.

"That you, Sam?" a woman asked, then came rushing out and hugged him. "Oh, what will I do without him?"

"He still breathing?" He looked over Lupe's head toward the lighted doorway and could see the figure of the middle

Ketchem man coming outside.

She swept the hair back from her face. "Yes, but the doctor says he may not live."

"Lupe, he's a tough guy. He'll make it."

"Oh, Sam, what will I do?"

"You've got more religion than the rest of us. Pray for him."

"I see you made it," Tom said.

"What do you know?"

"Someone killed Earl's yearling colt. I guess he found it."

"The big buckskin one," Lupe said, drying her eyes on a kerchief that Sam handed her.

"I know the horse. He wouldn't have taken a sack of gold for him. How did they kill the colt?" Sam asked.

"Best I could tell, they choked him to death on the end of a lariat."

"But why?"

"That's what we're all asking," Tom said.

"Steal him? Why would anyone choke a horse down till you killed him?"

"Maybe they were just going to maim him," Tom said.

"What for?" Lupe asked.

"Maybe Sam can answer that question."

Sam blinked at his brother's words. "You thinking the Wagners were behind it?"

"No proof."

"Come daylight we can go look at the tracks."

"They brushed a lot of them out."

"Not all of them." Sam put his arm around Lupe's shoulder to comfort her. "Let's go see that boy."

If those sons a bitches wanted war, he'd give 'em both barrels.

Chapter 5

God called Earl Ketchem up yonder at thirty minutes past midnight that night. Twenty-four years old, husband, rancher and drover, he slipped away in his sleep. Doc Sharp shook his head at the weeping Ketchem women, Lupe and Karen, holding each other. Then, after carefully cleaning his glasses, he looked up at Sam and Tom. "I did all I could for the boy."

"We know that, Doc. It wasn't your fault. I better go tell them folks outside," Sam said.

Tom agreed and clapped him on the shoulder. "I'll stay here with them." He meant the women.

"Well, folks," Sam said, standing in the lighted doorway, "our boy's gone. He's not in pain anymore. I'm sure he's over that divide where the water's cool and the grass is stirrup high. Thanks for coming. Reckon we'll bury him up at the schoolhouse cemetery unless his wife objects."

"I could ride over and get that padre at St. Anne's," Jason offered.

052687

"No offense, Brother Quarry, but it might be best for Lupe's sake if we asked him."

"I have no objection, Sam. I am here to comfort and help your people through this tragedy."

"I'll get him," Jason said.

"We'll have lunch here at noontime," one of the women piped up in the darkness broken only by the doorway's light.

"We'll all help you, Maude. My boys can go and tell the neighbors," another said.

"Has anyone sent for the law?"

"I better go tell Whit Stuart," someone spoke up. "That's all right, ain't it, Sam?"

"Sure." Sam gazed off in the dark and drew a deep breath up his nostrils. Why did he feel so sure this matter was his to handle — alone? If he'd only ended it with Harry in the Tiger Hole, maybe Earl would be alive. That buckskin colt hadn't been choked to death by accident. He knew it and every man over sixteen in that crowd knew it. It was part of a festering feud that would only end in more death and suffering.

"Tom," he said softly when his brother came out and joined him, "take your wife and kids to Fort Worth after the funeral."

"I can't run."

"Damn it," Sam hissed. "I know you can't, but I don't want to bury them, too."

The look in Tom's eyes would have melted a frozen lake. "They even try —"

"Not try, Tom. They will, 'cause your family would be easy. They would be like that colt, not hard to kill."

"Gawdamn it, Sam. I can't run."

"Take her and the kids up to her folks' place until we know what's happening."

Tom wet his lips and looked ready to fight him. "We can get them. We can get every mother son of them and not their colts, either."

"Get Karen and the children to safety first."

In defeat, Tom dropped his head. "You're right, if that's what this is. But what did one of us do to them?"

"Cut a pinto bull."

"God help us" slipped from Tom's mouth.

Him and a lot more. Sam knew he was going to throw up. Holding his hand over his mouth, he rushed down the stairs and rounded the corner before he heaved up his heels. The dry ones followed as he used the side of the house for support. Sourness ran out his nose, and the violence of the upset shook him. If he never did another thing in his life, he'd have to find his brother's killer. Earl lying up there on the white sheets reminded him of those two drovers who got shot up in Dodge. Their pale faces like Earl's. Life leaking out of them. The strong smell of disinfectant filling his nose that night. He shuddered and gagged some more.

A woman, Mary Gustoff, brought him a wet rag to wipe his face. "You better come around and sit down."

"I'll be fine."

"No. You come sit on the edge of the porch," the matronly woman insisted and guided him to the place. "Now there ain't nothing wrong with you sitting. Land sakes, you've been through enough. That fight and now Earl. Things get more than anyone can stomach."

He nodded like a wooden Indian. His throat hurt when he tried to swallow. No use feeling sorry for himself. It was the others who needed comforting. Mary finally left him, and he saw the last of the well-wishers were coming out of the house.

They'd need a coffin. Maybe they had boards enough in the shop. No, he'd get Raul to make it. The man was a good carpenter, and there were enough boards left over at the barn project. He rose to go and tell Tom his plan.

"You'll need sleep sometime," his

brother said, sounding concerned.

"I'll get some. Be back midmorning with the coffin. I think that everyone knows what to do. They've gone after a padre."

"Paw would die if he knew." Tom shook his head ruefully.

"I know Paw thought they was the devil's spawn. But Earl choose Lupe and accepted her religion as his own."

" 'Course her church never recognized Earl."

"Don't think it bothered him much. He told me she had hers and he had his."

"You couldn't put that boy down when he wanted something to work." Tom bit his lower lip and shook his head. "Had his whole life ahead of him."

"Cry if you can," Sam said and hugged him.

The task of building the coffin took Raul and his boys a few hours of hard work. But in the end, it looked more like furniture than a simple box. Sam was about to go hook up a team to a wagon when he saw the dust of a rig coming.

Standing up and whipping her galloping horse was Etta Faye Ralston. She swung the rig around in a circle. Sam ran out and caught the horse's head stall.

"My God! My God!" she said and rushed to him. He let go of the hard breathing horse and caught her in his arms. "Oh, Samuel, I am so sorry. So sorry —" She wept on his vest.

Lots went through his mind as he held her there in the midmorning sun. First, she was a real woman with her fine, ripe body pressed to him. Second, she wasn't putting this on. It was as if the unseen walls that kept her at arm's length from him all these years had fallen away like cracked eggshells and in doing so revealed another Etta Faye Ralston. Third, he didn't want to chase the new Etta Faye away.

He laid his cheek on the top of her head and hugged her. "It was a bad deal. But Earl would want us to go on with our lives."

"How can I help you?" She looked up and her wet blue eyes pleaded with him.

"I reckon we can load that coffin in the back and tie it down. It don't weight much and we can drive over there."

"Sure," she said and used her handkerchief to blow her nose.

He took his clean one out of his hip pocket, and gently as he knew how, dried around her eyes. Her reaction was a smile and the dullness in her eyes turned to sparkles.

"Thank you. I must look a mess."

"Etta Faye, you never look a mess."

She blinked at him. "Oh, you don't know. Sometimes I am a regal mess."

He swept her up and carried her to the side of the rig. When her feet were on the floor, he carefully righted her. The look in her face surprised him. It wasn't one of her usual indignation, but like that of a little girl taken back by something that awed her.

Raul helped Sam load the coffin and then tie it down securely.

"You and your boys better come. They'll have lunch ready by the time we get over there."

"Are you sure?"

"Sure?" Sam frowned at him. "Funerals are for his friends. Earl counted you as his friends."

"Earl did — but the others?"

"Won't no one say anything to you. You are my guests."

"*Gracias,* senor. He was a good man. We will be there."

When Sam climbed on and took a seat, he turned, and Etta Faye nodded in approval. But something else struck him. She was holding his arm like she was part of him. He didn't mind at all. He only worried that she might wake from her dream, bolt upright and revert to the Miss Ralston he once knew.

He clucked to her horse. Damn, Earl would have said, "I told you so."

Chapter 6

The schoolhouse needed a few window-panes replaced and a whitewashing on the outside, and the inside still bore the staleness of being closed up for so long. It had been swept clean by some children under adult supervision. All the cobwebs they could reach were gone and the benches lined up.

The padre went first and his Latin sounded like a simple song. Sam knew several people would not come inside while he preached. But Karen and Lupe were in the front row on their knees. Raul and his boys were in the second row, also on their knees. Sam, Etta Faye, Tom and Tom's two little children were in the next row. Over his shoulder, Sam could see many of the valley folks seated on the benches with their heads bowed. When the mass was over, the padre spoke softly to Lupe; then he went to Sam and Tom.

"Be seated, my sons. What you have done for her today is a very worthy thing. God will reward you, for I know I came today to a house divided. May God bless you and keep you." He bowed, made the sign of the cross, nodded to them and went out of the schoolhouse, his black robes trailing behind him.

Brother Quarry went to the front and asked everyone to stand and sing "Jesus Is Calling." In his deep voice, he led the hymn. Then he read from the Bible and asked everyone to come forth and be saved.

At last, Sam joined Tom and the others. They carried the coffin down the aisle and past the mourners on the porch. They went through the open gate by several white limestone markers that bore the names of earlier pioneers. There, on a high spot, was the fresh grave, and soon the box was lowered into the hole.

Standing between Tom and Karen, Lupe cried. Her plaintive sorrow tore at Sam's heart and crushed it underneath his breast bone. Emotions ran high as people walked by to pay their final respects. Sam and Etta Faye were the last to leave. Looking down on the box, he could still smell the fresh-cut pine boards. *God be with you, little brother. You have not died in vain.*

He hurried Etta Faye from the site. She had broken down in tears, and he wanted to somehow shield her from more anguish.

Friends and neighbors offered condolences. Whit Stuart rolled his hat around on his hand until the others had gone.

"Miss Ralston," he said in a cold, polite voice, then looked at Sam. "I'm sorry to bother you at a time like this, Sam, but I must warn you. This is not the old days. The State of Texas does not hold with lynching and vigilantes. They're criminal offenses."

"So is murder. You heard what Doc said: shot in the back, probably by a rifle."

"I heard all that. But I also know your reputation. Leave the law to me."

"What is that reputation?" Etta Faye asked sharply. "He just put his youngest brother in the ground. If you're the law, why aren't you out looking for his killer right now?"

"Everything in due time, Miss Ralston."

Sam shook his head at her. Stuart would not do anything. He served warrants that folks swore out. It wasn't his fault — he was only preserving the law.

As Stuart tipped his hat and left them, Etta Faye squeezed Sam's arm. "Sorry I lost my temper."

Sam pushed his hat forward and scratched the back of his head. "Looked good on you."

"Do you want to go home?"

"I better see about Lupe's plans. I'm going to ask her to go to her parents in San Antonio. She's not had time even to send them word. Things happened so fast."

"Will she go there?"

Sam looked around. Jason, Raul and his boys were filling the grave. Folks were leaving in their wagons and buggies. "She needs to go down there until we know what this is all about."

"You think her life is in danger, too?"

"She's a Ketchem."

"Oh, my, Samuel, you think this is a family feud?"

"I do."

"How will you survive?"

"Etta Faye, I will survive. The Wagners are the ones who better be buying funeral clothing."

She straightened her shoulders and raised her chin. "Perhaps I better drive home before dark."

The coldness in her tone told him enough. She had removed herself from him. In an instant, she had gone back inside her shell. The look in her eyes was one of aloofness and disdain. He took off his hat and beat it against his leg. Nothing he could say would change her. For a brief few hours, he had seen another side of her, which he liked.

But that real caring woman was not the same woman he helped on the seat, handed the reins to and thanked. Standing in the dusty road, he watched her rig disappear, and as she went, she took a piece of him with her.

Sam found Tom, Karen and Lupe on the schoolhouse porch. The two Ketchem children ran about playing tag.

"Tom says I must go to San Anton'." Lupe looked at Sam with her big brown eyes. "This place is mine, isn't it?"

"Yes, it is yours. The court may give you a guardian, but it is yours."

"Why must I leave it?"

"Because the Wagners killed Earl. They'll kill others of us, if we don't stop them."

"But why me?"

"You're a Ketchem."

"When can I come back?"

"I hope in a few months."

She straightened and nodded. "I will do as you say, but I want to live here. This is my home."

"And you will, I promise."

"Earl once said you were like a rock, Sam. I know you are." She dropped her head and fought back more tears.

"Why did Etta Faye leave?" Karen asked.

"Said she needed to get home before dark."

"Oh," Karen said in a know-it-all woman's way.

Sam spent the next day packing shingles with Raul and his crew. It was one of those hard jobs that took no thinking. He'd shoulder a bundle of shingles bound in cord, carry it up a ladder and dump it on the freshly covered surface. His roofers scurried across the next edge, nailing down row after row. His barn would soon be a reality.

Of course, rains had not been frequent. But one afternoon, clouds began to rise in great columns and thunder rolled across the land. Soon the shift in the wind sent Sam and his workers scrambling off the roof.

Lightning zigzagged across the sky and thunder growled like a lion overhead. Under the shed portion of the barn, out of the rain, Sam smiled at the sheets of water that ran off the eaves. His face was washed by a fine mist. The new barn would be a comfortable place for his saddle horses when it was completed.

"You put in window glass?" he asked Raul over the rain.

"Sure. Why?"

"I need some replaced at the schoolhouse

and I'm not very good at it."

"I can do that when I fix the roof."

"I'll pick some panes up next trip to town."

Raul nodded and they both ducked at a loud boom of thunder. Sam still planned a workday for the schoolhouse, but whatever he had completed beforehand was that much less to do then.

The rain soon passed down the bottom and they went outside in the cooler, fresh-smelling air.

"Be too slick to go back up there," Raul said. "I can make some doors for those stalls inside and fix bunks in the tack room."

"That would help," Sam agreed, grateful for the offer. "You're a lot better carpenter than I am. I'll leave you boys, I need to ride over to Tom's and see if the women are packed."

"You expect more trouble?" Raul asked with a frown.

"Shooting Earl was only the start."

"No way to stop it?"

"I doubt it."

"That is very bad business."

"Bad business."

Sam went to saddle Sorely. In a few minutes, he rode over the hill. Close to the schoolhouse, he met Jason Burns on the road.

"See you've been to town," Sam said, looking at the two pokes tied on Jason's horn.

"Got a few things Eva sent for. Word's out them Wagners want you and Tom dead."

"They willing to pay enough?"

"Huh?"

"They paid enough, I'd drop dead."

Jason slapped his saddle horn. "Ain't a serious bone in your body. I mean, they've put the word out."

"They backshot my brother. They'll have to backshoot me and Tom."

"I know they ain't above doing that. Why, you've ruined their good name telling Stuart that they killed Earl."

"I'll ruin more than that if I ever can prove they did it."

"Just keep an eye out. They're a sneaky lot."

"I will," Sam promised, letting his temper simmer.

He went past the schoolhouse and up the road. That brief time with Etta Faye beside him, before she went back behind her haughty facade, kept running through his mind. No changing that girl. Maybe growing up as the judge's daughter and going off to finishing school had made her like that. He'd never know. But how she would ever make it as a teacher was beyond him.

At his brother's house, there was a wagon packed and tarped down. Karen saw him and smiled.

"You came too late," she teased.

"Sorry. I got busy helping roof my new horse barn." He dropped out of the saddle, removed his hat and wiped his face on his sleeve.

"Lupe hired the Garcia boys to drive her and her rig to San Antonio. She didn't want to leave. Mrs. Hanson is taking care of her milk cow till she gets back. We will be able to come back, won't we?"

"Karen, I hope so."

"Good. I don't know how long I can stand Fort Worth."

"The minute it's safe."

"That's what Tom promised me."

"Where's he at?"

"The kid's pony, Star, wandered off. He told them they could take him. He's down the way somewhere looking for him. Hasn't been gone long." She turned and looked off down the pasture.

"I'll go help him." He stepped up on Sorely and loped down the flats. He spotted the bay horse and rode down in the live oak to where Tom's mount stood ground-tied.

"Don't go down there," Tom said, coming back uphill with an angry look on his face.

"What's wrong?" Sam stood in the stirrups and tried to see.

"They cut the pony's throat." Tom closed his eyes and shook his head. "What in the hell do I tell my kids?"

Sam twisted in the saddle to look back at the tops of the ranch buildings. They were less than a half mile from the house.

"Any sign?"

Tom shook his head. "Not that would help. Suppose they'll burn us out next?"

"Anyone who'd kill a pony would do anything. Get your family out of here. I'll be on the scout. Come back, and you and I will figure this out."

"Can you ever figure out a feud, short of folks dying."

"That's why I want Karen and the kids out of here. Karen said Lupe is gone all ready."

"They left late night and were going to stop at Soda Springs on the way to San Anton. Lupe has an uncle there."

"Go finish things. I guess I should have been more help to her." Sam shook his head ruefully. He couldn't find any resolution in this whole matter of Earl's death. "I want to look at this pony deal."

"I'll be at the house."

In the grassy draw, there wasn't much to find. The pony lay on its side. His throat was slashed wide-open, and the dark blood drew flies. No big thing to catch the quiet animal and then kill it. He dropped to his haunches and searched the ground for any sign: matted-down grass, heel marks or any indication that someone had been there.

He rose and walked down the draw. Buzzards had begun to gather. Three lit atop a nearby oak and peered down at the corpse. Sam came to the place where perhaps the killers had left their horses. He found a trampled-down spot under a tree and hoofprints, but the latter were too faint for him to follow. Still, the notion that the pony killers had been so close to Tom's house made Sam sick to his stomach.

He stopped under the canopy of a big tree and suddenly remembered that the same thing had gotten Earl killed. The killers had used his colt as bait. With the rawhide tie-down on his holster undone, he checked the skyline for shooters. His six-gun switching around on his hip, he kept to the cover and moved down the swale. If the horse killers were there, maybe he could draw them out.

He preferred to be the tracker rather than the tracked.

Some bobwhite quail scattered into the spiny brush, and he listened for any telltale sounds. Nothing. Maybe if he could reach the crest above him, he could see more. He followed a small slit in the vegetation and, keeping in a crouch, picked his way with stealth through to the steepest part. Seeing nothing, he scrambled to the top, where he caught his breath.

He saw nothing but did not feel alone. Making his way back toward his horse with a full view of the depression, he realized the brown body of the pony was in an open spot clearly in view from up there. The buzzards danced around it, arguing over their prize — a man in this spot with a rifle could have picked off anyone looking at the dead animal.

On his haunches, he saw the boot marks in the dirt from where the bushwhackers had lain on the flat rock and waited. Why had they not shot Tom? Maybe Sam's own riding up there had spooked the killers. Now Sam felt certain the dead pony was a trap intended for Tom.

Sam wet his sun-cracked lips and considered all the evidence and his speculation. The only way he could ever survive was take to the brush, become part Injun and beat the killers at their own game. Satisfied the backshooter was gone, he went after Sorely and rode back to the house.

"Paw said that Star died, Uncle Sam," Mark said to him when he dismounted. The boy's wet lashes showed his grief.

"I know that's a shame, but we can find another pony."

"Go help your mother now," Tom said, mussing the youth's hair. When his son was out of earshot, Tom asked Sam what he'd found.

"You're lucky to be alive. That was a trap just like Earl's colt to draw you into their sights."

"How in the hell did they get away without us hearing them?"

"Can't answer that but it was a trap. They might have left before you ever got there. But they were there."

"Damn, you be careful while I'm taking Karen to her folk's place. Maybe I shouldn't leave."

"Yes, you should. I'll keep an eye on your place. Get moving. You can make Frio by evening."

"Oh, Sam, this whole business has me so upset." Karen hugged him.

He patted her shoulders. "Me, too. But we'll work it out."

"Be careful." She hurried off to the loaded wagon.

"I'll be back in a week or ten days," Tom promised. Then he boosted his wife up on the wagon and handed the kids up to her. On the seat at last, he took the reins and kicked loose the brake. His mules stepped right out and Sam watched them head for Frio.

Lord, please let them make it to safety.

He made one more wide circle of the dead-pony area, looking for something to tie in the identity of the killer. At last, finding nothing, he headed back to his place.

Sundown painted the front of the schoolhouse blood red when he rode by it. Trying to ignore his concern over how Etta Faye would handle her rowdy students, he rode Sorely home.

One thing was certain. He would be alone until Tom returned. He'd have to rely on his rangering experience. As a boy of sixteen, he had ridden the countryside looking for the tracks of unshod horses used by the Comanches, for he had ridden in the colonel's Texas Ranger Company. He'd slept many a night rolled up in a thick cotton blanket. Soon he would be out with the coyotes, trying to outdo his enemies.

Chapter 7

At daybreak, Abe brought him word the colonel had died in his sleep. When the black man rode on to tell others, Sam stood with his shoulder to the doorframe and sipped on some coffee to reflect. He'd known lots of big men in his life, but the colonel was the biggest. From his leading the local guard forces to his importing Herefords cattle, the colonel always was the one folks looked up to for advice and help. Be hard for anyone else to ever fill his big boots. There would be a big void without him.

Shame, too, for Sam's intentions had been to talk to him about this Wagner thing and find an answer. He knew enough about feuds — it was the resolution of one that he wanted. Or any ideas the man might have shared.

The funeral would be the next day at two p.m.

"You get more bad news?" Raul asked, coming from his campfire.

"Colonel died last night."

"Had he been sick?"

Sam nodded; then he tossed down the last of his coffee. "Came on sudden-like. 'Course, he may have hid it from all of us for some time."

"He asked you the other day to take the cattle north next year, didn't he?"

"Yes, he did."

"What will you do now?"

"I'm not certain. This feud I told you about and all — lots on my mind."

Raul nodded as if he understood. "I have some sopaipillas as a treat. Come eat them while they are hot."

"Thanks. I'll be right along."

At the campfire, Sam grinned, sharing the dark honey and the puffy pastry with Raul and his pleasant teenage boys.

"What's the occasion?"

"Today we finished the roof and tomorrow we fix the schoolhouse and then we can go home."

"Maybe stay one day more. They may need the schoolhouse for his funeral."

"No problem. We can wait a day."

"Good. You and the boys can nail on the barn siding if you have time." That would complete the building. The fresh-cut lumber for that was stacked and spaced to dry, but it would be far better nailed in place. One less thing for Sam to do.

"We will do that if you wish us to."

"Yes, you and the boys can do it. I was going to do that myself, but since you're here and all, you can."

Raul smiled at him. "Fine. Is more work for us."

The next day, Sam dressed up: white shirt, celluloid collar, tie and brown suit coat. Feeling choked, he rode stiff in the saddle and arrived at noontime. Of course, the local wives had fixed a large spread of food outside the schoolhouse for everyone to eat, as was traditional.

Sam hitched Sorely and made his way to a knot of men. The mood was somber, as he expected, and they nodded at him.

"Sorry. I didn't hear about Earl until after the funeral," Oscar Mott said. Others gave Sam similar nods.

"Who did it?" Ralph Fears asked.

"I reckon one of the Wagners."

He searched the faces of the others. A few nodded; others looked down, in deep reflection.

"I'm kin to them, Sam. But I want you to know I had no hand in his death," Leroy Turner said.

"Thanks. I like to know who my friends are these days."

"Where's Tom?" another asked.

79

"Took his wife and kids to Fort Worth."

"Oh?"

"Whoever shot Earl set a trap for Tom."

"How's that?"

"They cut his children's pony's throat to draw him in."

"What happened?"

"I'm not sure, but they had the trap set."

"Why don't you ask for a Ranger to investigate?" Mott said. "That damn Stuart won't ever get off his ass. All he can ask is if you will swear out a warrant. Hell, it's his job to find them."

"I better go find Miss Thelma and pay my respects." Sam excused himself and headed for the schoolhouse. Coming off the rise he saw a familiar parasol. Stuart was helping Etta Faye out of her rig. Sam went on, hoping to avoid both of them.

"Oh, Ketchem," Stuart said loudly before Sam reached the steps to the schoolhouse. "Nothing has turned up on your brother's murder yet."

"Ain't too liable to either, is it, Stuart?"

"How's that?"

"With you warming that chair in your office, ain't much gets done."

"I've made inquiries."

"Good. I'll feel a whole lot better knowing that my brother isn't lying under six feet of dirt up there without someone caring about who backshot him." He nodded to Etta Faye and went on inside.

"Oh, Sam," Thelma said. Her face flush from crying, she came to him to be held. "I knew he didn't have long, Sam. But I didn't know it would be this short."

"We never know."

"I know how you and he were such good friends. You know, he always said you were his best ranger. My, my, what will we ever do without him?"

"Take a hitch and go on. He'd want that."

"Oh, he wanted so much for you to agree to take those cattle north next year."

"I know. I'm still thinking about it. But I have a lot on my mind, what with losing Earl and all."

Thelma nodded. "Guess we have plenty of time to think about it. I do hope you will drop by. I will need some advice. He wanted you to have the fancy Colt they gave him in Austin. The one with the steer head carved ivory handles."

"Oh, I could never —"

"He wanted you to have it."

Sam hugged her lightly and stepped back. "Others want to talk to you. I'll miss him. But he left us plenty to be grateful for."

"I know, Sam. I know."

He turned and started for the doorway. Etta Faye, standing at the end of the receiving line, stopped him.

"After all this, do we need to put off the schoolhouse workday?" she asked.

He shook his head, looking out the front door at two boys about to get in a fracas. "Business as usual. Excuse me."

With a few swift steps, he was out on the porch, then on the ground, and he had both boys by the collars before the first blow was struck.

"This is a funeral, not a sideshow," he warned. "Don't fight here."

"Yes, sir," the boys said, looking sheepish when he released them.

Matty Brooks, a large, earthy-talking woman married to Kell Brooks, took Sam by the arm and escorted him to the food tables. "You look like a wormy Mexican steer. You need to eat. Get a tin plate and fill it, or I'll fill it for you."

"Yes, ma'am, I certainly will."

"And that was nice of you to separate them two boys. I hope that Etta Faye can handle the likes of them when she teaches up here. There's some salty ones in that age group. Half ain't had much schooling either. Living way out here, they had no way to get to Frio."

Sam piled some barbecued ribs on his plate. "Guess she'll learn or they'll ride her out on a rail."

"You going to look after her?"

"Why me? I'm not on the school board."

"You set up the workday."

He took some German potato salad. "Just trying to help."

"More than that fancy deputy would ever do."

"I guess," he said, licking the barbecue sauce off his finger and trying to decide what else to take from the numerous dishes of food. "She likes him."

"No, I think she's with him to make someone I know jealous."

"Really?"

"You're damn right she is."

"Naw, you don't know Etta Faye. She don't want to be serious with no man, but she likes escorts."

"Say what you want Sam Ketchem, she's got a reason for everything she does, even coming up here and teaching school."

"I'll keep that in mind."

Matty threw back her head and laughed out loud. Then, recalling the nature of the day, she clapped a hand over her mouth and blushed. "I bet you do."

The Wagners arrived and a hush fell over

the crowd. Their women brought food in pans and dishes to add to the table. Harry wasn't with them. Bo, the next to the oldest, was a man almost as big as Harry. Sam knew him from roundup. Next came Frank, his wife and children. Frank ran a steam-driven sawmill.

The shortest Wagner, Tillman, considered himself a lady's man and a gunfighter; he wore leather cuffs studded with some cut-glass studs he told people were real rubies. He rode a fancy black horse, which had a saddle with some silver trim. He eyed Sam and then rode on. Sam was seated at the board tables set up for the occasion and enjoying his lunch when Whit Stuart came by.

"I know there's bad blood between you and the Wagners. But I'll have no trouble here today from any of you."

"Maybe you better go tell them that," Matty said, bringing Sam a cup of lemonade.

"I will." Stuart squared his shoulder and strode down the way.

"If there ever was a peacock contest in this outfit, Whit Stuart would get first place." She shook her head, looking hard toward where the deputy was confronting the Wagners.

In a short while, Tillman, who had shaken off Stuart's hand, came stomping down to where Sam ate his lunch. Boots set apart, he folded his arms over his chest and glared at Sam. "You got anything to say to me? To my face?"

"No. You got a guilty conscience?" Sam looked up at him mildly.

"Word's out you're saying we killed your brother."

A meaty rib in his hand, Sam motioned it toward Tillman before he took a bite. "I'd throw in a pony you killed, too."

"What in the hell are you talking about?"

"Someone choked Earl's colt to death so he'd go check on it. Then they shot Earl in the back. They tried the same thing on Tom. But they got spooked."

"Who are you saying did it?"

"I'm saying, if the shoe fits, wear it."

"Them's fighting words —"

"Wagner, get your hand off that gun butt!" Stuart came from the edge of the crowd with his own gun drawn. "I said there'd be no trouble here. You can claim your gun at my office."

He shoved Wagner's pistol in his waistband and backed up. "I want no trouble from any of you."

"I'm eating lunch," Sam said and dismissed Stuart.

Tillman stalked off.

"You better watch him," Matty said as she started to leave.

"I will." Sam wanted to say he was more concerned about the absence of Harry than anything else.

Sam left the funeral to ride home after they'd laid the colonel to rest. He'd promised Thelma to be by her place in a day or so, and he'd spoken to Matty and the other women about the workday and dance. With everything set, he went and drew the cinch up and stepped aboard Sorely. The horse acted humpy, but Sam scolded him and checked him with the bit. Setting out at long trot, he headed for home.

He came off Whitson Ridge, standing in the stirrups. Then he kicked the red horse into a lope and seated in the saddle again. Three rifle shots cracked the air. Sorely couldn't take them. He bogged his head down and began to buck out through the cedars. After crashing into one, Sam fell through the sticky boughs. On the ground, his hand reached for his pistol, but the holster was empty.

Had he lost it when the horse began to buck out on the road? He didn't need to become a target. Still, those shots were intended for him; one must have burned the gelding. He'd left bucking like a bee had stung him.

Sam would damn sure need that pistol for his own defense. Where was the shooter? That plagued him the most about being left on foot and with no gun five miles from home.

Chapter 8

It was an hour to sundown. Sam stuck close to the cedar boughs and worked his way toward the road. No more shots. He had heard a distant horse snort; he thought the sound came from further south. The rest of the noises were crow calls and the wind. If only he could find the six-gun he'd lost, he might be able to save his life.

Who was behind that rifle? Harry Wagner, no doubt. All set up and waiting for a man riding a horse to come down the road. If Sam lived through this day, he would never take the road again until the feud was settled. Backwoods trails and rangering around — no set patterns. Nothing any gunman could bank on about him or his travels.

He saw no sign of the six-gun. He had adjusted it only a moment before he set the pony into a lope. Maybe if he got close enough, he could spot it lying in the open near the road. But he did not know exactly where the gunman was situated, so such exposure made an effort like that hazardous to his life. No doubt, that was exactly what the would-be killer wanted: a clear shot at Sam.

Someone was coming on horseback. Sam could hear a man's grunts, his voice as he talked to the horse, and hoofbeats. Sam dropped to all fours and went under the nearest boughs. On the ground, he discovered a thick branch. Being the hunted was not his idea of a good thing.

Soon he could see out from under the boughs the horse's legs and hooves coming closer. The rider was out of his line of sight.

"I must've got you, Ketchem, you bastard. Where are you? Better yet where did you crawl off to die?" Wagner laughed aloud.

He was past where Sam crouched. When Sam moved, he scrambled out from under the tree and threw the stick as hard as he could at the back of Wagner's head. The glancing blow knocked Wagner from his horse. The pistol in his hand went off and wounded Wagner, who rose like a jackknife being closed and then went flat.

"I'm shot," he cried out.

"Better you than me." Sam went after Wagner's horse. When he caught the dun, he swung in the saddle and rode in the direction Sorely had taken, hoping against hope that his pony was acting ground-tied somewhere ahead and he could swap mounts.

When Sam found Sorely in an open spot, he smiled. Sorely raised his head in the fiery sundown. Sam dismounted from the dun, tied the reins over his neck and hit him on the butt.

"Go home, pony. Your boss might not make it." Like he even gave a damn whether Harry Wagner lived or died.

At the ranch, after Sam put up his horse, he went inside the house in the darkness. He lit a lamp and worried how he could get word to Tom that it wasn't safe to come back. Maybe with Harry shot up, the Wagners might quit. After stoking the range with kindling, he struck a match and stood back, then watched the fire catch in the shavings. He added some more small sticks and put the lid on the range. He planned to fry some bacon to eat, and he'd put on a pot of beans to cook all night. He placed the skillet over the heat. Then he set his hat on the back of his head and straddled a chair to sit on while he sorted the dry frijoles from the rocks. Deeply involved in bean cleaning, he heard the drum of a horse coming.

Who in the hell would that be at this hour? Before that Wagner bunch was through, they'd have Sam sleeping with the coyotes. He took the shotgun off the wall, broke it open and inserted two brass cartridges. The gun locked and ready, he blew out the lamp and stepped to the doorway.

"Don't shoot. It's me, Mr. Ketchem."

"Billy Ford?" Sam blinked in the starlight at a young man in his early twenties sitting in the saddle.

"Yes, sir. I got a late start, but I was coming by to see if'n you could use some help on the drive?"

"What drive?" Who in the hell told him Sam was taking another drive?

"Word's out you're going up the trail next spring."

"Word's out —" He shook his head in dismay. "Put your horse in the pen and wash up. It's too late for you to ride back home. We'll have some supper and then we can talk."

"Thanks. Be a long ride back home in the dark." The cowboy ran off leading his pony.

The boy's presence meant Sam needed to fix taters and some biscuits, too. The lamp relit, he unloaded the Greener and put it on the rack. Company might be what he needed anyway. An hour later, they were eating fried potatoes, bacon and Sam's soda biscuits.

"Jammer McCoy told me about the

drive," Billy said. "I was sorry to hear about your brother. Do they know who shot him?"

"You referring to the law?" Sam asked, running half a biscuit through some molasses on his plate.

"I guess."

Sam shook his head. "They won't do nothing less you file a warrant."

"Huh? I thought the law was supposed to —"

"Not in this county."

"You mean the killer's going to get off scot-free?"

"Looks like that."

"You know who did it?" Billy asked.

Sam sat back, licked the tangy sweetness from the edges of his lips, then wiped his mouth on a handkerchief. He blew his nose and considered how to tell Billy about his encounter earlier that evening with Harry.

"Let's say this. Earl's killer ain't going to no more dances."

"Good, and I savvy how that ain't for letting out."

Sam smiled at the youth's quickness. "Guess you're needing some work?"

"Got the corn laid by at home, so I could use a job."

"I could use some help around here. But you sure need your wits about you. They think you're some kin or even helping me, you might get on their death list."

"I savvy that, too."

"Good. Reckon we can get some sleep now and let them beans cook till morning."

He pointed out a bunk for Billy and toed off his boots. It would be good to sleep in a real bed for one night anyway. In his stockings, he went outside to listen to the night insects' concert and empty his bladder. He wondered about Lupe and how the girl was making it back at home. Seemed like only yesterday his cocky younger brother drove up at the home place with his olive-faced beauty on the spring seat next to him. Their old man sitting on a rocker on the porch about swallowed his tobacco at the sight of her. Cyrus Ketchem thought Catholics were part of an evil empire. But despite Lupe's religion, before Cyrus died later the next year, he had built a rapport with the girl that was deeper than many father-daughter relationships. Lupe made his last days ones of peace and smiles, despite his suffering from the things out of the past that added up to him dying at sixty-two.

Sam was asleep when his head hit the pillow. He woke before dawn, with the night's coolness penetrating the open house. Dressed, he restoked the stove, checked on the beans and put water on for coffee. Then he ground some beans in the grinder to use when the water boiled. His man was up stretching and yawning like a big tomcat.

"What have you got for me to do today?"

"Ride around my cornfield and be certain the rail fences are all up."

"I can do that easy."

"I've got a mare fixing to foal. I'll bring her in, since you're going to be here. I intended to take her over to the old home place and let Lupe's hands watch her."

"Who's over there?"

"Some Mexican boys. Anyway, she left them in charge, and I made her go to San Anton until things quieted down here."

"I've heard about feuds. What started this one?"

Sam fetched the pan of leftover biscuits out of the oven. They were warm. Wearing a pot holder, he gripped the pan, then set it on the table. "Near as I can tell, someone castrated a longhorn bull that belonged to Harry Wagner. He thought I'd done it."

"That's what your brother died for?"

Sam looked Billy in the eye. "That's it."

"Aw, damn. And Tom's took his wife and kids to Fort Worth over it."

"Couldn't take any chances after they backshot Earl."

Billy nodded his tanned face. "Don't make sense."

"Feuds never do. I'm just caught up in it."

"Yeah, I see that. When I get the fence checked, what then?"

"I've got three windmills need greasing."

"That should keep me occupied. What's that mare look like?"

"She's a stout gray. Wearing my brand. The Bar K."

"I'll keep an eye out for her."

Sam nodded and went to fill their plates with beans. They had better chow down. It would be a long time before they ate again. "I ain't here by suppertime, make yourself at home. You need to send word to your folks?"

Billy shook his head, his spoon poised and ready to dive into his frijoles. "I told maw I was going to try to find work and might be gone awhile."

"You need to go back home for anything, just let me know. The bucket of grease for the mills is in the shed, so are the tools. Just be careful and don't fall off."

Billy waved his spoon between bites. "I gotcha."

After Sam cleaned up the dishes, he set a new pot of beans on the stove and built a fire under them. They should cook before the fire went out, and the frijoles would be ready for Sam to reheat that evening. Maybe he needed a cook worse than a ranch hand.

Sam saddled Rob, and he and Billy parted company at the corral. Billy rode off to check the fence. Last time Sam saw her, the mare had been up in the Crow Springs country, so he set out in a long trot northeast.

The cured grass was in good shape to winter the cattle. Sam wanted to drill some oats for winter graze when the shortened days grew cooler. He spooked up a few cows and calves. Mother cows and white-faced calves — the improved breeding was making a mark. They watched him with suspicion riding past them. But they were not as booger minded as the longhorns Sam's father originally stocked the country with. He could recall the wild ones from his youth. The British crosses were much easier to handle.

Stopping in a branch, he watered Rob and then rode up the draw, seeing signs of loose horses. With his lariat shook loose, he kept an eye out for them in the live oaks. The mare might act a little foxy and have to be roped. Then he spotted the mare and three geldings grazing in a bunch. She threw her head up and eyed him like a hawk. The horses started up the draw and she went north, picking up her gait.

He pushed Rob hard and captured the mare with a long rope tossed over her head. She braked once the noose went tight. While she blew rollers out her nose, she let him get in to make a halter on her head. He and his horses were soon headed for home at an easy lope.

There was no sign of Billy when Sam put the mare in the trap. As he led Rob toward the hitch rack, he heard riders coming. He could see the deputy sheriff leading the pack. What did they want? The others he recognized as neighbors.

"Harry Wagner's dead. You know anything about it?" Stuart announced without even a hello.

"Why're you asking me?" Sam squinted out of his left eye against the bright sun.

"You two had an altercation a while back."

"You got a warrant for my arrest?"

Stuart shook his head. "I was just asking."

"Where did he die at?"

"Between here and Frio."

"Reckon he was drunk and he fell off his

horse and broke his neck."

"No, he was shot at close range."

"I'm asking again. Other than the fight I didn't start, why ask me?" Sam folded his arms over his chest.

"Well, he's dead. It's my job to ask questions."

"Maybe you'll find out who killed Earl while you're asking."

"That's under investigation, too. Harry's horse came home last night with the reins tied up. His brother found him this morning south of here."

"So?"

"Just asking and telling you what happened."

"Sure. Maybe you should ask in the bars around Frio who else had a fracas with him. I'm sure as even-tempered as Harry was he had other grudges going."

"Harry never rode over here?" Tim Youngman asked from his horse.

"No, why?"

"He told them in Gotham's Saloon he was coming out here and kill you."

"He never made it."

Tim nodded. "Yes, obviously he never made it this far."

"You had lots of reasons to kill him," Stuart said.

"I didn't kill him."

"You said that before." Stuart reined his horse around and spoke to his four-man posse. "Let's go back and see what else we can find."

"See you." Sam waved to them.

"Yeah, take care of yourself," Tim shouted as they galloped away.

Sam stood watching their dust and wondering if Harry's death was the end of the feud or if the other brothers would continue it. Family blood was always thick even over the loss of a worthless one. So Sam would still have to be careful.

Billy rode in. "Who was here? I saw the dust and wondered."

"Harry got shot last night. Stuart acted like he thought I did it."

"You tell them I was here all night with you?"

Sam chewed on his lower lip and shook his head. "No, I never thought about that."

"Well, I'd sure tell them that."

"I may need your alibi. Thanks."

Chapter 9

The schoolhouse workday rolled around. The evening before, Billy drove over with a wagonload of tools, boards left over from the barn construction they might need, and the whitewash Sam bought in Frio. When he'd gone to Frio, Sam had dropped by and seen the judge to leave word that the plans were on track. Etta Faye was not home that afternoon and he did not inquire about her absence.

Many others had camped at the schoolhouse that Friday night to be ready for the next day's work. Ralph Schrowder brought his fiddle and sawed a tune that made Matty Brooks come over and fetch Sam to dance with her on the edge of the campfire light. Despite her ample size, she was light on her feet and could dance well even on the dirt.

She curtsied to him at the end of the song and then laughed aloud. "If I didn't have Kell, I'd set my cap for you, Sam Ketchem. You're still the best dancer in the county."

"Thanks," Sam said, feeling a little embarrassed by her loud words, but Matty never was one to hold back what she thought. He was grateful when she went off to see about the meat they were cooking.

Jason Burns came by and spoke to Sam. "I heard about Harry being shot."

Sam nodded. "I didn't kill him."

"Oh, I never figured you did. He made so many folks mad with his bullying ways he got what he deserved."

"How's Thelma doing?" Sam figured Jason would know because he lived close by the colonel's place.

"Not real good. I saw her Monday just sitting on the porch. Her eyes don't twinkle anymore. You should go by and see her. She thinks the world of you."

"She also wants my word on the cattle drive."

"She thinks like he did. Figures you're the only one can do it."

Sam shook his head. After the last drive and all that went wrong, he had no urge to start a bell steer toward that old North Star. He shook his head at his friend over the matter and watched Billy go by holding hands with the Fisher girl. No wonder Billy had been so excited about the workday and dance.

"I think it's done," Matty said and delivered Sam a large hunk of meat with a bone sticking out of it.

"Not got one for me?" Jason asked, winking at Sam.

"Hell, yes, I've got one for you. Come on over." She waved over her shoulder as she headed back for the fire.

"But she ain't going to spoil me like she does you." Jason chuckled privately and set out for his share of the meal.

Sam sat on a bench and gnawed on his fire-flavored hunk of beef. Saliva flooded his mouth, and the tangy mesquite flavor pleased his taste buds.

"Don't stand up, Samuel," Etta Faye said and drew her full skirt under herself to join him on the bench.

"Didn't see you drive in," he said between bites.

"I came with the Fanchers. I'm staying at their place. Father said you were by last week. I can't believe all these people are already here." She shook her head, looking at all of them in amazement.

"They've come to work, even though some of them live half a day's drive away."

"How will their children ever get here for school then?"

"Most are serious enough about their kids' educations to send them, but they'll do lots of riding to get over here and home again. So go easy on the tardy ones."

"Oh, I will, but I am glad that you told me about the distance they must travel."

"That's why some never went to Frio to school. Too far."

"I see. Perhaps I should get a plate of food. You will be here for a while with all that meat on your plate."

"I'll be here."

"Oh, thanks." She hurried off in a swirl of her dress and petticoats.

The evening flew by and soon everyone was ready to turn in. Etta Faye, who had become the center of attention, waved goodbye to Sam and left to stay with the Fanchers.

He and Billy simply undid their bedrolls and flopped upon them near the wagon. In minutes Sam found sleep. It was the fragrant smell of good coffee brewing that filled his nose before daybreak. He grabbed a cup from his kit and set out for the source.

"Morning," Matty said. She bent over the fire, stirring a huge skilletful of chopped potatoes. "Guess you smelled my coffee, huh?"

"Morning. Yes, I did." He squatted down and let her pour him steaming brew in his cup.

"You think that fussy girl will ever make it up here with these hellions?"

"If you want to do something bad enough, you can."

She nodded and went to laying strips of bacon in another skillet; the strips sizzled when she put them in it. "Reba's making biscuits." She motioned toward the woman working the Dutch ovens, shoving coals careful like on the lids.

"Morning, Sam," Reba said. "We sure appreciate you getting this school session out here."

"Not me. It was the school board."

"Yeah, but you're the one gets things done up here."

Matty straightened up from her cooking, wiped her sweaty face on a rag and nodded in agreement. "Reba's right. Now we're hoping you agree to take them cattle to Ogallala."

He looked off toward the purple horizon and then blew on his coffee. It was all a conspiracy to get him involved in the damn cattle drive. They didn't know what it was like to tell mothers that he had buried their sons on the prairie where they could never visit the graves to pay their respects — graves with nothing but wind-swaying blue stem for tombstones because the crude

104

crosses he had left had been trampled by the next herd through or consumed in a prairie fire.

"Morning," Jason Burns said, joining him.

"Morning. I figured you could take some of the men after breakfast and repair the outhouses. I brought some lumber and nails. I'm going to shore up that porch and those stairs. The whole thing feels weak when I cross it."

"See someone put back the bell rope."

"Raul and his boys did that. They also think they fixed the leaks in the roof."

"You pay them out of your pocket."

"Wasn't much."

"Well, we have the money to repay you," Matty said. "Reba, how long on the bread?"

"It's about ready."

"Good, I'll go ring the bell and get them up then."

"Sure," Reba said. "You two want a couple?"

"Sure," Jason said. Sam nodded.

"Butter's over here and there is some peach chunky," Reba said.

"We're coming," Jason said, and both men were up and headed for her.

The bell began to clap when Sam took his first bite of the hot biscuit lathered in cow butter and thick jam. A taste of heaven — he could recall his mother's similar treats for her four cowboys.

Sleepy-eyed folks began to gather. Other wives and women put on aprons and joined in serving food. Almost too full to work, Sam went over and inspected the creaking porch. He sent Billy after tools and another boy to get a few boards from the wagon.

Matty had the whitewash crew of boys and girls lined up with brushes while a few adults stirred the mixture in pails. Things went fast and furious. Some worked on ladders and the whitewash soon was on the south wall.

Etta Faye took the more careful brush bearers inside to do the interior. Benches and tables were all taken outside and gone over by the men. Only after being tested for soundness and slivers were they stacked for their return inside. Tall grasses and weeds were cut back with hand sickles to the edge of the playground. By noontime, the outhouses were all they had left to paint.

Matty rang the bell for lunch and the barbecued beef was stacked on plates along with frijoles and Reba's sour dough biscuits. After the meal, everyone sat around in the shade and relaxed, except for a crew of teenagers sent to paint the out buildings.

With a frown, Jason walked over to where Sam rested. "Trouble's coming. I recognize that dun horse. That's Harry's brother riding him."

Sam sat up and nodded. "Why's he coming here?"

"He's either going to tell you the feud is on or it's off."

With his tongue tracing a shred of meat caught between his back teeth, Sam got to his feet.

Ken Wagner reined up the dun. With him were a couple neighbors. "Sam Ketchem?" Wagner looked over the crowd, like he wasn't certain of his man.

"That's me," Sam said.

"Oh, yeah. Well, you may have shot my brother, but you ain't getting a shot at me."

"I never killed your brother. I've got an alibi, too."

"I don't believe it. I'll see you in hell, Ketchem. Harry was my oldest brother and he never needed to die gut-shot."

"So what are you going to do about it?"

"I aim to clear all you damn Ketchems out of this country."

"Why don't we step out of here? We can settle this now, you and me."

"No, I want you to sweat when you're getting yours."

"That goes two ways, Wagner."

"Just 'cause you was a ranger once, I ain't scared of you. No, siree. You might've got poor Harry, but you ain't getting me 'fore I get you." His dark eyes tried to bore a hole in Sam as he checked his horse sharply.

"That all you got to say. Get the hell out of here," Sam ordered and waved him aside.

"This is school land. Public land. You ain't got no say-so."

"I say you're here disturbing the peace, and you don't leave, I'm making a citizen's arrest."

"You ain't heard the last of me, Ketchem," Wagner said through clenched teeth. He gave a head toss to the others. He and his neighbors trotted off the grounds. Wagner growled how he'd get even if it took forever.

"Have your funeral paid for," Sam said after them.

"It sure ain't over," Jason said, looking upset.

Sam agreed and he saw Etta Fay going back inside with a look of disapproval on her face. Either she intended it for him or the vanishing Wagner brother. He didn't know which.

Later, Sam danced with Etta Faye three times, then with Matty, Betty Jones and a host more of the women and young girls even. He was seated on a wall bench drinking lemonade when Etta Faye joined him.

"What will you do about that man?" she asked in a hushed voice.

"Ignore him best I can."

"But, Samuel, he will surely try to kill you."

He wanted so bad to tell her that his brother had tried the same thing and ended up dead. "I'll watch for him."

With a bewildered shake of her head, she looked at her hands in her lap. "I think you need the law up here."

"Stuart?" he snorted.

"He is the law."

"He is a slick-talking dude who has you all charmed. He won't do a thing about Earl's death. He won't do anything about today either."

"Well, I can see you have your mind so made up even good sense won't crack it." She rose in a huff and left him.

The night wore on, and soon everyone was exhausted. The dance and barbecue were such a huge success that everyone promised another in two weeks.

Sam went to find his bedroll after talking to several others who expressed their concern for his safety. He shrugged off their worries and toed off his boots before getting in his bedroll.

"Seen you made Etta Faye mad again tonight," Billy said.

"You keeping score?" he asked. "You sound a lot like Earl used to."

"Ah, boss, everyone in this country knows the only reason she took this teaching job was to be up here by you."

"First I heard about it."

"Well, now you know."

"She's as serious about any man as she was ten years ago when I first took her out. She don't want a man. She wants an admirer."

"Like old rose-oil Stuart?"

"Yes. Go to sleep." Sam found himself grinning at the new name for the lawman.

After church services on Sunday, Sam rode over to check on Thelma. He found her in the rocker on the porch underneath a blanket, despite the day's temperature hovering in the upper nineties.

"How did the schoolhouse thing go?" she asked, when Sam pulled up a straight-backed chair to join her.

"Went well, except Ken Wagner came by and accused me of shooting his brother."

"Oh, I see."

"This feud is burned into them like a brand."

"It sounds like it is. I'm sorry 'cause there won't be any rest until your side or theirs is dead." She looked across the shady yard as if seeing some distant object. "You understand that, don't you?"

"Yes, but I'm not sure I know how to handle it. Harry accidentally shot himself chasing me. Do I have to kill all of them?"

She closed her eyes as if in deep thought. "I would hope not, but perhaps in the end you shall have to. I fear you are dealing with some very ignorant people."

"Yes, they must be. How are you feeling?"

"A little stronger today. Did you come by to tell me today that you'd take the cattle drive next spring?"

"I knew you'd ask me."

"Well?"

"I've not decided. My memories of the last one are too sharp. I have neither the heart nor the mind-set to do it."

She laid her head back and shut her eyes. "Lots on your mind I know. The loss of Earl and all. This blasted feud and the deaths of those boys. But in memory of them and the colonel, you should go north."

"We'll see."

We'll see.

Chapter 10

Billy had been busy working the field for over a week, so the ground was ready for planting. He drove the drill down there, and Sam brought the wagon piled high with sacks of seed oats. They began in the early morning, with Sam opening the gunny sacks, and pulled up close in the field to where the hopper would run out. The sweet smell of the grain thick in his nose, Sam was ready when Billy drove up and they dumped the open sacks in the hopper. As they leveled the supply out with their hands, the rig was ready to plant more ground. Billy clucked to the team with the feeder disks slicing the ground and putting down the long kernels.

By evening the bottom field was planted and the doves had already found the stray oats. In the dying gasp of the day, the weary horses plodded back to the new barn. Sam lighted a kerosene lantern at the barn, and Billy and he rubbed down both teams and, after graining them, turned them in the lot on the shed side with the few saddle horses they kept.

"Should I start working up the next field tomorrow?" Billy asked.

"Probably. That would give us close to thirty acres of oats for hay next year."

"But if you go to Nebraska next spring . . ."

"You're thinking I won't be here for the harvest."

"Well?"

"I've not agreed to Ogallala. They'll find someone, but if you still want to go, fine."

"I've never seen nothing but Texas."

They stopped at the door to wash up. Sam poured water out of a bucket into the basin. "All you've seen is the hill country. It gets drier and hotter and closer to hell the farther west you go."

"Why did the Comanche go out there?"

"They had no choice. The only buffalo left were out there." Sam rinsed his soapy hands and then wet his heated face with handfuls of water before he dried off on a stiff feed sack.

"Were they really as mean as folks said they were?"

"Yes. They did things to captives that made me puke."

"You and the colonel?"

Sam lit a lamp. "Yes, and some others.

Some rangers got killed out there. Warren Hart died of a rattlesnake bite under the eye. He woke up and the snake was right there."

"More died than that?"

"Some others." Sam really didn't want to talk about them.

After taking two lids off the stove, Sam stuffed in kindling and struck a match. The fine strings of wood quickly ignited and he replaced the lids.

Billy filled the coffeepot from the water pail. "What else happened?"

"We traded six horse and three mules for two girls and a black boy."

"Why did the Comanches trade them?"

"I think the prisoners were slowing them down."

"Didn't the Comanches usually just kill them?"

"Usually, but they had lots of loot and must have needed the horses and mules to help carry it."

"So how were the prisoners?"

"They gave them to us naked and nearly out of their minds." Sam shut his eyes as the gruesome pictures of the three came back. "The girls had been raped many times, and they weren't even teenagers. The black boy had been gelded. We made them clothing from our blankets and brought them back. All you had to do was touch them, and they went into convulsions, thinking they were going to be abused some more."

"It must have been hell?"

"It was. We brought back a Mrs. Mossel. Some trader had bought her from the Comanches hoping her family had lots of money and would pay him a big ransom. But the Comanches had wiped out the rest of her family. So a church in Fort Worth offered a hundred dollars for her."

"You went after her?"

"The colonel and six of us rangers went out there to get her. She had an Injun baby at her breasts and she feared the whole time we'd take it. She screamed a lot at us and gave an Injun chant all day as we rode. It was spooky."

"What happened to her?"

"She committed suicide they say. Ran out in front of a three-team hitch and was trampled to death."

"How did those people live? The Comanche?"

"They killed buffalo and made raids. Their camps stunk bad, and there was no water, so I guess that's why they never bathed. The women cut their hair short with sharpened shells and dressed in dirty rags.

The colonel said they were not supposed to look tempting to another man."

"That sounds bad."

"Those little girls were wives to men."

"Were all the other Indians like that?"

"I only chased the Comanche and some Kiowa who lived in teepees."

"What do the Comanche live in?"

"Lodges of skins. Not big, there's no timber out there. Just willows to make frames."

"I guess I ought to be proud to sit at your table, but we've sure ate lots of beans lately."

Sam looked at the pot of cooked down beans he'd taken off the stove to slop on their plates with a wooden spoon. "We have been eating them a lot. Tomorrow I'll go to town and hire a cook for this ranch."

"Who?"

"Hell, I don't know. But I won't come back till I find one."

"Fair enough. But you better put on a pot of them berries before you go, 'cause you might not be back till after dark."

Sam had always sworn he needed a cook. He'd never married one, so he would have to hire one. A cook would probably be cheaper than a wife or a woman to please, anyway.

The next morning, he arrived at the Tiger Hole at nine o'clock and went in to talk to Marty O'Brien, who was busy polishing glasses.

"We still got cold beer," O'Brien said, when Sam bellied up to the bar.

"Draw me a big schooner and then tell me where I can hire a cook."

"A cook. Ye need one now, huh?"

"Yes, I want a cook. I may hire a horse breaker this winter and I need a couple Mexicans to split out more rails. Besides Billy and I are tired of our own cooking — mostly mine."

"There's a woman with four kids needs a job, Kathy McCarty. Her man was killed in a wagon accident going to San Anton about three months ago."

Sam visualized a big fat woman with snotty-nosed kids hanging on her skirts. "Are there any men?"

"Vibby Leach got drunk and fell in a well and drown."

"That's a shame." Sam took a big sip of the wonderful cold beer.

"Worse part is the poor folks whose well he fell into still can't drink the water."

"Any trail-drive cooks out of work?"

"Might be in San Anton."

"Mexican?"

"Juanita — no, no, she married Jesus and they went to El Paso." O'Brien shook his head. "Kathy is the only one I know."

"Four kids. How old are they?"

"They all can walk."

"Good. Where's she?"

"She lives in a shack down behind the wool warehouse."

"Is she clean?"

O'Brien nodded. "Oh, you'll see."

Sam finished the beer and considered threatening the other man if he was sending him on a wild-goose chase. He rode Rob around to the wool warehouse and saw several jacals sitting along the potholed street. He observed some white children playing; they stood up to stare bright eyed at Rob. Horses like him didn't come down their street often and they looked impressed.

"Your name McCarty?" he asked and the children searched one another, as if mystified at this stranger's question.

"My name's McCarty. What did you be needing from a McCarty?" asked a woman in a doorway, her hands on her hips. She looked defiantly at Sam. Her blue eyes were the color of the sky, and her hair, as dark as velvet, was swept back and pinned up. Less than five feet tall, she had a trim figure underneath a pressed dress that buttoned to the throat.

"I understand you need work." He had removed his hat and held it in his hand.

"If you come looking for a whore, ride on, mister."

He shook his head to dismiss her stern warning. "I came looking for a cook. I own a ranch west of here. One cowboy and I right now, but I may have a crew before long and need a cook and housekeeper."

"Where would I live?"

He put the hat back on. "I guess in the house. Me and Billy can live in the new barn."

"You've seen my young'uns?"

"Yes, they can come along."

"What do you pay?"

"Twenty a month and food for all of you."

"How will I get there?"

"I'll have Hack Smith come by with his freight wagon and deliver you."

"I know Hack."

"Here's ten dollars to defray your expenses."

"That come out of my first month's pay?" Her eyes hooded with suspicions, she waited for his answer.

"No, it's a bonus."

"What else?"

"I want you to meet me at Hazelgood's

119

Store in an hour. You can pick out what you'll need to feed us, and Hack can haul that, too, unless you have lots of furniture." He leaned forward in the saddle and peered in the door.

She laughed aloud. "He can haul it and all the supplies. I'll be at the store in one hour."

"Nice to meet you, Mrs. McCarty." He touched his hat and eased Rob around.

"Whatcha call him?" the smallest boy asked with a bold look on his freckled face.

"Rob."

"Hiram," his mother said sternly.

"Boys got to ask questions, ma'am. I'd judge that he has lots more."

"Maybe ten thousand," she said and looked at the sky for help.

Hazelgood's Store was where a person went for everything: farm machinery, harnesses, tools, seed, potash fertilizer, feed, clothing, material, lace, thread, shoes, guns, ammo, pots, pans, lamps, dishes and food.

Gustoff Hazelgood was a walking dynamo. He employed several young men who were not only pleasant but resourceful. At the sight of Sam entering the front door, Hazelgood left his huge desk and came off the platform to meet him.

A burly man who looked more like a lumberjack than a storekeeper, he wore a smile plastered on his face and shot out his hand to shake. His hair was the color of wheat and his complexion bore a tint of pink.

"How have you been?" Gus asked. "I was saddened to hear about Earl. And I heard his wife left right quickly."

"Don't worry. If she owes you anything, she'll pay you. Until this feud simmers down, she needs to be in San Anton. Same for Tom's wife and kids."

"I knew that you'd see her debt was taken care of. It was why she left that bothered me. But I can see what you mean. What do you need today?"

"My new cook is coming to select supplies and I'm to meet her here."

"And who may that be?"

"Kathy McCarty."

"Ah, the young widow."

Sam nodded.

"That should liven up the ranch. She has four children."

"Might not hurt a thing. The boy I've hired and I are so tired of our own cooking, I figured we needed a cook."

"Don't blame you. How about a small drink?"

Sam, looking around the store, saw no sign of Kathy, so he agreed. "How's business?" he asked.

"That's what I really wanted to talk to you about." Gus took a wheel-back chair that squeaked when he turned in it to reach down in the drawer for a bottle of bonded whiskey. He set the bottle and two glasses on the counter.

"Oh?"

"Several small ranchers have accounts with me. If they sold their steers, they wouldn't get nothing for them. But if they could be included in a drive and they got a good price for 'em, they could wipe their slate clean."

Gus poured the glasses three-fourths full. "Now they pay me, but they never get completely out of debt. You know what that would mean to small ranchers?"

Sam nodded woodenly. Most folks considered what they owed as their inability to succeed. To be out of debt was worth bragging over. "And we don't owe a soul." He'd heard many a rancher's wife say that to others at gatherings. Glass in hand, Sam knew what would come next.

"You're the man to deliver them," Gus said.

"Big gamble. Their stock could drown in the rivers or die in a freak snowstorm. There could be a stampede and the whole herd would be lost for ever."

"And they could find a good market and bring forty dollars a head."

"Or get there and the market be two dollars." Sam shook his head. "There're lots of risks in sending cattle up the trail."

"Lord, Sam, lightning could strike, too, and kill them all. But a man like you could get the herd through and not rob these men."

Sam clinked his glass to Gus'. "You and the colonel's wife been talking?"

The storekeeper nodded. His brown eyes did not leave Sam's. "We've talked, but so have my customers. Have you even considered heading a drive?"

"Not seriously."

"I know what happened on the last trip you made, but that was just fate."

Sam rose when Mrs. McCarty swept inside. "My new cook has arrived. I better get started."

"Sam?"

"Yes."

"Think real hard on it."

"I hear ya." Sam finished his whiskey and set the glass down. Then he met Mrs. McCarty at the counter.

"What do you have out there?"

"Some frijoles and chili peppers is about all that's left."

She made a pained face. "What would you like to eat?"

"We don't care so long as we don't have to cook it."

"Do you have a cow? Chickens?"

"No, but I can get some. You want a cow?"

"It would help."

"I ain't sure that Billy would milk her for you."

She nodded. "I can do that if you get one. Besides, that brood of mine likes milk and I like butter, don't you?"

"Yes, ma'am."

"I'm Kathy. Call me that, Mr. Ketchem."

"I'm Sam." He removed his hat. "Nice to know you, Kathy."

"What can I get for you today?" asked a tall young man with glasses. Arthur Martin was one of the more knowledgeable salesmen.

"Mrs. McCarty is my new cook. Get her what she needs."

"Yes, sir, Mr. Ketchem. I mean, Sam."

"A barrel of flour," Kathy began. "Two pails of lard —"

Sam stepped back and braced his butt on a counter with high-top shoes. Arms folded, he heard Kathy call out, "Raisins, dried apples, canned peaches, tomatoes, baking powder, sugar —"

She turned and looked at Sam from top to bottom as if she'd not seen all of him before. "Do I need to cut back?"

He shook his head and motioned her on.

"I didn't want you to be in the poorhouse over my ordering all this."

"Not a problem today."

"Good." She turned back and continued her list.

"You have cooking pots and pans?" she asked over her shoulder.

"You see something you need, put it in this order."

"A Dutch oven and a large cast-iron skillet too much?"

"No." He could use them if he ever went north again anyway. He'd sold his cooking gear, chuck wagon and all in Dodge after the two boys' funeral. That drive was meant to be his last and final drive.

"My heavens," Kathy said, turning while Arthur went after some thread for her. "This will cost a fortune."

"Get a big jar of hard candy to hand out as rewards for them young'uns."

"I can see you want to spoil my children."

"I doubt I can do that. But get them each a pair of shoes, an everyday outfit and a Sunday outfit. There's dances and social things, and school will start this fall."

"Do you know what that will cost?"

"Kathy, they won't need to hide at the social gatherings 'cause they're ashamed of what they have to wear."

"Still —"

He put his finger to his lips. "They can earn it doing chores."

"I should hope so. But it will cost —"

With a head shake, he dismissed the concern written in her look.

"Hack will be by later and haul my order to the ranch," he told the clerk. "I'll be outside when you get through, Kathy."

"Better send the kids in, so we're sure this all fits," she said.

"I will." Sam pushed outside, and there on the bench, with their legs swinging, were four McCarty children.

"I know you," he said to the freckled-faced youngest. "You're Hiram."

"Yes, sir." Hiram beamed.

"And you are?" he asked a girl with pigtails.

"Rowann's my name." She was perhaps eight or nine.

"Nice to meet you." Sam looked at the oldest boy. "What's your name?"

"Darby, Mr. Ketchem, sir."

Sam guessed the boy might be twelve. He

126

turned to the second boy. "What's your name?"

"His name is Sloan, but he can't talk," Rowann said. "He can't hear you either. He's my twin."

The youth nodded and swallowed hard when she gave him an elbow and motioned toward Sam.

"But he's no trouble and he's a good worker, Mr. Ketchem," Darby put in quickly, as if Sam might reject them over the boy's handicap.

"That's fine. He can't help it. Your mother wants all of you inside," Sam said.

Their eyes wide with amazement, the children looked at one another and scrambled off the bench. Rowann took Sloan by the hand.

Hiram stopped and looked up at Sam. "I guess us being Gawdamn Irish don't bother you none?"

Rowann put her hand over her mouth in shock at his words. "Hiram! Mother will whip you." Her fingers shot out and she jerked him after the others.

"Don't bother me a bit, Hiram," Sam said with a grin.

"Good!" the boy shouted over his shoulder as his furious sister propelled him inside.

Suddenly a man shouted, "You no-good bastard!"

Sam saw the man come wading out of a saloon across the street. In reaction, Sam's hand went for his six-gun, and he used his thumbnail to flick the rawhide thong off the hammer that held it in place.

"You backshooting trash!"

Ken Wagner wasn't as big as his late brother, but Sam had no intention of taking another beating. The rage on Wagner's bearded face as he started across the near-empty street would have matched Harry's the day he tore into the Tiger Hole. Wagner must have been drinking firewater for a while.

Sam looked back and hoped that the children stayed inside long enough for him to solve this matter. Then he stepped into the street. Folks on the sidewalk began to run for cover. One man driving along saw the confrontation coming and lashed his buggy horse into a frenzy. The rig went swaying from side to side as it tore out of town.

"You shot my brother! Get ready to die!" Ken's hand went to his gun.

"I never killed your brother —" Sam's draw was faster and the cocked Colt in his hand belched fire, smoke and death.

Wagner shot his own gun into the dust.

Half spun around by the bullet in his chest, he fell in the dust. Sam went over and kicked the weapon from the other man's grasp in case he tried anything. But the man's eyes already looked glassy, and his life was evaporating.

"Hold it right there," Stuart shouted.

Sam holstered his gun. "Got here five minutes too late, didn't you?"

"I ain't having your feud in my town."

"Tell it to the Wagners. That's the second or third time they've jumped me."

"You ain't welcome in Frio, Ketchem."

Sam wanted to laugh at the man with his big silver star. "Tell Gus that and you'll be unemployed in a minute. This sumbitch came out of that saloon on the prowl. I bet he's been in there all day, drinking and bragging how he was going to take me."

"I said —"

"You want to call a coroner's hearing, do it." Sam had had enough. None of the customers that came out of the saloon to stand on the porch and gawk acted hostile. Satisfied that they were no threat, he turned on his heel and headed for Rob.

"Listen to me, Ketchem. I don't want your feud in my town."

Filled with pent-up anger, Sam jerked the cinch tight. He was upset enough over the shooting, and he didn't want any more words with Stuart. "Then mind your business. That dead drunk should have been locked up or run off over an hour ago." He took the reins and stuck his toe in the stirrup. "Stuart, you're on the wrong side."

In the saddle, Sam checked Rob and looked at the furious marshal standing in the center of the street, clenching his fists. Words would only fuel the flames. Sam reined Rob aside and booted him out to leave. This feud would never end. Sam's life would never return to normal either. Damn that Wagner bunch anyway.

Chapter 11

Past sundown, Sam dropped heavy out of the saddle and undid the girth. He led Rob over to the tack room, where Billy lit a lamp and joined him.

"You find a cook?" Billy asked.

Saddle and pads in his hands, Sam stopped. "You know a Kathy McCarty?"

"No. Who's she?"

"Widow woman. Four kids. Says she can cook." Sam put the saddle on the rack in the new room. "Guess you and I are bunking in here."

"You taste her cooking?"

"No." A smile on his lips and about to laugh, Sam said, "But she ain't bad to look at."

"Look at? Four kids? We're sleeping in the bunkhouse?"

"For now."

"Aw, hell, Sam, why didn't you hire some trail-drive cook?"

"There wasn't one to hire. Besides, you ain't seen her nor ate her food."

"You ain't either."

"I seen her. What's to eat?"

"Frijoles. Remember? That's why you went to town."

Sam shook his head. "Her and them four kids were the highlight of my day. Ken Wagner jumped me before I left town." He looked at the stars and wondered how many more Wagners wanted to die.

"Sorry. What happened?"

"They're having his funeral."

"Oh, damn, I'm sorry, Sam."

"Never mind. Hack's bringing Kathy, her kids and all her things out tomorrow, along with plenty of food. Who's got a cow?"

"I ain't milking no damn cow."

"Didn't ask you to. Marty will know where one is and we've got to build a chicken house."

"Chicken house? Next you'll want a pig pen, too."

Sam stopped in the lighted doorway and laughed. "Going to be different around here."

"What's Etta Faye think about you hiring a widow woman for a cook?"

"Hell, I never asked her."

"You'll hear about it."

Sam reflected on Billy's words. Etta might object, but he did so few things that pleased that woman, he didn't care.

Hiram was standing in the back of the freight wagon, on top of a barrel, waving his felt hat over his head and shouting, "We made it! We finally made it!"

Hack Smith had a mild smile and a handshake for Sam before he helped Kathy off the spring seat. She straightened her calico dress and nodded in gratitude at Sam.

"That's Billy Ford. Billy, this is Kathy McCarty."

"Pleased to meet you, ma'am."

"The pleasure is all mine, let me assure you. That's the house?" she asked, and they headed for it.

"Yes. Billy and I moved all our junk and beds out to the barn this morning."

"Oh, you have a real stove," Kathy said when she walked into the kitchen.

"We're close to civilized here," Sam said.

She smiled at the three men, who were standing with their hats in their hands. "I think it can sparkle. A few curtains and some of my things, and this can be a cheery place."

"Ma'am, can you make pancakes?" Billy asked.

"Sure. Why?"

"We tried that a few times and they never quite worked out," Billy said.

"We can have them in the morning."

"Wonderful."

"Let's get the wagon unloaded first," Sam said, getting back to reality. "There's a lot of stuff out there that needs to come inside."

Two hours later, Kathy was making bread dough. Soon she had baked five golden loaves. Rowann was peeling potatoes while the boys helped bring in their furniture.

"Sure hope we don't move again soon," Hiram told Billy as they went back for more.

"Why's that?"

"Too much damn work."

"Hiram McCarty, watch your foul mouth unless you want your tongue polished with lye soap again," his mother said.

A wooden box full of canned peaches in his hands, Sam smothered his amusement as he came inside. He watched Kathy shake her head in disapproval at him for even thinking about laughing. "He's not funny, Sam Ketchem."

Later, seated at the table, eating a slap of fresh bread, Sam watched Kathy fix supper: ham and potato casserole. Billy and the boys had gone to the creek for a swim.

"I'm going to find a cow tomorrow," Sam said.

"Wonderful," she said, pushing a wisp of

her black hair from her face with the back of her hand. "I sure hope we please you, Sam Ketchem."

"You will."

She looked around to be certain that Rowann was outside at the moment. "The man you shot in the street yesterday was a Wagner?"

"Yes, why?"

"I wanted to know. I heard something about a feud?"

Sam nodded and looked into her blue eyes. "I never started it. But yes, I guess they want one."

"Two men are dead?"

"Three counting my brother."

"Bad things, feuds. Not much can be done about them either."

"I'll try to be certain nothing happens to you and your children."

"Thank you." She chewed on her lip. "And all this food and this house. I may have to cry."

"I'll leave you alone."

"No, Sam. I feared the whole lot of us might starve this winter before you rode up." She blew her nose in a rag from her apron pocket. "Now I can see lots of pain in your eyes, too. Maybe we both can find a new way."

"I'm ready, Kathy."

"So am I."

The next day he set out for a cow. At the Brooks' place, Sam dropped out of the saddle and spoke to a collie dog that was barking at him.

"That you, Sam Ketchem?" Matty Brooks asked, coming out of the wood frame house, drying her hands on a sack towel.

"Ain't no one else. How have you been?" he asked as she ran out for a hug.

"Fine, just fine. What can I do for you?"

"I need a cow."

Taking him to the house, she looked up vexed at him. "What on earth for?"

"I have a cook and she needs a cow."

"You have a cook and she — oh."

"Her name's Kathy McCarty. She's a widow woman with four young children."

"She does need a cow. Now who has a fresh one that they'd sell?" She directed Sam to a chair and soon brought him coffee and apple pastry while she went over all the possible cow sellers in the neighborhood.

"Stokes. Armand Stokes would be the best one to try."

"Thanks. He lives on Dogget Creek, right?"

"Yes, and he has some good cows."

"I'll have pens built in a few weeks and need a half dozen nice shoats."

"My, my, nothing like the hand of a woman to turn a ranch into a farm." She threw her head back and laughed out loud.

"I've got Billy Ford on the payroll and intend to hire a few more hands, so I need a cook."

"Why not a trail cook?"

"Weren't any around here," Sam said.

"Good reason. My boys got a sow with six pigs. Would you pay two bucks apiece for them shoats when they're weaned."

"If they'd deliver them."

"Oh, they will. What else do you need, farmer?"

"Chickens."

"Laying hens, huh?"

Sam used the side of his fork to cut the delicious strudel. Waiting for her reply before forking in the next bite, he considered the prospects of all the things he would need for the additions.

"I'll get busy looking for some."

"Thanks. I better go see Armand about that cow." He finished his coffee and prepared to leave.

"I guess they asked you already?"

He paused ready to put his hat on and

looked at her for the answer.

"About taking the cattle north next spring," Matty said.

He shook his head mildly. "They're looking for a man to do it. But I won't."

"You told them no?"

"I've been up there, and I don't want to go again."

"You still blaming yourself for them boys' deaths?"

"Probably always will."

"Why?"

"They were my responsibility. I let them down."

"Nonsense."

"Matty, I have to live with my own ghosts."

"Let's change the subject. You have any intentions toward this woman you hired as your cook?"

He shook his head in disbelief. "Why ask that?"

"Just wanted to know where you stood. I have more of that apple dessert."

"Thanks, but I've got to run." He kissed her on the forehead and went out the door.

"And think about the cattle drive!" she shouted after him as he rode off.

The cow he purchased was a dish-faced

Jersey. With the cow and her small heifer calf, he arrived back at the ranch after dark. Holding a lantern high, Kathy came to pass approval on his purchase.

"The baby's a wee one," Rowann announced as it suckled its mother.

"She looks like a real cow," Kathy said, sounding impressed.

"She's real enough. A little tired from the long walk but she's young and healthy."

"I'll milk her early in the morning," Kathy said. "We best put that calf up when she gets through."

"One of the horse stalls will work."

"So you found a butter machine," Billy said.

"She's not a butter machine," Hiram said. "There's lots more work than that to get butter."

Everyone laughed.

"How did your day go?" Sam asked Billy.

"Fine. I'll talk to you about it later."

"Supper is still warm. You should come and eat," Kathy said and gathered all the curious children to leave the cow and calf alone. "And thanks for the cow. You won't regret it."

After supper, Sam, picking his teeth, walked to the bunkhouse with Billy. "What went wrong today?"

"Nothing, but they're spying on us — on me, anyway."

"Who?"

"A Wagner, I guess. I seen him twice in the live oaks while I was working."

"Man or boy?"

"Boy."

"I'll ride out tomorrow and circle back. You go to work like normal."

"What does he want?"

"Damned if I know."

"He can't be fifteen."

"A spy is a spy and he can shoot, too, I bet. You want out?"

"No, but I want a gun."

Sam rubbed the stubble around his mouth. "I have a small thirty caliber Colt."

"I'd feel a lot better with it than no gun at all."

"We can load it tonight. Just be careful."

"I will. Thanks."

Sam listened to the night insects; it would be fall in a few weeks. The Wagners had spies out. Sam had hoped that the feud was over when Ken had died in the street. Sam decided to show Kathy the shotgun and how to use it.

When he got to the house before dawn, Kathy was already back with a pail of milk. Actually the ring of her efforts on the side of the pail had awoken him.

"Coffee will be ready in a few minutes," she promised, slinging things around.

"Slow down. No rush," he said.

At last, she dropped in the chair opposite him and pushed wisps of hair back from her face. "You don't have to be so nice to me, Sam. I work for you."

"I hope you enjoy the work. I think you fit our life style well."

"Good." Kathy looked relieved.

"Six shoats enough to feed out?"

"You bought some pigs already? Oh, yes. That means a smokehouse."

"I may need another section to put the farm on."

They both laughed.

Sleepy eyed, Billy joined them. "What's so funny?"

"A chicken house, a smokehouse and a pig house — that's what we've got to build."

"Don't sound like ranching to me." The cowboy made a sour face.

"Armand told me about a Mexican who has a whole herd of goats he needs to sell. We could butcher one, and it would last this crew two days. So till it's cold enough for meat to keep, I'll have him bring by a few head each week."

"That sounds great. You like goat,

141

Kathy?" Billy asked her.

"I cooked one that stunk bad once."

"Aw, that was an old billy goat. Kids are good eating."

"Really," Sam said. "They're good barbecued."

"If they don't stink when I cook them, we'll eat goat," Kathy said.

"I better get ready to ride out of here," Sam said.

"Not till you have your breakfast," she said, looking shocked at the notion.

"Yes, ma'am," he said and settled back down with a wink at Billy.

His plans to try to catch the spy were made. What he would do with the spy was something else: a mere boy involved in a plot to harm him or his man or even anyone. This feud was madness unleashed.

Chapter 12

Sam left Sorely on top of the canyon in some brush and could see the second oat field from the heights through the trees. Using a brass telescope, he detected some movement in the bordering brush. First he thought it was deer, but the sight of something blue like pants convinced him the spy was down there. With all day to observe him, Sam moved along the rim, looking for the horse the boy must have ridden over there and had hidden. At last, he found the tracks and a cow pony hobbled in a small glen. It wore the WC brand they used on their horses.

Squatting on the ground, Sam watched the animal snatch mouthfuls of grass, then look his way. He wondered how to make the animal unavailable for the spy's escape. His decision was to move him the half mile to where Sorely was hitched.

At last, the horse was hobbled with his own and Sam went back to the rim to keep an eye on the spy. The boy had a gun. No telling the caliber, though it looked like a

.22. Still he came armed and not for hunting game. When Sam noticed Billy taking a lunchbreak, the spy moved around toward him. The motion worried Sam about Billy's safety, so he set out to capture the spy.

With stealth, Sam made the bottom, eased himself through the thick live oaks at the field's perimeter and at last saw the boy trying to work his way closer to Billy. In a few steps, he had the boy by the shoulder and jerked the rifle out of his hand.

"What?" said the boy.

"That's what I want to know?"

"I was hunting. Ain't no law against that."

"There is when it's humans. What's your name?"

"That you, Sam?" Billy shouted.

"Yeah, and I've got the bushwhacker."

"I ain't no bushwhacker."

"What's your name?"

"Delmore Wagner."

"About ten years in Texas prison and you'll think you was hunting."

"I ain't going to no damn prison." Delmore tried to kick at Sam, but Sam jerked the boy to his toes.

"You're going to rot in prison. Now why were you spying on us?"

"I ain't saying."

"Let me have him," Billy demanded. "I'll teach him to spy on me."

"Were you supposed to shoot Billy?"

"I don't have to —" the boy started.

Sam strung him up by the collar. "Were you?"

"Yes."

Sam shook his head. The kid didn't have the nerve — that was all that had stopped him. He was fixing to get his courage up that day; and he'd crept around to be close enough to Billy so that the shots would count.

"Let me have the little bastard. I'll fix him so he don't ever have a family," Billy ranted.

"Let the law send him off for ten years," Sam said.

"You taking him to town?"

"Yeah, and swearing out a warrant for his arrest. You sit there on the ground." Sam made sure Delmore was seated.

"Want a sandwich. Kathy sent an extra." Bill held up the gallon-size lard bucket.

"No, I'll get him in jail and be back late."

Billy stretched his arms over his head. "I'll have this one disked by tonight. Plant tomorrow."

"Sure. You get everything ready for in the morning and we'll start early."

Billy agreed, then looked at Sam. "That oldest boy of Kathy's, Darby, wants to come help seed this field."

"Be fine with me. I need to hike up on the hill and get the horses. You watch this kid till I get back. Don't mistreat him or shoot him unless he tries to run away."

"He's safe with me."

Sam nodded and set out for the horses. He wondered if Stuart would hold the kid for a while in his jail. The deputy wasn't prone to do much for Sam. Still Sam needed to have Delmore held long enough to make an impression on him. If those Wagners got word he was in jail, they might storm it. At least then they could all be arrested for jail busting. Sam was thinking too far ahead as he scrambled over the rocks to reach the ridge. Riding Sorely, he let the smaller horse trail behind.

"Get on that horse," Sam ordered and then he tied the boy's hands to the saddle horn. Billy made a lead, and in minutes, Sam was headed for Frio in a short lope. The sooner this business was over, the happier he would be. Besides, all this would make him late for supper.

"You with them when they shot Earl?" Sam asked as they walked their horses for a breather.

"Who shot who?"

"You want your tongue cut out?"

"No!"

"Then talk and talk fast."

"I swear I wasn't there. Honest, mister, I wasn't there."

"Who did it?"

"Harry and them came back and said they got one, is all I know."

"How did he say it?"

" 'We got one of them Ketchem bastards tonight.' "

"You tell everything to the law, they might only give you ten years."

"Ten years?"

"Be better than hanging."

By midafternoon, Sam reined up in front of the marshal's office. Stuart came out, putting his suit coat on.

"What did you bring him in for?" Stuart made a disgusted face at Sam and Delmore.

"Trespassing, attempted murder and a witness to Earl's murder. I'll swear out the warrant."

"You know who killed his brother?" Stuart asked the youth.

"Yes — sir."

"Who?"

"My uncles Harry and Ken."

"Who else was with them?"

"Farley."

"Who else?"

"That's all."

"Who set you up to kill Sam here?"

"My aunt Josie, Ken's wife."

"Are all you Wagners crazy?"

The boy dropped his head and wouldn't answer.

"Get him off the horse and inside." Stuart looked up and down the quiet street. "Folks heard what they've done, they're liable to lynch him."

"Want me to sign the warrants?"

"Yes, you better. Damn it, Sam, this is serious."

"So was Earl's death."

Warrants signed, he swung by the Ralston house and Etta Faye came out on the wide veranda to talk to him. He told her about capturing the boy.

Etta Faye had the maid bring out tea, and she arranged the area where she planned to serve it to him. "Samuel, do you think that the feud is over then?"

"I wish it was. But there's no way to know. I hope his testimony will end it, but if the women are in it, maybe not."

"Sounds so barbaric."

"I agree."

The maid served the tea and some cookies on a tray. "Will that be all?" she asked.

"Yes," Etta Faye said and poured Sam a cup of tea, then one for herself. "One or two lumps of sugar?"

"One's fine."

"Very well," she said and dropped the cube in his cup. "I shall have two."

He stirred his tea with a very small spoon. He figured if he ever had to eat with such fancy silverware, he would starve to death before he could ever shovel enough inside.

"The cookies are from Scotland," Etta Faye said and he tried one, which was a little dry and flat tasting, but he nodded in approval at her.

"Will you be at the dance this Saturday?" he asked.

"Oh, yes, I had not thought about the event. I better plan to stay at the Fanchers' then."

"Save me a dance."

"Save you a dance? Why every woman in that region dances with you. I suspect I need to be on your card."

"How many dances do you want?"

"A half dozen would be a good round number."

He pursed his lips and agreed with a nod. "So be it."

"Good, that's settled. Samuel, have you ever considered going into politics?"

"Etta Faye, I am so busy farming, ranching and looking out for backshooters, I don't have time. Besides, Tom has been staying in Fort Worth with his in-laws and I need to check on his cattle and his place, too."

She put a hand on his forearm. "You can't be a small rancher all your life."

"I'll think on that," he said and finished his tea. "Due back and I'm late. See you Saturday."

"Six dances. I want all of them." She bounced up and skipped along beside him, across the veranda and to his horse. When he finished checking the girth, he turned and kissed her on the mouth.

Acting dazed, she threw her other hand up to her lips and looked out of her blue eyes in total shock.

"You — you kissed me —"

"That happens, they tell me, when two people of opposite genders hang around together."

"But I am not some cheap harlot —"

"I only kissed you."

"I'm not engaged to you —"

Sam shut his eyes. Then he threw his arms around her and drew her tightly

150

against him and kissed her hard on the mouth. Her eyes opened so wide, he thought they might pop out.

"I've been wanting to do that for ten years." With a final squeeze, he released her.

"Oh — you —" She brushed off the front of her dress, as if he had soiled it.

"Aren't you going to run and hide?"

She drew her shoulders back, as if she had been involved in something revolting, and then trembled all over. "I don't know what to say, but you are not the gentleman I thought you were."

"It don't matter. You still don't understand, do you?"

"What's that?"

"That you really are a woman behind that facade."

"Why did you do this to me?"

"To show you what it was like when two people are in love — well, one maybe."

Etta Faye closed her eyes as if to regain her composure.

Sam stepped up into the saddle. "Saturday at the schoolhouse." He sent Sorely dancing off for town. After one check of the low sun, he knew he'd miss supper.

Chapter 13

Tom came back on Friday and agreed to stay with Sam and Billy at the Bar K, since Sam had hired a cook and he wasn't much of one himself. With the oats planted, all Sam needed was a good soft rain on the seed to keep the doves away. Clouds came in, but no rain had fallen before they saddled up for the ride over to the dance at the Lone Deer schoolhouse.

"You sure you don't want to go?" Sam asked Kathy for the fifth time.

"No, we'll be fine. I have some sewing to do, and I'm really happy as a lark to have an evening just to rest."

"Can't tell if some cowboy might take a fancy to you," he teased.

"Oh, Sam, I'm not ready for that. In time maybe, but my loss still runs too deep in me."

"I was only kidding you. Getting out and meeting others wouldn't hurt though — might even help."

"Later."

He looked around the yard. "I don't

expect any trouble, but you do know all about that shotgun on the rack in there."

"Yes, and I can use it."

"Good, I hope you don't ever have to. I guess all the kids are school age."

"Yes, I'd love for them to go."

"I'll tell the teacher she'll have four more that will be there when she opens the doors."

"Oh, that would be so good. Chauncy moved us around a lot to find work. So they've missed lots of schooling. I hope she can catch them up."

He wanted to say that the kids might catch Etta Faye up. But he kept his comments to himself. "I think she'll try hard."

When Sam, Tom and Billy crossed the branch, they could see activities around the schoolhouse were booming. Plenty of cooking smoke was swirling around on the afternoon wind. Women were stirring pots and tending some beef quarters on spits over hot coals. A dozen kid goats were also being barbecued.

"We're going to eat anyway," Tom said and laughed. "Hate my family missing all this."

Sam realized his brother was not happy being separated from Karen and the children. In the end, he figured Tom would sell out and move away, if things didn't soon improve. Sam couldn't blame him.

From the cooking crew, Matty Brooks rose up at the sight of Sam, scrubbed her wet face with a rag, then came to meet him. "Well, they say you had one of them arrested and he told all."

Sam dismounted, hat in hand, and looked at her hard. "He said the two dead men shot my brother."

"That settle it?"

"Matty, I am not certain of anything."

"Here give me the reins," Billy said. "I'll put your horse up."

"Thanks. See you boys later," Sam said as Tom and Billy rode on with Rob in tow.

"See Tom made it back. Come along with me," Matty said and took Sam's arm in the crook of hers. "I have some fresh biscuits and peach jam. Tell me more about that widow woman cooking for you at the ranch."

"Kathy McCarty and four nice children. They liven up the place."

"Her husband got killed? I hear she was pretty desperate for work."

"Yes, she must have been to take on feeding Billy, Tom and me."

"She as pretty as people say she is?"

"She's very nice looking. What?"

Matty gave him a shove. "You big oaf. You're the prize catch up here."

"Or the worst one. I have no interest in Kathy McCarty. In fact, we tried to get her to come up here tonight, but she said it was too soon after her husband's death."

"Fine."

"Of course, it's fine. There was not a cook available in the county. Billy and I were tired of our own beans."

Matty laughed aloud. "I would be, too. Let's get those biscuits and jam out for you."

After his treat, Sam went over to where men had congregated in the afternoon shade. Squatting in a loose circle, some smoked while others chewed tobacco and spat in the dust. Rain and cattle prices made the rounds, until Jason Burns spoke up.

"Looks like us little ranchers are going to sink or swim over a cattle drive."

"Yeah" came a mixed chorus, accompanied by bobbing heads.

"I know the colonel asked you, as well as several of us, Sam, so will you take our cattle up that western trail to Nebraska for us?"

The other men had Sam cornered and were playing on his conscience by acting as if he was their only chance for success — a weighty load on the back of a man in the midst of a feud. Sam had his own troubles to worry about. Besides, bad memories of his last, ill-fated drive still haunted him. Over and over, he saw those two boys dying on their backs in the dust of Front Street in Dodge City.

"Boys, I went to Abilene ten years ago. Made seven or eight trips. What the hell am I telling you boys about it for? Jason was a cook's helper on that first trip. Mr. Mott rode point. One of the Cotter brothers horse wrangled." Sam shifted his weight to his left boot. "You all know there's been drives that brought nothing — lost it all."

"That's why we want you," Mott said, flicking the ash off his cigarette. "It's the only chance we've got."

"There's got to be someone besides me in this community who could do this."

"Sam, you're who we want," Mott said.

"You know if Howard was here this afternoon," Yancy Pike said, pointing at the pale dirt between his dusty boots, "he'd say, 'Sam, let me go with you.'"

Sam chewed on his lower lip. Somewhere under the waving grass up in the Indian Nation, the crude cross long gone, rested a freckled-faced boy who would have whooped alligators bare-handed for Sam. He recalled the sadness in Lucy Pike's face the day when he rode up to her yard without her boy and paid her the four months' wages, the money that was going to buy him a hand made pair of boots and a new saddle.

Why me, Lord? Sam closed his eyes. "Boys, ain't no guarantee I can do it —"

"But will you?" Jason insisted.

"Yeah," Sam finally surrendered with an exhale, "I'll take them north next spring."

"Amen," Mr. Mott said and the cheer went up. Hats sailed in the air. Buck Saunders shot his pistol off. Everyone went to clapping each another on the back.

Skirts held high, the womenfolk came running over to hear the news. Children ran to the celebration.

"He's gonna do it!" someone announced loud enough to hear back in town.

Matty Brooks, with her dress in one hand, began to dance a jig with Sam despite his reluctance. Hands went to clapping to keep time, the suspense was over — word was out Sam Ketchem, trail boss, was going north with the herd.

A fiddle and bow soon joined in and folks were scuffling up dust in celebration. Matty passed Sam off to Eva Burns, who threw her head back and whooped out loud. Her jubilance forced a smile on his face. When a rancher's somber wife felt that good, his decision must have been the right thing to do. But could he deliver the herd?

At last, he managed to ease out of the hugs and handshakes, and saw Etta Faye drive up under her parasol. He felt good he'd made his decision. Maybe this time, things would go smoother. Perhaps the last time he'd had bad luck.

Sam took Etta Faye's hand and helped her down.

"I'll put your horse up Miss Ralston," a freckled faced boy offered.

"Thank you, Clarence," she said. "I have two baskets in the back."

"I'll get them," Sam offered.

She nodded and gave the boy instructions about her horse's care. The boy drove Chelsea off to the back of the schoolhouse.

"Well, how are you?" Etta Faye asked as she turned to Sam. "I heard the news. Stuart has your brother's killer in jail."

"A witness anyway."

"Will there be more arrests?"

"Maybe you should ask him?"

"I can see I have gouged you, Samuel. May I apologize?"

"None needed."

"What's all the excitement about? Everyone looks worked up into frenzy."

"Oh, we're going up the trail next spring to Nebraska."

Etta Faye swallowed hard. Her blue eyes widened in disbelief. "Samuel, you aren't going to be the trail boss, are you?"

"Yes."

Her gloved hand clapped over her mouth, she paled. "But after all you went through . . ."

Chapter 14

Fiddle music carried on the cooling breeze that swept hints of the dying cooking fires to the schoolhouse. Night bugs joined the songs, mingled with laughter and the excitement of the gathering. Little ones were tucked in wagon beds to sleep and infants suckled on their mothers' breasts in the shadowy world beyond the Chinese lanterns. Inside the coal-oil lamps made the waxed floor shine as couples waltzed around the room, as their parents had in Tennessee, Georgia or Arkansas before braving the wagon drive to the south central Texas hill country. Scotch-Irish people for the most part, Baptist or Methodist, they blended with the German colonists who lived by the Lutheran doctrine.

Sam was caught by several men to discuss some details. How many men would he need to hire? How much money needed to be raised for expenses? When would he leave? All questions he put off until he knew the number of cattle to be driven. Trying to get in the front door, he felt as if he was swimming an ocean. The tie, the celluloid collar and the brown suit made him feel stiff.

Etta Faye was in the schoolhouse, and he had promised to dance with her. She was upset about the deal and acting like a spoiled child who did not get her way. But she never said a word in the past about Sam going on the drive. Times like this, he wondered why he even tried to make something spark between them. He made the doorway and spotted Etta Faye in a starched blue dress. She was talking to two teenage girls. The music had stopped. Sam put his hat on the rack, then crossed the room to where Etta Faye stood. He hoped his hair was still combed down. He felt naked without his usual head gear in place.

"I hope both of you attend class," Etta Faye said to the teens. "To be able to read and write is helpful to anyone, especially young ladies."

The girls thanked her, as if uncomfortable to be out in the spotlight, and left.

"Samuel." Etta Faye studied him. "You look very nice in your suit and tie. Perhaps when you return, you should go and see a tailor in San Antone and get a new one."

"Oh, yes, I wear one so often."

"You will in time. You'll see what I mean.

Since you have all these ranchers' gratitude for accepting such a thankless job, the least you can do is solicit their votes."

Sam shut his eyes and shook his head. Then the music began. He took her hand and they waltzed around the room. With her bow-shaped back in his arms, he guided her easily around the dance floor, as if no one else existed in the schoolhouse. The soft strains of the music mellowed and the sharp look on her face mellowed. Sam wanted the song to last forever.

When the set was over, they stood in silence. At last, Etta Faye said, "I could use some lemonade."

"Lemonade you shall have."

He escorted her to a table where Eva Burns served them glasses of the drink.

"When will you start school?" Eva asked Etta Faye.

"October first. Do you have children who will attend?"

"Two younger ones, but the older boys say they don't need any more."

"I know how that is. But if they are ever going to be more than cowboys, they need a good education."

Eva shrugged off the comment, as if getting her older boys to school was more than she could do. "But I'm afraid they don't want to be anything else. And they'll pester you to death to join you, Sam, now they know you're going up the trail."

Sam agreed with a nod. "Good lemonade." Finished, he handed the glass back to her.

Etta Faye thanked Eva and carried the drink in her hand. She and Sam went toward an open space on the benches along the wall. Seated at last, they had little time to converse with each other because well-wishers were coming by to thank Sam. At last, the music began, and feeling grateful to escape the limelight, Sam excused himself and took his partner to the center of the room. If the world was a dance floor, he felt that he could own Etta Faye, lock, stock, and barrel. Then they were gone again into that flowing world of their own, where no one else existed.

The musicians took a break. Sam left Etta Faye with a group of women, including Matty, who wanted to help her during the first week. Sam went outside and joined Tom.

"Billy's found him a girlfriend, I believe," Tom said as they walked leisurely down the dusty road.

"The Fisher girl?"

"I didn't think you noticed a thing. You

and that Etta Faye looked like you were both moonstruck on that dance floor."

Sam glanced up at the stars. Moonstruck? Was that the word for it?

"I wanted you to be the first to know. I'm going to sell out." Tom shook his head wearily and both men stopped walking. "I can't bring my family back here and risk them being shot. There's a dozen more of them Wagners. Vindictive women like the one who sent that boy out to shoot Billy. Hell, he's not even a Ketchem. I can't take it."

"You have to do what you have to do for Karen and those kids. I sure can't offer you any kind of assurance this thing is over."

"But we've worked so damn hard to build us places here."

"Paw would have been proud." Sam clapped Tom on the shoulder. "We took what he left us and built on it."

"I know it won't be the same as the hill country but I've been out to see Buffalo Gap. I plan to move up in that country."

Sam closed his eyes. Earl was gone, and now Tom was leaving. Maybe he needed to make a move, too. There was a lot of country opening up north. Real grassland.

"I know you'll help me close the deal and get everything packed," Tom said.

"Sure," Sam said with a knot that would

be hard to swallow caught in his throat. The two hugged each other. Sam patted Tom on the back. "I know that was hard to tell me, but thanks."

"Hell, if I didn't have Karen and the kids, I'd ride down there tonight and stomp everyone of their asses to kingdom come."

Sam chuckled. "That was what the old man was always going to do to us when we messed up: stomp our asses."

"Yeah, but I mean it."

"I know you do."

Some of the wind in Sam's sails was gone when he went back inside the schoolhouse. He looked around the room for Etta Faye and didn't see her. He went and talked to Mr. Mott, who stood off to the side.

"Sure pleased about you coming around. I know the colonel would have been proud. He was a big fan of yours."

"I was one of his, too."

Matty Brooks made faces at him; she wanted to talk to him. Sam excused himself and crossed to where she was serving pie and cobbler.

"You know she left?" Matty hissed.

"Left?"

"Yes, when someone told her that you'd moved in that widow woman in your house."

"Huh?"

"It wasn't me. I couldn't help it either. The gal blurted it out. Etta Faye left in tears. You hadn't told her?"

"No. So damn much going on, it never crossed my mind as important." He exhaled in distress. What next? "She go back to the Fanchers?"

"I really don't know. I'm sorry, but it sure upset her to hear it like she did."

"Thanks," he said in defeat.

"Want some pie?"

"No, I couldn't swallow a bite," Sam said and left the dance.

Chapter 15

Rain came — the kind country people prayed for: a slow soaker that swept in over the hill country, washing the small, waxy oak leaves clean of dust. It was the rain that would sprout Sam's oats — bring them up like turnips and greens. The runoff would make the stream and creeks so dingy for a while the small schools of minnows would be hidden.

It rained hard the first day the school bell rang. Huddled in his wagon under a tarp to stay dry, Sam drove the four McCarty kids over to the schoolhouse. He locked the brake and tied off the reins. Grateful the downpour had let up, he unloaded them one at a time and sent them splashing for the front door.

The last to come off was Sloan, who looked very vexed by the situation. Halfway to the door, Rowann looked back to check on him and blinked.

"He's fine," Sam reassured her. "I'll bring him."

She needed no more encouragement and,

with a flush of excitement over what waited ahead, ran on. Darby and Hiram were already through the door and waving for her to hurry and catch them.

Sloan closed his fingers tight on Sam's hand. To encourage the boy, Sam nodded, and the rain dripped off his brim when he did so. When he and his ward entered the room, he saw Etta Faye look up from talking to a small girl. It was their first meeting since the dance. She strode across the floor, the picture of composure. But the coldness of her manner vibrated off the room's walls.

"These are the McCarty children?"

"Yes, that's Darby. He's twelve. Hiram is six. Rowann is nine, and this is Sloan — he's her twin."

"Hello, Sloan," she said, her attention centered on the boy.

"Oh, Miss Ralston," Rowann interceded. "Sloan can't speak. But he's very excited about coming to school."

"Is he mute?" Etta Faye asked.

Sam nodded.

"Oh, what a shame. Can he be reached?"

"We don't know. He and Rowann can communicate. Maybe you can learn him some things."

"He ain't no dumb knot on a log," Hiram said. Then realizing he had spoken out, he put his hand over his mouth.

"Oh, Hiram, we know he is not that," Etta Faye assured the boy.

"Yes, ma'am."

"Their mother didn't come?" Etta Faye looked around past Sam.

"Rain and all. She had things to do and sent me."

"If she looks at all like her daughter, she must be a very lovely person."

Sam wasn't about to step into that trap. He simply nodded. "If Sloan gets to be too large a task or you feel he's not getting anything from your teaching, his mother says she will understand."

"I'll have twenty-two students. That's more than the school board thought."

"Big job."

"Samuel, thanks for bringing them today. I will do what I can for him and the others."

"Everything is working?"

"One small leak in the roof." She indicated the tin can on the floor. "But we are doing fine for now."

"Need anything, send word."

"Oh, I will, Samuel."

He excused himself and left the building, which was full of kids from Hiram's age on to a tall boy in his late teens, who tried to look inconspicuous in the background. Several, Sam noticed, had bowl haircuts. The newly exposed skin was snow-white either from the clipping or the children wearing hats all summer.

On the wagon seat, with a fine rain in his face, Sam took a last look at the door. Etta Faye must have sent someone to close it to prevent any more water from being blown inside. Sam undid the reins around the brake handle and wet his lips. Sure not too warm a reception from her. He wondered about silent Sloan and if school would help him adapt more to life. The boy always looked so heartbreakingly alone to Sam, even when he walked across the yard.

Sam released the brake and clucked to the team, then headed home for the dry barn and some horseshoeing he needed to catch up on.

Billy and Tom had built a fire in the forge. When Sam reined the team inside the alleyway, the other two men looked up from rasping away at hooves. Sam nodded to them and began to unharness the horses.

Concerned how things had gone, Kathy hurried out from the house under a shawl. "How did it go?"

"Good enough. Rowann spoke up for Sloan and Hiram told Etta Faye that Sloan wasn't a bump on a log."

"Oh, that boy and his smart mouth."

"Don't be hard on him. He meant what he said."

"Darby was embarrassed. I really thought he might run away last night. He's seen less school than any of them."

"There's a bigger boy than him there today. Maybe they can strike up a friendship and be buddies."

Kathy clutched the shawl. "I'm grateful for all your help. I guess I should have gone, but I don't have very much education and felt insecure even to enroll them."

Sam nodded. "Maybe you can learn, too."

"How much education do you have?"

"I went to school six years."

"That's something."

She looked at Tom, who nodded at her.

"It didn't make me a whiz." Sam gathered up the harness from the off horse and put it on the rack.

"He was Mr. Patrick's pet," Tom said. "That was our teacher the last three years."

"How's that?" she asked, acting interested in learning about their past.

"You don't even want to hear," Sam warned her. The horses unhitched, he led them through the gate into the pen under the shed roof and turned them loose.

"Someday you can tell me, Tom." She ducked when the thunder rolled over head.

"Rain will really come now," Billy said from working on the hind hoof of a dun horse.

"I'll bet it does. I'll call you all for lunch," she said and put up her shawl, then ran for the house.

"I'm going to let you take my steer with yours to Nebraska," Tom said while beating on a red-hot shoe to form it. His blows on the anvil rang like a church bell.

"I can do that. What about the cow stock?"

"I'll need to drive them up there to my new place when I get one. Do it this winter before they drop calves or I'll lose them on the trail."

"Good idea. You've got a buyer for the place?"

"Mr. Mott says he'll buy it for his daughter and son-in-law. I'm supposed to meet him at the bank tomorrow. You know his son-in-law?"

"Yes, I do. And the less I have to do with Glen Martin, the happier I'll be, but you sell to whoever and I'll get along. He's a bag of wind."

Tom nodded. Then he went to try the fit of the shoe on the bay. He came back to heat the shoe and pound on it some more when the steel became cherry red.

"I've got some corn in the field over there. Reckon I could sell it?"

"Sure," Sam said.

"Good. I don't want to haul it clear up there."

"I'll check in town for buyers, next trip," Sam said, straining on the handles of the nipper to pry the shoe off Sorely's right hind hoof. The shoe gave at last. It was too worn to put back on the horse, so Sam discarded it. At once, he was filled with dread over all the work he must accomplish before the drive.

He looked up from holding the hoof when Tom said, "I'm going to go see Karen tomorrow after I close the deal."

"Fine. Billy and I can handle things."

"Then I'll go and see about a place."

"Sure."

Tom was leaving the country faster than Sam liked. But Sam could not blame his brother. Tom had a lovely wife and two smart kids who would be up on the hill attending school if they weren't in Fort Worth.

In a short while, Sam would be the only Ketchem in the county — if some Wagner didn't backshoot him. Sam had never thought he and his brothers would separate. Their paw brought the family there from Washington County, Arkansas, way before the war. His Southern roots were threatened by the antislave talk around him. Though he had never owned a slave himself, he respected other folks' rights and their property.

"They're going to bust this whole country in half one of these days with a big chopping ax, and when the smoke clears, I want to be south of that line," Paw said. That was also the day he sold the Arkansas farm and hired an auctioneer to cry the sale. His keen blue eyes never stopped looking toward the Texas hill country again until he found the home place that Sam owned.

After shoeing Sorely's hind feet, Sam went to stand in the doorway to see the rain clouds rushing in. Maybe it was time for him to search for a new country. He could do lots of looking on the trail.

Then he saw Kathy in the horse's doorway, waving for them to come. He waved back. "Lunch, guys. If we hurry, we can beat the next shower coming up the valley."

They broke and ran for the house, laughing as the rain drops began to strike them.

"Sure won't hurt the oats," Billy said.

"Yeah," Tom said. "Ever think about planting rice, Sam?"

"No, but I once knew a Chinese cook couldn't cook nothing that didn't have rice in it," Sam said.

"You been thinking about a cook for the drive?" Billy asked, putting his hat on the rack by the back door.

"Yes, but I haven't made a decision yet."

"Drive to where?" Kathy asked.

"Ogallala," Tom said, drying his hands.

"Where's that?" she asked, putting bowls of potatoes covered in gravy on the table. Then she headed back for the fried pork and biscuits.

"Umpteen miles northwest of here," Sam said, taking his place at the head of the table.

"Two thousand miles?" Tom asked, ready to bow his head.

"More or less. Let's say grace." Sam waited for Kathy to be seated. Then the four clasped hands.

"Lord, bless this food. Thanks for the rain and be with all our loved ones. Amen." Sam raised up and nodded to Kathy. "A long ways up there and even longer coming back."

"I'd like that job," she said, "cooking for them."

Sam blinked at her in disbelief. "You serious?"

"Why, there's Injuns, rustlers, and filthy, sweaty cowboys who can't find enough water to bathe in. And there are river crossings that would scare a saint." Tom frowned at Kathy and shook his head. "No, you wouldn't."

"Well, I sure would."

"I don't know how a crew would take to a woman cook," Sam said.

"You three eat my grub."

Sam laid down his fork and grinned. If Etta Faye hated him for hiring Kathy for a housekeeper, she'd sure enough be pissed over him picking the other woman for the drive. "I'm taking that under advisement."

When Tom gave Sam a questioning glare, Sam asked, "You're eating her grub, bro. Had any like it on the trail lately?"

Tom snickered and shook his head.

"I ain't said she was hired either. It's only under advisement. All of you hear me?"

"Yes" came the mixed chorus.

"Good. Billy, you go fetch the kids from school this afternoon. I'm going to ride to town with Tom. He's leaving us tomorrow. We'll spend the night in Frio and he can leave from there."

"We will miss you, Tom," Kathy said.

"When you have these two guys fat enough to butcher, send me word," Tom said.

She blushed. "It's fun to feed hungry men who like my cooking."

"Nice meeting you. Best this place has looked since our maw was alive." Tom motioned around the house.

"You should see where I lived before in town. The only jacal that anyone lived in in that block behind the wool warehouse. So bad even the Mexicans had moved out of them."

"You did good here. Take care of these two." Tom excused himself to go pack.

"You'll miss him, won't you, Sam?" Kathy asked when Tom left.

"I won't miss all the work he's left for us to do," Sam said. He and Billy laughed.

Gathering up the dishes, Kathy scowled in disapproval at both of them.

That evening after boarding their horses at the livery and reserving a bunk in the back room, Sam and Tom headed up the boardwalk to the Silver Moon Café in the twilight. Frio looked and sounded quiet at midweek, with a few horses standing hip shot in front of the two saloons. The lights were still on inside the restaurant when Sam pushed the door open. Pearl was gathering dirty dishes.

"Well, if it ain't the Ketchem brothers," she said and grinned big. "Be with you two in a minute, 'less you know what you want?" She hurried for the kitchen door at the rear with a load of plates. Some said Pearl had come from a house of ill repute in Dallas, but the lanky woman in her late thirties had become a fixture as the waitress and Donny's common-law wife.

"Steak, taters and bread," Tom said and Sam agreed, as they sat at a table in back of the empty room.

"You heard them, Donny. Better get to cooking. They look hungry enough to eat a bear," she said, fussing with her hair. "We had a big run at supper and I got behind. Coffee suit you two?"

"Fine. Any good gossip?"

"Yeah," she said, "you're selling out." With the coffeepot grasped with a pot holder, she poured Tom's cup and set apart the other one to fill Sam's. "And you're living with a widow woman who has four kids and you are going to drive a herd north come spring."

Tom looked pained. "Sam ain't living with no one but Billy and me in the bunk-house."

"She's out there, ain't she?"

"Yes," Sam said, "she's cooking and taking care of the house."

Standing above them, holding the granite pot, Pearl nodded. "You two always were gentlemen. I'll buy that story. But it sure put a burr under Miss Ralston's backside."

"Some folks can only think the worst," Tom said, spooning sugar in his cup of coffee.

Sam blew the vapors off the top of his cup. He wondered how Etta Faye was getting along with those kids.

Wearing an apron with the evidence of his labors on the front, Donny James greeted the men. "They tell me you're leaving," he said to Tom.

"Yeah, going to try some new country."

Donny dropped to a chair and rested his elbows on his legs. "Damn shame. I knew your paw. He came here with my dad and worked damn hard. No-accounts like them Wagners should have all been drowned when they was born."

"Tom's got to do what's best for his family," Sam said.

Donny closed his left eye and critically rolled a cigarette, then lit it with a kitchen match. He puffed on the flat cylinder in the corner of his near-white lips until smoke escaped from the corner. "If we had any real law here, you wouldn't have to move."

"Law can't prevent much in a county the size of this," Sam said.

"Aw, hell, that pretty boy we've got for a deputy sheriff couldn't prevent nothing. He shot at stray dogs with his pistol for thirty minutes yesterday, and never hit a blessed one. Ended up hiring the Sims boys to do it and buying the shells." A grin exposed the spot where Donny was missing two teeth. "They shot the asses off them curs and cleaned up the damn place. Must have got a dozen of them worthless whelps."

"Business doing good?" Sam asked.

"Aw, we get by."

"Getting by, he says. Why, I would, too, if I had the help he has." Pearl winked at the brothers as she slid in front of them plates heaped high with pan-fried potatoes, large steaks and golden biscuits. "That ought to fill you."

"It will," Tom said and Sam agreed.

"Hate to see you leave here." Donny rose with some stiffness. "I'd better go help her do the dishes or she'll gripe all day tomorrow about it. Good to see you. Good luck, Tom."

"Thanks. Shame we can't go swimming in the Frio like we did years ago."

"Catch catfish long as my arm." Donny

nodded, standing in the kitchen doorway. "Man, there used to be lots of fun. Now it's all work, no play."

"You get back here and play with these dishes," Pearl said from the kitchen. "I don't want to spend much longer in this joint."

"All right, all right."

"Burr under her butt," Tom mused aloud. "You and Etta Faye. Sam, one day you'll need to find another woman. That stiff-backed sister won't ever marry you."

"Hell, I never asked her to." Sam busied himself eating. Why in the hell was everyone so worried about him and Etta Faye?

The brothers left the Silver Moon full and satisfied. Pearl even gave Tom a kiss on the cheek. They were walking two abreast in the shadowy light on the empty boardwalk, heading for the Tiger Hole, heels clunking and spurs ringing, when a figure bolted out from beside the harness shop, holding a gun.

"You sonsabitches —"

Sam grasped the barrel of the pistol. He ripped it from the assailant's hand, then used the butt for a club and sent the man to his knees. Using the gun, Sam repeatedly battered the man until he was facedown on the boardwalk. Then Sam realized Tom had ahold of his arm and was trying to make him stop.

"He's down. Stop!"

"Which one is he?" Sam asked, out of breath and trying to recover his composure while Tom turned him over to see his identity.

"It's Tillman Wagner. He's still alive."

Sam looked off down the dark street at the outline of the false-front buildings against the inky sky. "What a damn shame."

"Where's Stuart?" Tom asked as he rose. "Guess we can drag Tillman over to the jail."

"How in the hell should I know where Stuart's at? Let Tillman lay there for the buzzards."

"Get his arm. We can deliver him," Tom said.

"I hate to waste my time on such garbage."

"Come on now."

They lugged Tillman's skinny figure over to the jail. Then they locked the moaning outlaw in an empty cell. Sam saw the face of the Wagner he'd brought in pressed to the bars, looking hard at their activities.

"What happened to Tillman?" Delmore asked.

"He ran into a brick wall," Sam said.

Then the brothers wrote Stuart a note and placed Tillman's pistol on top of the paper.

Make out a warrant for attempted murder by Tillman Wagner. Sam Ketchem.

"Let's go get a beer," Tom said.
"Or two," Sam added.

Chapter 16

Sam reflected on the circumstances that had forced his brother to sell his place and move away. He used his tongue to test the edge of a molar. He couldn't decide whether he should ride out to the ranch or spend another night in the livery bunkroom. Somehow Tom's leaving Sam was even tougher on Sam than Earl's funeral had been. Sam shoved his empty beer glass at Marty O'Brien and rose from the stool.

"The last two times I've been in town — no, make it three — I've had trouble with those damn Wagners," Sam said.

"Aye, laddie, them worthless devils will soon get tired of you beating them up," O'Brien said.

"Whatever I do only makes them meaner."

O'Brien served Sam a fresh glass of beer. "Doc Sharp said Tillman was beat senseless. Hell, he never had any sense to start with. What will Stuart do to him?"

"Turn him loose I guess. I swore out the damn warrant. I ain't got no sympathy for him. He tried to kill me and Tom and would have if I hadn't jerked the damn gun away from him."

"You were mad, too?"

"Yeah." He raised the mug to sip on the foam. "Damn mad. They killed Earl and Tillman tried to kill the two of us."

"Damn shame they're that stupid."

"It is."

Sam left the saloon an hour later and went to bed in the bunkhouse. Some freighters who were up early rummaging around woke him. He was in the Silver Moon before sunup eating breakfast.

"What about Tom's things?" Pearl asked him.

"Hack Smith's going to haul the furniture up to Buffalo Gap when Tom finds a place. Tom's got possession of his old place until January. I'm going to move his stock up there before Christmas."

"Guess he left you some work."

"I can handle it. I just hate him having to move off."

Pearl refilled Sam's coffee cup. "Bad business. You be careful. Did you move that woman in to make Etta Faye jealous?"

"I never had her in mind when I did it. Billy and I needed a cook, period."

Pearl shook her head in disbelief. "You could have fooled me." Then she laughed out loud and winked at him.

The rain was over when Sam rode home, and the country sparkled in the clear weather. It was a pleasant time of year, not too hot or cool. Sam would need a bunch of boys to gather Tom's cows. He'd better go find some.

First, he would collect Tom's horses and see how many more they'd need for the drive, besides his own, to come up with five horses to the man. That way they could rotate the animals and not have to haul grain for them. Sam would need a wagon anyway and someone to cook. It was off season, so he should be able to find help for the drive, including a swamper and a night-hawk for the horses. The trip would take three weeks up and a week to come home.

Sam arrived at the ranch and found Billy busy fixing a pen. "What's that for?"

"You have pigs coming, right?"

"Right."

"This is for them."

"Good. Start thinking of boys we can get to make the drive up to Buffalo Gap." He dismounted heavily and began to undo the girth.

"You had lunch?" Kathy called from the house's doorway.

"No."

"You two get cleaned up. This goat in the oven is about ready."

His saddle in the tack room and Sorely out in the lot, Sam and Billy headed for the house.

Billy was using his fingers to count. "Mayberry, Tom Jacks, Toddle, Cristian Webber and Pacho. That's five."

"Five what?" Kathy asked when they came in from washing up.

"Hands he thinks we can hire to drive Tom's cows up to Buffalo Gap next month I guess."

"Who's going to cook for you all?"

"We'll get someone in San Antone, I guess."

"What about me?" Hands on her shapely hips, Kathy looked at Sam with resolve in her blue eyes.

"Cows, pigs, kids in school and, oh, yes, the chickens I'm supposed to get."

"I guess," she sighed and brought the big roaster over to the table. Inside, with onions and potatoes floating around, was the cooked kid goat.

The two men set in to eat and Kathy filled their coffee cups. Then, after fetching a platter of fresh biscuits, she joined them. Sam decided she would spoil him and Billy to death.

"How's school?" Sam asked absently between bites.

"Fine. You must ask Rowann."

Sam frowned at their snickers.

"What's so funny?" He searched them for an answer.

Billy buried his head in his eating, shaking it in disbelief. Kathy simply smiled. "She can tell you."

"What about Sloan?"

"Oh, from what I can tell, he likes it."

"Good. Maybe they can teach him."

"It won't be easy, but Rowann has him writing his first name. You know that new colt?" Kathy asked.

"Yes."

"Sloan has him broke to lead."

"What? Why, he ain't a week old," Sam said.

"I never knew a thing," she said, "till Billy came in and told me."

"I saw him doing it. Couldn't believe my eyes," Billy said.

"I scolded Rowann for letting him do it. But she said, 'Mother, Sloan has a way with animals.' And he does."

"Just so he doesn't get hurt. Colts can kick and bite you in a second," Sam said.

"You will have to see him do it." She rose. "Save room for some apple pie."

"I'll be too full to work," Billy complained.

"When you two are eating some old man's cooking on your way to Buffalo Gap, you can recall it."

"Yes, ma'am. No pie for me this time," Sam said and wiped his mouth on his kerchief.

"Why not?" She had a disappointed look at him.

"I don't want to get too spoiled here before we go on that drive," he teased.

Billy broke up and slapped his legs in laughter.

"You'll see who gets the last laugh around here," she said and gathered up plates to wash them.

Sam put on his hat and stopped at the doorway. "Can you drive over and get the kids this afternoon? Bill and I need to round up some ponies."

"Sure. I want to meet their teacher anyway."

"I can hitch the horses for you —" Billy said.

"No, Billy. You two go on. I'm a teamster's widow, remember?"

"Sure?" Sam asked.

"Of course, I am."

Horses saddled, the two set out across

country. Sam knew an area the ponies liked to gather, and in an hour, the two men were on the rim rock. Setting their horses, they viewed the ponies in the timber and open glens.

"Let's get them up. There's a trap at Tom's place where we can keep them for a while," Sam said.

Billy and he swung their horses down a steep trail and hit the bottoms. Sam sent Rob flying off to the east. The horses fled southward but soon the ones Sam drove in joined the herd and they dropped to a trot.

A wise mare in the lead needed little coaxing to head for home. The men stood in the stirrups and let their mounts trot at the back end while Sam counted heads.

"Forty-two head. With mine, we should have enough."

"We taking mares?" Billy asked.

"I hate to, but they need to get up there. That stud can stay here for my part."

"Won't Tom want him?"

"What he wants and what he gets are two different things." Sam undid his lariat and pushed Rob around the outside of the herd. He had the loop ready at his side, but he didn't want the foxy stud to see it. Then he pressed Rob on.

At the last minute, the stud realized

Sam's intentions and broke to run, but too late. The hard-thrown noose sailed over his ears and head. When Rob set down, Sam swung the big horse sideways and shut him down. The stud rose on his hind feet in defiance and pawed the air. For a long second, Sam considered charging off and busting his butt good, but reconsidered.

He rode in close. The stud acted hostile to Rob, but it made Sam no difference. He popped the slack in the rope a few times to show the stud he meant business, and soon they were off after Billy and the rest of the herd.

The horses finally in the trap, Sam recalled the corn he had to sell for Tom when they rode by the yellowing stalks.

"You hire some boys ahead of time and we can gather that corn and yours too before we go to Buffalo Gap," Billy said as they went up the wagon tracks beside the rail fence and led the stud. Sam was taking him home so he didn't lead the mares astray.

"Good idea."

When the two men were home at last, the kids ran out to see what they had brought back with them.

"He yours?" Darby asked, climbing on the corral.

"Naw, he's Tom's stud," Billy said.

Sam noticed Rowann wrinkle her nose. No doubt she could smell the male's musk.

"He'd be a handful to ride," Hiram said, looking impressed as he grasped the tall post and squatted on the top rail.

"Don't get in the pen with him," Sam said. His arms full of saddle, he went for the tack room.

"I guess he's some horse. I like Rob better," Rowann said, accompanying him on the way.

"He's all right, but I agree. How's school?"

"Fine, we are really busy."

"You like Miss Ralston?"

"Oh, yes." She ducked under his arm. "She asked me again today how you were."

"You tell her I was all right?"

"I told her you were fine and she could come see for herself."

"Oh, why is that?"

"Well, she asked where you lived. I said in the bunkhouse, of course. We lived in the house. I think it upset her or she was worried for you. She asked me again, 'Doesn't he live in the house, too?'" Rowann shook her head. "I told her there simply wasn't room for you in that house. Besides, you have a nice new bunkhouse in the new barn."

"Glad you told her the truth." He patted her on the back. That should settle Etta Faye's concern about him living in sin. "Come on. We'd better go wash up."

From the corner of his eye, he saw Hiram on the top rail holding his finger to his mouth for them not to talk. Sam frowned. What was going on?

"Oh, no —" Rowann said in a soft gush.

The stud horse grunted with a squeal and stomped his front hoof. Through the corral rails, with dread stabbing his heart, Sam could see Sloan with his hand held out, advancing on eleven hundred pounds of impatient fury.

Chapter 17

The next five minutes, the onlookers stood frozen. There was no way Sam could climb that fence and snatch the boy away before the stallion could fatally strike or bite the small boy. The stud made suspicious grunts. Then he stomped his front foot like he was impatient with this small invader. With its nostrils quivering and wide-open, rollers came out of his nose. He peeled his lips back and showed his long, powerful teeth. His short ears rose in seconds, then fell back again. The horse could not decide if the boy was a threat.

At last, the small hand stroked the horse's nose, like that of any child who reached out and petted a newfound puppy. The stud made gurgling sounds in his throat. His head was so low that he blew small puffs of dust up from the dirt around the boy's feet.

Sloan began to pull the burrs from the stud's forelock. The horse nudged his head against Sloan's stomach. For a long moment, Sam wondered if he would butt the boy hard enough to hurt him. But the smile on Sloan's face told the tale. He was tickled by the horse's action.

They played a game, which was not what Sam expected from a pawing defiant stallion. Then Sloan patted him on the forehead and, as if satisfied, turned and headed for the fence. Sam and Billy rubbed their sweaty palms on their pants. Each step Sloan took drummed like thunder in Sam's chest. The stallion squealed and pawed the ground, but made no effort to pursue Sloan. The boy looked back at his new friend from the fence, then ducked underneath it. "Sloan, don't you ever do that again," Rowann cried. His bland face beaming, she shook him. "I know you can't hear me. Look at my face. I don't know what we'll do with you." She dragged him toward the house.

"Son of a bitch," Billy swore and sagged against the fence. "I knowed he was dead. How did he do that? He can't even talk."

"Oh, he can talk to them," Hiram said, coming off his perch. "I don't know how, but they savvy him. That new colt sure does, too."

"You're right," Billy agreed.

"Mexican woman said Sloan had God's gift." Darby simply shook his head. "No mean dog ever bit him when we lived in town. He could catch a loose burro anywhere."

"Boys, all of us have to watch him closer," Sam warned them. "That horse ain't no dog. One kick and your brother will be dead."

Chapter 18

When the word went out Sam needed trail-drive help, the hands began to drift in.

Lacy Mayberry rode in on a dish-faced bay horse with a long running walk that made Sam's mouth water when he watched. In bat-wing chaps, the teenager swung down and took off his new white hat.

"You Mr. Ketchem?"

With a nod, Sam hung his hammer on the fence, then stripped off his gloves and shook the teen's hand. "Billy and I are building a chicken coop today. Got word we have some pullets coming."

"Oh." The youth shifted his weight from one boot to the other and wet his lips.

"You do farm work?" Sam asked.

"I thought this was a trail-driving job?"

"We have about forty acres of corn to harvest first."

With a perplexed look on his face, Lacy slapped his hat back on and shook his head. "I can do that at home. Reason I rode over here was I wanted to get off the damn farm."

"Damn farm or not, we have to get some things done around here before we can make the first drive."

"First drive? There's more than one?"

"First drive is taking my brother's cows and calves to Buffalo Gap, Texas."

"That ain't fur."

"Take a month to get the cattle up there, then come back."

"When you leaving?"

"After we get the corn gathered."

Mayberry rubbed his nose. "You're saying I've got to pick corn to go along?"

"All pays the same: twenty and found."

Lacy nodded. "Where we going up north? I hear Kansas was closed to Texas cattle."

"It is. We're going up the eastern side of Colorado to a place called Ogallala, Nebraska."

Mayberry's green eyes looked confused. He wrung his hands and started to speak twice.

Sam folded his arms over his chest. "Lacy, you want a day or so to think on it? Come back then. We ain't filled up yet."

"What if you are and I can't get on?"

"Well, then I won't need your help."

Lacy wiped his palms on his chaps. "Can I leave Jeepers here while we're gone on the drive?" He indicated the bay horse.

"Sure. But why?"

"Aw, 'cause my stepdad would sell him if he got the chance."

"Meet Billy Ford. He's my foreman."

"Well, damn, Sam, I just got a promotion. Nice to meet you, Lacy. Put your stuff in the barn. We've got new bunks in there. Put Jeepers in the lot till we ride out."

"Thanks."

"Nice to have you on the crew. We're working on this coop. Come help."

"Sure and, Mr. Ketchem, sir, thanks."

"Sam'll do."

At lunchtime, Tommy Jacks Riddle rode up. He was in his early twenties, a tall drink of water with a shock of gold hair, a deep tan, and bowed legs. He wore a red silk bandana with a vest that lacked half the buttons and was frayed at the edges. On his head was a Mexican straw hat.

"Buenos Dartes," he said in a Texas drawl. "You Senor Ketchem?" He dismounted and made two giant steps to clasp Sam's hand in a rock-hard, callused one.

"Yes, I'm Sam."

"Tommy Jacks Riddle. Applying for work, sir." His deep-set blue eyes looked like polished coal.

"Let's go eat lunch and we can talk at the table."

"Nice place you got here," Tommy Jacks said, looking around.

"Thanks." Sam introduced him to the others.

Inside, Sam spoke to Kathy. "Two more strays to feed." He gave her their names.

"You'll have to build a bigger table next," she said, going by Sam for the rest of the food.

"Always something." Sam chuckled and drew a disapproving look from her.

"Mighty fine food," Tommy Jacks said as he prepared to fill his plate. "Where I've been, you get sand-filled tortillas and hot peppers twice a day."

"Where's that?" Billy asked.

"Well, me and a federale had us a misunderstanding in Chihuahua. Him being a colonel, I lost. So he told me I could stay in his hotel awhile."

"How did you get out?" Billy asked, swapping a gravy bowl for some green beans.

"Made me a new door and let myself out. That's why I got this straw sombrero. The wanted poster showed me wearing a big felt hat."

"Was there even a trial?" Kathy asked.

"Trial? I didn't have no money for a lawyer." Tommy Jacks shook his head with his lips pursed out.

"Don't pay to get in trouble in Mexico, does it?" Billy asked.

Tommy Jacks waved his fork at him. "You are exactly right, amigo. I ain't ever going back either."

After lunch, the four-man crew finished the chicken house and began planing boards for the new tables and benches. Sam cut them and Billy assembled them. With knives and rasps, Tommy Jacks and Lacy worked on the surfaces. Kathy went after the children with the light wagon.

Later that afternoon, Toddle Karnes came in on a thin pony. The gray about fell over when the teen dismounted. "You needing drovers, mister?"

"How far you rode that poor thing?" Sam asked.

"San Antone to here. Why?"

"He looks weak."

"That's what I told the guy that sold him to me. He said he was tough. Guess he is — made it here anyway."

"You been on a drive before?"

"No, sir, I've never been up here before either, but I can ride and rope and I ain't afraid of a grizzly bear."

"Might pay to be cautious around one though."

"What's that, sir?"

"Be careful around a grizzly bear. Sam's my name. That's Billy, the foreman, and you can introduce yourself to the others. We've got some work to finish. That bother you?"

"No, sir."

"Billy, show him the bunks. We pay twenty and found."

"That mean I'm hired?"

"You want the job, you are."

Toddle sailed his hat in the sky and whooped loud. Billy waved for Toddle to follow him.

"What do they call you?"

"Toddle Karnes."

Sam wrote his name in the tally book, wondering how the hell he had got that handle.

New tables and benches were moved inside in time for supper. Kathy's children stared wide-eyed at the strangers. And the new hands worked up their nerve and flirted with Kathy.

"You need to go and buy supplies tomorrow," she informed Sam at the end of the meal. "And I like the tables. They'll work fine."

"You wish to go?"

"No." She frowned at him, like he was

strange. "I have way too much to do."

"All right. I'll drive the kids to school and go from there."

"If you don't get back in time should I go after them?"

"No, I can make the trip easy."

"Unless you shoot another Wagner while in town."

She glanced over at him with a wary mother's face.

"I'm not looking for any trouble."

Her head back, she looked at the open rafters over head for heaven's help. "I keep thinking it will be you and not one of them the next time. I guess, like most men, including my departed husband, trouble simply finds you. Anyway, I'll make a list."

After conferring with Billy about the crew's plans for work that day, Sam loaded the kids in the wagon and headed for school. Rowann was standing behind him holding on to the iron rod over the seat.

"You better stop and see Miss Ralston today."

"Why's that?"

"Well, like I told you, she was sure worried about you getting enough sleep."

Sam flicked the team with the reins to keep them trotting and suppressed his amusement. "I'll do that when we get there, Rowann."

"I know she will be glad to see that you are fine, even though I told her so."

"Yes, ma'am," Sam said.

"Mr. Ketchem?"

"Yes."

"I sure wish you had a daughter so I had someone to play with." The wagon ran over a rut and made both of them sway. "Besides, taking care of so many boys is lots of work and now you've hired more."

"Big job, but I appreciate you."

"I know."

"How can you appreciate anyone who talks your ear off?" Hiram asked from his seat on the crate in back.

"Oh, don't be so harsh. She means well," Sam said.

"Maybe for you, not for me."

Sam drew up before the school. Kids came running to greet them and look hard at Sam.

"Can I go up the trail with you, Mr. Ketchem?" a young redheaded boy asked.

"No, you can't, Nealie. You're like me: too damn young," Hiram announced.

"Watch your tongue, Hiram McCarty," Rowann said with Sloan in her tow. "Mother hears you've been swearing, you'll get your mouth washed."

"And who's going to tell her?"

Hat in hand, Sam walked up the hillside, and Etta Faye came out on the porch in a starched dress. Her hair was different. It was down and cut shoulder length, instead of pinned up with flowing curls. Strange how she even looked the role of a schoolteacher.

"Samuel, how are you today?"

"Fine. Had a great night's sleep. Looks like you've settled in and they haven't treed you yet."

She found a small smile for him. "The session is not over yet."

"Oh, I think they like you well enough they won't burn you at the stake."

"That is a precious relief to know I will be spared burning."

He looked hard at her willowy figure standing above him and regretted stopping. Something about seeing her always made his stomach roil for a long time afterward. It struck him like that since his school days, she had bothered him.

"I better get to town. Anything you need from there?"

"I have some letters. Would you post them for me?"

"Sure." He waited while she went to get them.

"Here," she said, handing them to him and then giving him the money for postage.

"I could have paid that." He looked at the nickels and pennies in his palm.

"No, I am a workingwoman now. I can afford my own postage."

"I'm coming back this afternoon, so I'll bring your mail with me."

"Oh, yes, that would be so nice. Have a good day, Samuel." She began to ring the bell. "Time to start classes, children!"

He put on his hat and headed for the wagon, feeling not unlike a schoolboy who had been dismissed for the day.

Frio sat in the sleepy splendor of the yellowing cottonwood leaves. Driving up the main street, Sam decided there would be no glorious fall colors. The last dry spell had ruled that out. Frost, when it came, would paint a picture on the hill country. Driven about like lost souls, the leaves tumbled across the road, caught in pockets along the boardwalk and against buildings and on the porches of the various businesses.

Sam carried Kathy's list in his vest pocket and the letters Etta Faye had sent in the inside one. When he stopped at the post office, he drew out her letters and looked at them. One was addressed to Sears and Roebuck, Chicago, Illinois. That was a mail order, no doubt, from the catalogue. Another was going to the Texas State Education Department in Austin. One for Lucille Vandergrift, Mason, Texas. He didn't know her. The last one was addressed to Whit Stuart, Frio Springs, Texas. Hell, he damn sure wasn't delivering any of her love letters.

Still upset, he stormed into the small post office and saw Clem Sparks under his green celluloid visor behind the grilled window. "Howdy, Sam. Guess you want your mail."

"Yes, and I have a few letters to post."

"Hmm," Sparks said, looking them over after Sam handed them to him and also put the change for postage on the counter. "You could save yourself three cents carrying this one across the street."

"Mail them."

"Yes, siree, that's my job. Just the same, I wanted to save you some money. My daddy said a penny saved was soon a dollar earned."

"That's fine. I also need any mail for Kathy McCarty, Billy Ford, and Etta Faye Ralston?"

"How is that girl doing up there anyway? I never figured she'd take the job way up there. Could have taught here in town," he rambled on, going through letters in search of theirs. "Did that make sense to you?"

"Never thought about it."

"I always kinda figured you and her — well, guess it never worked out, huh?"

"What's that?"

Sparks glared over the top of his reading glasses at him. "Why everyone in town expected you and her to get hitched. Guess you bolted the notion, huh?"

"I never asked and she never did either."

"I see. Here's one for Mrs. McCarty. Got a card for Billy Ford. And two letters for Miss Ralston, one's from Troy Blackstone. Remember him?"

"No."

"He lived around here a few years back. Big lawyer in Austin now. They say he's rich."

Good, maybe he could afford her.

"Letter here for Tom — from his wife."

"She can tell him herself. He's on his way up there."

"Don't see nothing for you. Check back later. The stage comes at noon and there may be mail on it."

Sam put the mail in his vest and left the post office. Ten minutes with Clem was ten minutes too long for Sam. The postmaster knew everything about everybody, and what he didn't know he would ask until he found out.

Hazelgood's Store smelled of harness oil and spices. A bell rang over head when Sam went through the front door and closed it. He touched his hat for an older lady coming down the main aisle to go outside.

"Hmm," she snuffed. "I would think that Marshal Stuart would bar ruffians like you from the city."

Unsure what he'd done to the older woman, Sam removed his hat and turned sideways to see her better. "He would, ma'am, if he was worth his salt."

"Oh, when will civilization ever come to Texas?" she said with disapproval. She lifted her skirts and fled the store.

"Can't come soon enough for me," Gus said and laughed. "Mrs. Shoemacker thinks we should be like New York City out here."

"Being the ruffian I am, I need a list of things." Sam had to stop and laugh. "First Sparks got on me at the post office and now Mrs. Shoemacker. It ain't my day."

"We'll try not to aggravate you." Gus called to an assistant to fetch some supplies on the list. "Four cases peaches, four cases of canned tomatoes. You must be hiring."

"I am. Put the word out."

"Oh, yes, but why so early?"

"Taking Tom's cow herd to his new ranch next month, I hope."

"Where's that? Can you read this?" Gus handed the list to Sam.

"You know that red hat that's faded from the sun in the front window?"

"I'll make you a deal on that."

"Good. I'll take it. Got any high-heel button-up shoes?"

"What size?"

"Don't matter."

Gus looked around. "I have a pair that is two different sizes in the same box. Can't send them back either."

"Good. You have a fancy dress you've had in stock a long time?"

"Yeah."

"These are little girl things?"

"Yes, they will be. Sam, if you want to spend another dollar, I have a china tea set for a little girl I forgot all about."

"Put it in. Rowann will love it all. And I'll need three jackknives, too."

All Kathy had ordered — raisins, dried apples, a barrel of flour, lard, sugar, baking powder, canned peaches and tomatoes, potatoes, lemons, frijoles, chili, vanilla, cinnamon and salt — was secure in the wagon with the other things, when a Mexican youth came running as Sam took the seat.

"Senor. Senor."

"Yes?"

"I am a vaquero and out of work, senor."
Hatless, in his road-soiled shirt and pants,
he hardly looked the role.

'What is your name?"

"Pacho Morayes."

"Where is your sombrero, hombre?"

A pained look crossed his swarthy face. "I
sold my horse to feed my brothers and sisters. I traded my sombrero this morning for
some burritos."

Sam considered his words. "Does your
family live near here?"

Pacho broke into Spanish and motioned
with his arm that the casa was on the river.

"Stay here," Sam said and went back
inside the store. He stopped by the pile of
beans in hundred-pound sacks. "Put one
more on my bill," he said to Gus.

"Sure, but my boys can pack that."

"I've got it," Sam said, shouldering his
load. Outside, he put it in over the tailgate
and told the boy to get on the seat.

"Do I have the job, senor?"

Sam nodded. "First, we'll need to give
this sack of beans to your family so they
don't starve while you're gone."

"Really? Oh, thank you, senor."

"You can pay me out of your wages."

"Thank you, senor."

Sam shook his head. One more lost soul

to take with him up the road. He bet the boy was good horse man.

Hours later, Sam drove up to the Lone Deer schoolhouse and dismounted, stiff from the drive.

"I'll go get the kids," he said to Pacho.

Sam walked uphill to the front door, hearing voices reciting inside. He checked the sun and knew it was close to four. The picture of Pacho's short mother holding her hands out as if praying still upset him. They had no food, and all of them talking in Spanish at once was more than he could translate. So he had set out a case of tomatoes and peaches, too.

"Oh, Mr. Ketchem, you are back," Etta Faye said.

He stood in the doorway until she waved him inside. "We are through with this lesson. So you may take the McCarty children home with you."

"Thanks. I figured you'd had such a good day today and all these children were so nice to you. Well, in this poke is some candy for everyone. You dole it out please." He gave her the sack, then fumbled for the letters he carried inside his vest.

"Candy?" the children cried.

"Oh, how very nice of you, Samuel." Etta

212

Faye's face brightened. He swore if there had not been two dozen children there, she would have hugged him. "What should we say, class?"

"Thank you, Mr. Ketchem."

He nodded and followed the four McCarty children out.

"We ain't missing any candy, are we?" Hiram asked.

"No, sir. I have some for you, too."

"Good or I was going back."

"Who's with you?" Rowann asked, looking suspiciously at the Mexican boy on the seat.

"Pacho, another cowboy."

"He don't look like a cowboy to me," Hiram said.

"He is, trust me," Sam said, loading them in the wagon.

Kids with hard candy rushed out of the schoolhouse, shouting and waving.

"Rowann, give everyone, including Pacho, a piece of candy from that poke."

"Yes, sir, Mr. Sam."

He climbed on the seat, undid the reins, released the brake and looked at Etta Faye standing with her back to the door. With a nod of approval at him, she waved, then delicately put a piece of hard candy into her mouth.

She still made his guts roil.

Chapter 19

Corn, corn and more corn. To reach down, twist the shuck loose and then toss it with accuracy against the back board on the wagon so it didn't miss the bed took practice, and his crew had lots of that from sunup to sundown. The stack in the barn grew higher after backbreaking shoveling and hurrying back to the field so the crew never ran out of something to load.

Sam had hired Mike Quarry, the preacher's son — a round-bottomed boy who looked stout enough for the job. The first day, Sam kept Mike with him, and they broke a single tree pulling a load up the grade out of the second field. Sam held the horses from bolting and quickly he locked the brakes. Knowing the boy had been brought up in a strict Christian home, he asked him for a good cuss word to use.

"Oh, Mr. Ketchem, I never use them," Mike said.

"Good," Sam said, about to spout some of his own, fighting the left-side horse to get the broken single tree off his hind legs.

"Whoa. Whoa."

Billy drove up. "Hard on equipment, aren't you?"

"Hard enough, thanks. Hey, take Mike along with you. He can pick corn now he knows all the things we do."

"Thanks, Mr. Ketchem." Mike climbed down and went over to Billy's rig.

"You need help?" Billy asked when Sam had an argument with one of the horses, clapping him hard on the rump with his hand to make him stand still for the recoupling process.

"I got her." Sam straightened. Getting in and out of wagons was not as easy as it had been when he was a young boy. He was grateful he had a good size crew to help. In their youth, it would have taken him, Tom and Earl two months to gather in the patches of corn on his place alone. They'd be done if the weather held before Thanksgiving.

After the noon meal, Sam could see the Quarry boy straightening and holding his hip, instead of firing shucks at the wagon. Sam figured the boy would be sore for a day or two. Finally, when Sam came back from the barn, Mike walked over.

"Mr. Ketchem, I think I'm going to quit," Mike said.

"Something wrong, Mike? First day or two in the field is always the hardest."

"Naw, I'm quitting."

"Well, if you'll wait till I go back to the house, I'll get you some money."

"Mr. Ketchem, you don't owe me one damn dime." He then stepped over downed stalks and found his way across the field. Never looking back, he was headed for home.

At supper, Billy, still amused by the tale, went over it for the boys. "So he said he never cussed?"

"That's what he said," Sam said.

"What did he tell you when you offered to pay him for his work?"

" 'You don't owe me one damn thin dime.' "

"Guess he found that bad word, huh?" Tommy Jacks asked.

"I've heard worse," Sam said.

"Who wants some apple pie?" Kathy asked, holding one up for them to see and smell.

"All of us," Billy said.

"Oh, Sam," Kathy called later, as he started out after the crew. "Jason Burns wants two wagon loads of corn. He stopped by today and said the Phillipses want some, too."

"They can have Tom's corn. I need to sell it for him. Start a list so we don't sell more than we have."

"I will. Sam" — she crossed the kitchen — "I've wanted to thank you for what you did for Rowann. She tries so hard to help Sloan and mind him, and she hardly has a life of her own."

"Oh yeah, I've been to two tea parties already. You've done a wonderful job getting meals and everything for these boys."

"They're a nice crew."

"Get this corn in, we'll see."

"You found a chuck wagon yet?"

"May have to go to San Antone to find a good one."

She rubbed her hands together and wet her lips. "I know one thing. I'm sure proud you needed a cook."

"So am I, Kathy. So am I."

The barn was full of corn and most of Tom's sold. Sam hired a quiet, bowlegged boy from Jackson named Thirston Cones. Riding a mule and carrying a guitar slung over his back, Jammer McCoy arrived at his front door.

"You hiring, mister?"

"I was yesterday," Sam said.

He slumped down in the saddle. "Lordy, mister, I was born a day late and been ten dollars behind all my life."

"You play that string box?" Sam asked, indicating the instrument.

"I sure do. Thought you'd never ask me." He swung the guitar around, tested the tune and broke into playing.

" 'Down in Tennessee where the cotton grows —' " Jammer plunked away, singing four verses to his song.

"Charles Goodnight, who was one of the early ones in this cattle-trail business, hired a boy one time who could hardly ride a horse, but he played a mean fiddle. Jammer, you're on."

"Thank you, sir." He whipped off his hat and bowed to Sam. "You won't regret it, sir."

"I pray not." Sam looked at the high clouds. There might be frost over night — nothing like a frigid daybreak to saddle up a spooked horse and go to roundup.

Chapter 20

Bawling cows and calves rang in his ears. Sam set a dun horse called Soapy off the ridge toward the bottoms. He could see the yellow canvas top of the chuck wagon, which to his relief had made it. Joaquin Sanchos, the cook he'd hired in New Braunfels, was a hard-faced whiskey drinker who claimed he'd been on six drives, including one for Major Strom, whom Sam knew. But Sanchos said he never drank on the trail.

Without time for much more searching, Sam had hired Joaquin at fifty a month and sent him, a used wagon and four spooked mules westward to meet him in three days at Lost Horse Creek. The supplies Sanchos needed to pick up would be waiting at Hazelgood's.

The smoke from the trail branding was sharp in the air. An acrid smell of scorched hair filled every worker's nose. A large oak fire ring in between the two squeeze chutes had branding irons heating. Cows and calves were being stamped with a sideways

S for the drive. Animals bawled as the red-hot iron was applied to them. Then they struggled to be released before others ran in for the same treatment.

Billy pulled off his heavy gloves and shouted above the loud noises of cattle and men, "We'll be through branding by evening. That Mexican going to cook tonight?"

"I'll tell Sanchos to get something ready."

"You know, boss man, we're pretty spoiled by Mrs. McCarty's cooking."

"She can't go with us. Kids in school. All that livestock at home. Besides, it's no place for a lady out there."

Billy never said a word. He just stared at Sam. He fished in his pocket and then handed Sam an envelope. "Rowann sent this along for you. It's from the teacher."

"Thanks. Go over and meet the cook. Tell him I said — tell him yourself to have supper ready. You're foreman."

Billy stepped in the stirrups of his saddle. "I met him once today and wasn't impressed."

Sam, busy opening the envelope, never looked up. "Next time you can hire the sumbitch. Damn hard to find one. I looked for four days." He shook open the paper and could see Etta Faye's fine handwriting.

Dear Samuel,

Why are we always so brusque with each other? We can't wait to see each other, and then we snarl like angry dogs fighting over a pile of bones when we finally are together. What is this love-hate relationship we seem to drown ourselves in? There are nights I could scream at the moon and stars wondering if you are safe or dead. Oh, yes, Mrs. McCarty's children tell me that you are working hard. They said they weren't leaving your place. Before you go on the drive, please come by either the school or the Fanchers' place and see me.

Sincerely yours,
Etta Faye Ralston

Sam closed his eyelids tight, but he couldn't drown out the cattle and shouting around him. The wind had shifted while he stood there, and his eyes were full of smoke. He blew his nose in his handkerchief. He stepped in the stirrup and swung a chap-clad leg over Soapy's rump, then headed him for the Lone Deer schoolhouse.

Chapter 21

Sam hitched Soapy to the rack out in front of the schoolhouse at the base of the slope and used his hat to brush off some road flour. He had no time for a bath or cleaning up with all he had left to do. Etta Faye would have to take him like he was. Besides, she had written he should drop by.

"Oh, Samuel, you did get my message," Etta Faye said from the doorway. Then she turned and told her pupils to behave and do their lessons.

He turned the hat in his hands. "I have lots to do. We leave in the morning with Tom's cattle."

"Tom here yet?"

"No. I guess he'll find us on the road."

"He's put all this work off on you?" She looked upset over the matter.

"I guess. I'm the oldest. Maw said the oldest do the work."

"You are" — she raised her chin — "generous to a degree that exceeds one's own welfare."

"I see. Well, I'm not sure why you wrote

to me. I thought you mailed Stuart a letter saying you would marry him."

"Marry him?" She looked aghast. "I severed my relations with him in that letter. I've come to realize he was not what I wanted in a man."

"Shame I didn't deliver it myself," Sam mumbled.

"What?"

He shook his head. "Nothing. I'll be back in a month, before Christmas, and we can talk more then."

She nodded and looked sad. He couldn't stand it any longer. His spurs jingling, he ran up the four steps, took her in his arms and kissed her. When he moved a little back from his deed, her eyes flew open and her jaw dropped.

"Samuel," she gasped. "You be careful." She closed her eyes as if the cool afternoon wind was telling her something.

"I will." He clunked down the stairs on his bootheels and turned back to see her in the doorway. This time she waved at him. He grinned big as any fool could, then spurred Soapy for the ranch.

Kathy came to meet him at the corral when he dismounted. "You have any sleep the past few days?"

"No, ma'am, not much."

"And you're leaving tomorrow. Billy sent word that the cook arrived."

"A day late."

"I guess the boys will eat down there then tonight?" she asked.

"Yes. Sorry I'm so late getting here." He set the saddle on its horn and went to the horse tank to soak his face. A stallion in the pen acted spooked, grunted and ran around the pen at the sight of him. His actions drew a scowl from Sam, who considered the stud worthless. On the far side of the pen, the big horse threw his head back, snorted and pawed the dust.

"What about him?" Kathy asked.

"I can't take him up there with the cattle. We'll have enough trouble taking a mixed herd." He swept off his hat and dunked his face in the water.

Her hand on his shoulder, she drew him up. "For goodness' sake, come to the house. I'll heat you some water and you can clean up. You're a mess, and dunking in this tank isn't going to help."

Cool water ran down his face, shirt and vest. He rubbed his week-old whiskers and laughed. "I accept your hospitality."

Later, bathed, shaved, dressed in clean clothes and fully fed, he sat in the kitchen drinking fresh coffee and eating a second piece of apple pie.

"I have all the people on this list who owe Tom for the corn that you delivered to them," she said, handing Sam a piece of paper.

"Good. They'll be by to pay sooner or later."

"Fine. What else?"

"If anyone else comes by about adding their cattle to the drive to Ogallala next spring, tell them I'm near full up, but get their names, in case someone cancels."

"I'll do that."

"I bought two fat hogs from Schlousinger for us to butcher when I get back. He's trading me them for some corn. He may bring them over and get his corn."

"Darby and I can handle that."

"Good boy, but everyone pulls their load around here. I don't know what I'd do without all of you."

"I need to run and get the kids. I'm sure they've started for home, but that's a long walk." She stood up, then reached across the table and kissed Sam on the cheek. "You're the nicest guy, Sam Ketchem. We'll have supper at six. Will you eat with us?"

"I guess."

"Go take a nap. You look too tired to start on such a long journey."

"Fine, I will," he said and followed her out.

Kathy led the harnessed team out of the barn and he hitched them for her. Minutes later, she had the horses trotting off to get the kids, and he went to get some sleep, but restful slumber never came to him. Stampedes trampled through his brain. Bad hailstorms beat down on him. Graves dug in the prairie ground haunted him. The ring of a shovel pounding down a handmade cross echoed through his nightmares. When Kathy awoke him with a shake, he bolted up in the bed.

"Sorry to jolt you so, but I have supper ready."

He swallowed hard, feeling depleted and shaken by his dreams. Were they the future or was he only borrowing more trouble?

"I'll be there soon as I get my boots on."

"You all right?"

"Sure, I'm fine." He bent over and pulled on his right boot. He watched Kathy reluctantly go to the doorway. He waved her on to assure her that he was fine.

The children asked lots of questions during the meal.

"Where do you get water to drink?" Darby asked.

"Strain it from a river, a creek or lake, if you can find one," Sam answered.

"Ooh," Rowann said, "can you drink it?"

"When it's all you've got, you drink it."

"I don't think I'd like it on a cattle drive," Rowann said.

"I would," Darby said about to fork in a bite of food. "What're you looking at me for, Rowann? Beats the heck out of milking cows and slopping pigs."

"Yes, Darby," Sam said. "But night herding and little sleep can get old, too. Rain, even sleet, without a roof over you can get real old in a hurry."

"I'd go along in a minute if you needed me," Darby said.

"There will be time for all of that when you're older," his mother said crossly.

"How old were you when you went up the trail, Mr. Sam?" Darby asked.

"Sixteen," he lied.

"Been lots of guys fourteen went up there."

"Darby, let Sam eat, please," Kathy said. "He has enough to fret over without all your talk about something that isn't going to happen."

"Yes, ma'am."

"Several of the neighbors will be coming by to check on you," Sam said, taking a second helping of potatoes and creamy gravy. Sanchos came to his mind. He hoped the man was as good as he said he was. Cowboys traveled best on full bellies. And his crew was spoiled by Kathy's cooking.

After supper, Sam told Kathy he was going to turn in. He asked her to get him up by three so he could be over there when the crew got up for breakfast in camp.

"I'll set the alarm clock."

He told the children good night, then went to the bunkhouse. As Sam walked by the corral, the stallion blew hard and squealed at him. Then he snorted out of his nose like Sam was a spook. For the moment, Sam thought nothing of the horse's behavior.

But hours later, Sam sat up in bed, wondering what that worthless stud horse had been all upset about. He could hear the horse galloping around. Something was amiss. Sam reached for his Colt in the dark room. A sliver of moonlight shone in the open double doors when he slipped into the alleyway. Dressed in his underwear, he walked in the chill of the night to the barn door, listening to the rhythmic drum of hooves.

His shoulder close to the board and bats of the siding, he worked around to the

228

corner until he could see the horse going in a short lope around the pen. Something — no, someone, was riding him. Sam's heart stopped.

Sloan, in his nightshirt, sat on the stud's back, holding a hank of his mane. The boy was straight-spined as some army cavalry sergeant.

Sam stood back and out of view. It wouldn't do to try to get the boy off. Anything he might try would only get the boy hurt. This drama had to play itself out. All Sam could do was observe.

His heart in his throat, he watched the boy bring the big horse to a halt, then jerk on its mane until the stallion was beside the fence. Sloan reached out and looped his arm around the tall corral post; then he quickly climbed onto the fence. After a pat on the forehead from the boy, the stallion gave a deep snort and bobbed his head.

Like a squirrel, Sloan eased down the rails. Standing on the ground in his knee-length nightshirt, he peered around to be sure the coast was clear. Then his bare feet churned up dust as he ran and disappeared inside the house.

How long had Sloan been riding the horse? Sam wondered, as he headed back to his bunk.

Chapter 22

Lacy Mayberry and Tommy Jacks were the point riders. Sam put Pacho, who he figured was the toughest roper in the outfit, on the right flank because an occasional critter needed to be roped and busted. By hook or crook they were going up the trail. Jammer on the left. Thirston and Webber on the drag. Toddle was the wrangler in charge of the horses and helping Sancho.

"You boys on drag will have your hands full today," Sam warned them in the pre-dawn coolness. "Some of these foxy old cows will want to break out for their old country. They'll lay back and try you all day. In fact we may have several days of that."

"I'll be back here, too, to help you boys," Billy said.

"Everyone shake hands," Sam said. "It's one for all and all for one in this business."

"Never heard it said that way before, boss, but that fits it," Tommy Jacks said.

"Something a schoolteacher said to me once," Sam said. "And please, guys, be careful. Let's pray.

"Dear Lord, guide and protect us on our way. We're grateful for your guidance, Father. Help these boys as they ride to make a safe journey and return home in one piece. Amen."

"Amen." They all nodded and went for their horses.

Riders in place, Sam swung his hat over his head. "Move 'em out, boys!" Something grabbed Sam's guts and squeezed. He hoped it was Providence and not the devil, who had ridden with him last time.

Bawling so loud they hurt Sam's ears, the herd began to line out. The lead bell steer, a tall red roan with antlers six feet wide, headed north. The cows began to fall in, as the riders coaxed them with shouts and Pacho's bullwhip cracking the air. Two hundred twelve cows, a hundred seventy big calves, a hundred-forty yearlings and a hundred-twenty two year olds, plus fifteen bulls from mature to long yearlings — Tom's herd was bound for Buffalo Gap.

Despite the coolness, the horses quickly worked up a sweat. The contrary nature of the cattle on the first day kept the riders pressing hard to force them to stay in the herd. One mostly longhorn cow and her three-hundred-pound red roan calf threw their tails over their backs and lit a shuck. Jammer and Billy, swinging lariats, soon disappeared in the brush after them.

The cowboys rode back empty-handed in a short while, and Billy turned up his hands to show that they had gotten away. Fighting with another crazy cow that wanted to get away from the pack, Sam nodded.

By midafternoon, they let the cattle spread out and graze for a couple of hours. Sam felt grateful for the fall rain, which provided some feed. He hoped that Sancho had made camp on Woolie Creek all right. It would be a good place to bed the herd down.

With no noon meal, the drovers would be starved. A good cook would have sent along bread or fried pies for them to snack on. Sam had to talk to the man about that when the boys got to camp. The cattle were hard enough to line out without eating all day.

Sam heard the two bulls bellowing. A big fight was about to break out, and that could send the cattle running. He rose and Pacho headed for his horse.

"I will separate them, patron."

The Mexican boy on a fast bay loped off to handle the bull matter. Sam decided to trail along to be sure Pacho's plan worked. He caught Soapy and set spurs to him. He could see from the dust being pawed up that two or more studs at war were in the center of the herd. He short loped into sight and reined Soapy up.

A thick-necked Hereford bull coated in dust over his hump charged at the challenger, a short-horned red bull of Durham ancestry who held his ground despite the fast rushes by the bigger bull. Pacho's whip began to crack. Many of the onlookers moved aside and some younger bulls ran off. When the two challengers acted unfazed by his whip, Pacho looked back at Sam.

"Bust 'em. They need to be separated. Let them fight another day."

Pacho nodded and drove the cowpony in close. The Hereford bull ran sideways, but showed no intention of leaving the scene. Then the sharpness of the whip changed his mind, and he soon fled with Pacho on his heels.

His lariat unstrung, Sam rode in, standing in the stirrups and sent the Durham bull the other way. After receiving a few welts on his back from the hemp rope, he doubled his speed to get away. Sam reined Soapy down to a trot. The cattle looked unvexed by the whole thing and chewed grass in reply.

A day or so and the drive would be well on

its way. Sam rested on his horse at the edge of the herd. Where was Tom? What was keeping him? Then he remembered Etta Faye waving from the schoolhouse doorway, and he felt warm despite the sharp edge to the wind. It would be a cold night to sleep on the ground.

They found Sancho on the banks of Woolie Creek. After watering the cattle, the men bedded them down as the sun spread a bloody light over the open country around them.

Billy drew up the night guard. Sancho acted like a bulldog with sore teeth. He grunted and grumbled as the cowboys came to fill their plates in the twilight. Sam came last and frowned when he fetched a cold biscuit left over from that morning out of the tub. He ladled up the beans on his tin plate and looked for anything else to eat in the growing darkness.

Seated on the ground, he knew the hands were awfully quiet. He shrugged it off. They were all tired from the first day. Then he took his first bite of the cold beans. He spat them out.

"Gawdamn it, Sancho, did you even cook these fart berries?" Snickers rose up from the cowboys sitting around in the darkness.

"Sure, why?"

"You try to eat them?"

"They wasn't bad."

"The hell they aren't. Jammer, you and Pacho go out in that herd and find a fat calf. Don't let him bawl. We're having beef for breakfast and supper tomorrow. And, Sancho, you can cook it decent or you can walk back to San Antone on foot. You hear me?"

"Yeah, but —"

"That's your worry. You can't cook beans and make fresh biscuits for the meals, load up now."

"All right, but it's dark. How in the hell am I going to see to butcher?"

"Use some one of those coal-oil lamps in the wagon."

"I guess they work." Sancho scratched his head.

"They'll work. We'll all pitch in and have the calf skinned and butchered in thirty minutes."

"Right," Webber said, taking a round wet stone to his knife. "Thanks, boss."

"And another thing. When this crew rides out, they need some food to go in their saddlebags."

"Hell, they're babies?"

Sam had to hold back his temper. His first thought was to take his fists to the man.

"No, but they're working damn hard in the saddle and need the food."

"All right, but I never —"

"This is my outfit. We do things my way. Is that clear?"

"Clear enough — bunch of snotty-nosed kids is all you've got."

Sam held up his hand to stop Tommy Jacks from plowing past him. "Easy, boys. We've all got a job to do. We will get it right."

Dawn brought a crystal glaze to the land. Sam's gritty eyes fought the darkness; his cook had used the lanterns to cook by. They hung under the fly, where he worked. Maybe the cook would serve decent food. A shiver went up Sam's spine — it was freezing cold. He wrapped up in a blanket and, full of dread, went to see the cook.

At breakfast, Sam named Billy Ford chief scout. Sam wanted to be close to the herd until they were lined out better. Shaping a herd usually took several days, and mixed herds were even worse than all steers. Cows and calves were hard to manage when some stubborn old cow came back through the entire herd on the prod, hooking and fighting to find her offspring.

"I think there will be plenty of grass up on

236

the Cedars," Billy said, sitting on his haunches under a wool blanket and eating his beef and beans.

"Find us a place, get Sancho some water and wood if you can and we'll be along. Meet the herd about midafternoon." The food on Sam's plate was palatable — not wonderful, but probably as good as it would get.

The cattle were on the move at daybreak. With ten-hour days, light for travel was precious, and not much was left for grazing time. It would make the drive a long one. The only good thing would be the river crossings. The rivers should be shallow at that time of year. But a winter storm could change everything.

Sunup didn't warm the air very fast. The cowboys' horses had bucking fits, and Tommy Jacks had to catch and rope Webber's pony after he unceremoniously dumped his rider. Brushing off his pants and coming to his horse, Webber laughed. "Least he didn't throw me in a patch of pear cactus."

"He's saving that," Billy said and rode out on his mission.

"Sure beats shucking corn," Lacy shouted. Standing in the stirrups, he rode at a trot with the others toward the herd.

They'd all survived the first night with little sleep, but they had not been challenged yet. Stampedes, storms, even rustlers could all be up the trail as they went. One thing Sam felt confident about was he would know when this was over if his outfit had the salt to make it to Ogallala.

The men headed the herd up and moved it out. With wing riders in place, the cattle acted better. In another day, they would be in unfamiliar country and the cattle wouldn't feel so anxious to "bust out" — especially the foxy old brush cows who'd learned how to hide back in the live oaks and let roundup crews ride by them in the past. There were plenty of them in this long river of horns and continuous bawling.

At midday, Sam sat on a high point and could see Billy coming back. A wave of relief settled in. Billy must have Sancho set and a place for them to light. Sam booted his horse off the hillside to meet his man.

"How is it up there?"

"Fine, 'cept the guy wants ten cents a head for grazing."

"What?"

"Some guy named Schade, says he owns all that country."

"Is it fenced?"

"No."

238

"No way I can pay ten cents a head every night for cattle to graze from here to Buffalo Gap. Does he have any backing?"

"I don't know. He was by his self. He's kind of a tough-acting guy in his forties, I'd say." Billy looked concerned.

"Guess we'll meet this Schade later." Sam looked toward the horizon over the rolling cedar-clad hills. He didn't need any trouble, but he wasn't standing for "fee grazing" on unfenced range when he was only passing through with a herd.

By late afternoon he would know all about this man and his demands. "You picked out Sancho a place and all?"

"Right and I told him where it was."

"Good. He ain't going to make a fancy cook, but he will have to do until we get through this drive."

"Next spring?"

Sam smiled. "We definitely ain't taking him to Nebraska, but don't let him know that or the food might get even worse."

"I'll go spell the boys some. See you this afternoon. We're headed pretty well right for that place."

"Keep us on course."

"I will. I told Tommy Jacks about it coming in."

Later, they watered the herd strung out

on a creek, then drove them up on the flat and let them graze.

A rider came burning the ground and reined up a ewe-necked Morgan that looked like a stud. Unshaven, the man had eyes like coal chunks, and he spat tobacco to the side, trying to settle his hard-breathing horse.

"You Sam Ketchem?" he demanded.

"You must be Schade?"

"Yeah, and I own all this land." Schade made a sweep with his hand in a wide arc.

"Nice spread."

"I want ten cents a head for you trespassing on my land."

"Guess you're new to Texas."

"What the hell does that mean?"

"It means you don't have this land fenced, and I can drive my herd through here and not damage you."

"You a damn lawyer?"

Sam shook his head. "In the morning we'll be up the road. You can sue me, but it won't do any damn good. No Texas court will give you any relief — and if you reach for that gun butt, consider yourself dead. Am I clear?"

"You think you can come in here —"

Sam shook his head warily. "It ain't worth dying over, mister."

"I can stampede them cattle off my place."

"You better have a box and a new suit picked out if you try it."

"You ain't getting by with this." Schade spat again.

"Mister, tomorrow I'll be gone. Ride out of here and forget this ever happened."

"I won't, by Gawd!" Schade went to whipping his horse around and left in a huff.

For a long moment, Sam watched the man's back as he rode away. Fortified with liquor, Schade could be a real problem. Sam would be wise to keep an eye out for the next few days.

"He back down?" Billy asked, riding over to join Sam.

"For now," Sam said. "Keep your eye peeled for him. He said he might stampede the herd."

Billy shook his head in disgust. "You figure he owns all this country?"

"Might, might not. Be a good bluff any way to collect ten cents per head per night."

"I can't count that high."

"I couldn't pay it either."

"I figured your brother would have caught up with us by now."

Sam looked around. "So did I."

They moved on without a stampede, the herd becoming more of one flow rather than individuals jammed into a group. Still, settling the order caused head butting and fights between the cows. Some had so much gusto that they almost broke up the herd's northward motion. Cowboys waded in on horse back with lariats and bullwhips to separate the lusty fighters. Their mouths open, bawling mad, the cattle hooked and fought to see who was over the other in social standings.

The Colorado River proved shallow; the water came up only to their horses' knees. Sam wondered how the Brazos would be. Forced to detour west to avoid farms, they camped for the night on a muddy creek stirred up by the herd getting water.

Sancho burned the beans and the smoked ham bought from a local farmer. Out of words for the man's lack of concern for his job, Sam forced the food down, knowing he would need his strength for the long hours in the saddle the next day.

"This the right place or am I lost?" Tom shouted out in the night.

"Get in here, you devil. Where've you been?" Sam was grateful for some good news.

"Hell, bro, you know everything takes time." Tom dropped out of the saddle, and they hugged and clapped each other on the back.

"How's Karen and the kids?"

"Fine. They're at her folks', and they're ready to move out there."

"Good. Get some food. We can talk later."

"Man, you guys've been making tracks with this bunch."

"We've tried," Sam said, grateful to at last have his brother along.

With food on a plate, and seated on the ground next to Sam, Tom explained about all the trouble he'd run into while buying the new place.

"Get most of the cattle?" Tom asked between bites. Then he stopped and looked around with a frown. "This sure ain't good grub."

Sam shook his head. "You want to cook?"

"No."

"Neither do none of them. So shut up and eat it."

"Boy, I savvy."

"We got most of your cows and calves. We lost a few but here's the tally book." He handed the small pad to Tom.

"No, you keep it. I trust you."

"Good since I been taking care of your business for two months now, it seems."

"Didn't say I didn't appreciate it. Oh, yeah, I've got two letters for you from the women in your life."

"Women in my life?"

"Yes, from Etta Faye Ralston and that nice Kathy McCarty."

Both envelopes in his hand, Sam headed for some lantern light to read them.

Dear Samuel,

I hope this letter finds you in good health. I am concerned about your welfare. Sleeping on the ground during the recent frosts we experienced down here must be hard. Exposure to such conditions is not good for one's body.

School proceeds well. I know it runs smoother than you ever expected it to go for me. We will have the final program the night before Christmas Eve. I do hope you will be able to attend it. That will, of course, end my contract, too, and the school session. I have not heard any word about the school board's plans for a winter session or if they would hire me for that term.

Rowann told me when I wrote you to tell you that Sloan can write his whole name. A wonderful achievement for someone afflicted like he is. He has been aided by the efforts of his determined sister.

*I shall pray each day for your safe
return. God bless you, Samuel,
    Etta Faye Ralston*

He opened the second letter. It was in
Kathy's daughter's handwriting.

*Dear Sam,
    I collected the money for Tom's corn,
except from Joe Leonard. The pigs the
German brought are fat and will be
fatter by the time you return to butcher
them. No problems here. Jason said
that the Wagners are going to be ready
for your return, they claim. So be
careful when you come home. Sloan
wrote his name this week. We had a
party. Darby is checking on the cattle,
and they all seem fine. See you about
Christmas, I hope.
    Kathy*

"Good news or bad news?"
Sam tucked the two letters away inside his
vest and shook his head at his brother.
"Good news. My fighting roosters all sur-
vived the frost."
"You got fighting roosters, boss?" Tommy
Jacks asked, coming by to dunk his plate and
silver ware in the tub of soapy water.

"No, just joking. Brother, we better talk about the directions we need to take to get to your new place."

"Why, you're doing fine," Tom said.

Sam shook his head. Like he thought would happen, Tom was going to let him do all the work. That's how it had been all their lives — why change now on a cattle drive?

Chapter 23

Billy was on the scout for the night camp. Tom was there to ramrod the drive for the day, though the boys knew how. Sam decided to drop over to Lynnville and pick up a few things for grouchy Sancho, and he'd be happy to get the never-ceasing bawl of cattle out of his head for a few hours.

According to a handwritten sign and arrow nailed to a tree, the town was five miles to the east. Sam had been through there before and knew that there were several stores and saloons in the village, so he set out on Rob for some shopping and relaxation from the pressures of the drive.

He found the place by midmorning — a cluster of buildings and stores on a small creek. Several women in proper attire went about on the boardwalks, visiting and gossiping as they made their purchases in the various businesses. On the opposite side of the street from where Sam stood, two horses waited at a hitch rack in front of the two-story Gunderson's Saloon. A dove waved to him from the second-story window and he nodded, uninterested in her wants and wishes.

He stopped Rob before Gurley's Store and dismounted heavily. With care, he pried the wet latigos apart and loosened the girth. Two men in dusters rode up and dismounted stiffly across the street. Their keen interest in something on Sam's side of the street forced Sam to look to the right of the store, where he spied the First National Bank of Lynnville.

The notion struck Sam hard that the men were bank robbers. He needed to do something and quick. He entered the store. Once inside, he stopped two ladies. "Don't go out there."

"What's wrong?" one lady asked.

"Bank robbers, I think. Give me that shotgun and a box of shells," he said to the clerk.

"How can you stop them?" The clerk handed over the scattergun, then ducked down for a box of shells, which he slammed on the counter.

"There's more of them now." One of the ladies pointed over the stack of brogans. Sam's heart quickened as he saw through the front window three more riders in dusters rein up outside.

"I'll help," a fresh-faced boy in an apron

said, poking brass cartridges in a Winchester's receiver.

"Be careful who you shoot," Sam warned him, headed for the front door.

"Where's Marshal Greiby?" the storekeeper asked.

"Hold up there!" came an order from outside.

"That's him," the woman, who was now on her hands and knees, said as Sam rushed by her for the doorway, jamming shells in the two chambers. The scattergun snapped shut with a tight newness when he came out the door and heard a hail of gunshots aimed away from him.

"Drop 'em!" Sam shouted.

A rider on a dun whirled with his smoking pistol, but buckshot from Sam's left barrel took him off his horse. A second rider tried to shoot at Sam, but he, too, met his fate when Sam shot him. Sam broke the gun open and reloaded. The fresh-faced boy was on his knees, using the doorframe for a brace. He fired his Winchester at two men across the street. Beside him, the store's left-hand front window crashed into pieces. Sam raised the shotgun, but too late, a third rider was already boiling out of town.

Sam, the storekeeper and the boy rushed to where they saw Marshal Greiby lying on his back in the street. The young woman from the store, her skirts in her hands, hurried to keep up, moaning, "Dear God, make him be all right."

The lawman forced a smile for her. He had plenty of blood on his white shirt. "I'm fine, Audrey darling."

"We better get him to Doc's," the storekeeper said.

Sam agreed and raised the man by grabbing under his arms. The storekeeper and the boy took the lawman's feet.

"Oh, be careful," Audrey said and trailed along.

"Who stopped the robbery?" asked a red-faced man in a fine suit.

"The boy and this lawman did," Sam said.

"Ain't so. This man saw it minutes before it went down," the storekeeper said, indicating Sam.

The boy agreed. "He saved us all."

"I owe all of you," the red-faced man said.

"Biggest ones are this marshal and that large plate-glass window," Sam said as they hurried along.

"Doc's home. Good," the storekeeper said, directing Sam to a small white house.

"Bring him in," the physician said. "Are there any more?"

"All outlaws we think. Don't worry about them," said the red-faced man.

"Put him there on the table," Doc said. "Then everyone clear out."

The young woman went around the lawman and placed a kiss on the man's cheek.

"You can wash up," the doc said to Sam. "How many wounds?"

"Three that I could tell," Sam said, then excused himself to join the others.

"Alex Peabody. I run the bank." The red-faced man stuck out his hand.

"Sam Ketchem. I came to town for some supplies. I have a herd west of here on the trail."

"What did you need?"

"Some raisins and some vanilla."

Everyone laughed.

A big burley man in a soiled apron came up the street. No doubt he worked in a saloon. "We got them, 'cept the one run off. Two's still alive. They say they're the Tanner Gang. Bruce Tanner's dead, but his brother, Coil, got away."

"There's rewards on them guys," the boy said, looking impressed about the deal.

"Miss Moberly, I'm sure the doc can patch the marshal up," the storekeeper said to the girl, who was sniffling in her kerchief.

251

"He looks plumb tough to me," Sam said. "I figure he'll make it."

"You gents want to come to the saloon. The drinks are on me," Peabody said.

"It wasn't easy shooting them two," the boy said to Sam.

"It ain't ever easy to shoot anyone, but when it's do or die, sometimes you have to do it."

The boy nodded, "Mr. Gurley, do I have time to drink a beer with you all?"

"Yes, you do, Sherman. Your mother may whip both of us, but one beer won't hurt a boy who just became a man."

A barefoot youth of perhaps ten brought back Rob, who had been spooked off by the shooting. Sam paid the kid a quarter and hitched Rob with a lariat, taking the bridle and reins into the saloon to repair them while he had a drink.

Later, Sam left his name and address with the banker, who promised to divide any rewards among them. Then Gurley wouldn't let Sam pay for the raisins and vanilla.

At supper that night, Tom asked, "Anything happen in town today?"

Sam shook his head. "They had a little ruckus. The Tanner Gang tried to hold up the bank. But the townsfolk stopped them."

"You get in on it?" Billy asked.

"Naw."

"Must've been lots of shooting," Tom said.

Sam looked off into the night. "You'd been surprised how quick it was over."

Chapter 24

Days stretched into weeks, and the crew crossed into the shorter grass country with few farms. The weather held, save for some light rain. They reached Tom's place and Sam could see some cottonwoods the previous owner had planted and watered. The property had corrals, sheds and a nice frame house that had probably replaced an adobe jacal. A few hills off toward the town showed where the migrating buffalo were once forced to funnel through the cut.

Tom's cattle spread out. All the men ate their fill of beef, potatoes and onions.

"You know that lazy Sancho slept all day. Toddle cooked this," Tommy Jacks said, going after another plate. "But he didn't want you to know 'cause he wants to move up to drover on the big drive."

"Tasted better than most of our meals," Sam said.

"He could cook for us going home."

"You boys help him, and we might make it home eating good." Sam set the plate aside and went over to Tom. "Give me fifty bucks."

"Sure what for?" He dug in his pockets.

"I'm going to find that damn Sancho and fire him."

"He won't be hard to find. He's sleeping in the tack room." Tom gave Sam the money.

Sam walked over to the tack room, opened the door and shouted, "Here's your damn money. You're fired!"

"Huh? How do I get back?" The man sat up on his cot.

"I don't care if you crawl. Stay out of my line of sight." Sam tossed the money down on Sancho's lap and went back to eat.

"The crew's been thinking," Billy said.

"That would be dangerous. What's on their mind?"

"We want to fix up the chuck wagon so it's comfortable enough for a woman. Then, well, Kathy and the kids can go with us to Ogallala."

"Lord, no. The trail isn't any place for a woman and kids."

"We'd sure eat good."

"Hell, I'll find a good cook next time."

"I don't know why you're so dead set against her going along."

Sam closed his eyes. How many times did he have to tell Billy no?

The crew loaded up the next day, after Toddle cooked a good breakfast, and then they headed south. Sam shook his brother's hand and told him to hug Karen and the children for him. He promised to drop by to see them on his return from Nebraska late the following fall. Huddled in jumpers and underneath wool blankets against the sharp north wind, the cowboys rode south. They hoped to celebrate Christmas at home in a week.

No one was home at the ranch when Sam and Billy and Tommy Jacks arrived. It was the night before Christmas Eve, and Sam knew there was a party at the schoolhouse, so they rode over there. Tommy Jacks, Billy and he dismounted in the schoolhouse yard, which was packed with rigs.

Folks looked up when the three men came inside. Sam hoped they hadn't disturb Etta Faye's program. He spotted her up front, in a starched blue dress. She was giving stage directions to her students. The sight of her made his guts roil.

Rowann recited a poem about flowers and never missed a beat. Her warm smile was directed at the three cowboys in back. Her mother, seated at the end of a row of chairs, nodded to Sam in approval.

At the end of the program, several people came over to shake Sam's hand and to ask about Tom and his new place. At last, after the crowd moved away to eat cake and drink warm apple cider and cocoa served by the mothers, Etta Faye walked over. "Well, Samuel, even away from home, you seem to get involved in all sorts of heroics."

"Heroics?" He frowned at her.

"The Fort Worth paper, of course, carried the entire story on how you stopped the Tanners from robbing that bank in Lynnville, Texas."

"Boss, you said —" Billy clammed up when Tommy Jacks elbowed him.

"You can't believe those newspapers," Sam said with a small smile. "Lovely program. We tried to get here on time, but weather held us back."

"Were either of you gentlemen with him at Lynnville?" Etta Faye asked.

"No, ma'am, but shucks," Tommy Jacks said, "it was only one gang."

Sam closed his eyes. His face felt hot. The room had suddenly grown warmer. Etta Faye's arm slipped into his. "Come and enjoy some cake. I bet they didn't feed you any in Lynnville."

Christmas morning, the children opened

gifts Sam had brought home for them. Rowann got a new doll, Darby spurs, Hiram a cowboy hat and Sloan a fat yellow-and-white collie pup. Rowann instantly named the pup Bob. Sam gave Kathy a bolt of blue checkered cloth, thread and some lace. He also gave the family a large sack of hard candy and some big oranges. He even surprised Billy and Tommy Jack with a new shirt for each for them.

"What can we give you?" Kathy asked, fighting back tears.

"You have. You're my family. I am the richest man in the world."

"You better get going," Kathy said, taking his hat, coat and scarf off a hook. "You told Miss Ralston you would have dinner with her and the judge at noon today."

"Guess I better make tracks."

When he put on the wool coat, Kathy threw her arms around him and hugged him. "Don't freeze. It's cold out there."

"Lordy day, girl, those presents aren't that big a deal." He raised Kathy's chin and looked into her sparkling wet eyes.

"They are, Sam."

"I'll probably board in town tonight, so see you in the morning. Merry Christmas."

Everyone but Sloan waved. The boy held

tight to his pup. With a smile and a wave, Sam was on his way. Soapy, fresh, full of hay and grain, trotted quickly along the trail.

When Sam crossed the creek and started up the far bank for the schoolhouse, something sharp struck him in the back. Then he heard the rifle report. He pitched forward, then hit the ground hard enough to jar him for a second. The next shot hit in the dirt and spooked Soapy. Sam scrambled for the cover of some cedars. He dove into them. Stiff boughs jabbed him in the face and body. More shots cut through the flat needles and showered down on Sam as he hugged the earth and tried to unholster the six-gun under his coat.

A searing pain in his right shoulder told him the bullet was high. He wouldn't be able to use that arm, and he couldn't hit a bull in the ass at close range with his left hand. But that shooter out there did not know that. If he had the nerve to come in closer, Sam would get off a shot or two. The shooter was located beyond the creek in some cover. He'd let Sam ride past.

Sam couldn't find Soapy. After the second shot, he had rushed away. If the gunman didn't catch the horse, he'd run home. Of course, cold as it was, he might freeze before he got there.

"Damn it to hell," Sam cursed. He was supposed to be at Etta Faye's for dinner. How bad was the bleeding? He had no way to know. He listened above the wind. Someone was coming on horseback. He could hear him ordering others to go around. Sam cocked the Colt, but his right arm wouldn't go up.

Then a woman said, "No! Come on. He'll die in this cold if you didn't kill him. If you'd only caught his Gawdamn horse —"

A woman was leading them? Sam wanted to see her, but he heard a buggy going west, then more horses leaving. He didn't dare leave the cover. His main concern was his attackers would return to finish him off later. Good thing Tom was at Buffalo Gap. He was out of harm's way up there.

The next thing he knew it was late afternoon. The cold air was murderous. His eyelids were heavy. No way could he keep them open.

"Here he is!" Billy shouted from a mile away.

"How bad's he been shot?" Kathy asked. "Is he alive?"

Of course, I am.

Chapter 25

The ride to Frio in the wagon, despite all the blankets swaddled around Sam and Kathy holding his head in her lap, was a rough one. He felt as if he was being shaken to pieces. Billy drove in wild-man fashion. Tommy Jacks kept looking over the seat back at Sam, then laying the whip to the team. At last, they were at Doc Sharp's house and drew him out of the wagon, with Kathy giving orders on how to handle Sam.

"Where's he shot?" Doc asked.

"In the back," Kathy said and they gently rolled him over.

"When did it happen?"

"This morning, I guess, when he set out for town. His horse came back about noon. We started looking for him right away and we didn't find him for hours."

"Who did it?"

"Doc, we don't know. He hasn't talked since we found him."

"That's not new. Sam never talks much. I'm going to cut this shirt off him."

"Fine. You think he'll live?"

"Yes, I do. If they'd hid his head from him, it would be different."

"Good, I must go find Etta Faye," Kathy said.

"Why?" Doc asked.

"He never made it to her place for Christmas dinner."

"Oh."

"Do you need me for anything?"

"No, I'll be fine. Tell those two cowboys to stay close. I may need them."

"They'll be right here and I'll be back in thirty minutes or less."

Sam wasn't sure of anything when he opened his eyes. His right arm felt stiff and the fire in his shoulder was intense.

"Are you coming around?" Etta Faye asked.

"How did I get here?"

"Someone shot you on your way to my house."

"Oh," Sam said.

"I wondered about you all day. Then, late yesterday, Mrs. McCarty came by and told me where you were."

"Kathy? Billy? The others all right?"

"Quit worrying. They're fine. They've gone back to the ranch to take care of the children and chores. Tommy Jacks — I believe that's his name — said they would rehang the door on the schoolhouse that they used for a stretcher to get you in on."

"I remember someone shooting me and then falling off the horse."

"Deputy Stuart was by earlier. You were asleep and I wouldn't let him try to wake you."

"You've been here all night?"

"Yes."

"You better go home and get some sleep."

"I am fine. It is you we all are concerned about. Doc said the bullet didn't go in far, but there is always the danger of infection."

"I'm already beholden to you for sitting up with me."

"Are you trying to run me off."

"No. You must need some sleep."

"Can I tell you a wonderful thing?"

"Sure, I need some wonderful things to happen."

"If you are going to be sarcastic —" Etta Faye raised her brows and frowned at him.

"I'll behave."

"The parents asked the school board for another three-month session and they want me back."

"Why not? You're the best they ever had out there."

"The condition is every family must furnish a cord of wood since there's no money available until the legislature meets next year."

"They'll do that. You really won everyone over out there."

"Now you get well, and I'll have a grand and glorious New Year." She frowned again as he tried to rise. "What's wrong?"

"Just thought of it. Your present."

"My present?"

"Yes, it was Christmas yesterday. I was headed for your house." He lay back. "It's in my saddlebags."

"Oh, you'll have plenty of time to find it."

"I won't have plenty of time. I've got a cattle drive to organize."

Etta Faye shook her head. "I swear, Samuel, you'll sit up at your own funeral and direct people to do things you didn't finish."

Sam laughed at the notion. He reached over and squeezed Etta Faye's hand with his good one. There was a lot that needed to be done. . . .

Chapter 26

His arm in a sling, Sam was back at the ranch in three days. Billy drove him home in a borrowed buckboard. When they pulled into the yard, the McCarty children ran out to greet him and Kathy, drying her hands, joined them.

"Don't ask him a lot of fool questions," she said to her brood.

"They wouldn't do that," Sam said. He was stiffer than he thought he would be.

"They would," Kathy said. "Did the trip wear you out?"

"It was far enough," he said and smiled at Sloan holding his puppy. "That thing know how to walk?"

"He don't get much chance," Hiram put in.

"Come on in. I have supper about ready," Kathy said.

"Good. I've missed your cooking. Doc's housekeeper is a nice lady, but she makes portions for small people."

"Doc is not very big."

"He won't get bigger on her food either.

Won't get enough." Sam went into the house, which was full of the tempting smells of her cooking.

"Sit down. Rowann get Mr. Sam some coffee. I hear Tommy Jacks coming in, too. Guess we can eat."

The meal was hard for Sam. Kathy cut up his food, and he felt helpless feeding himself left-handed. The sling had to go, Doc or no Doc.

Over supper, the kids talked about the small pigs, and the men talked about the preparations for the drive.

"There ain't enough grass anywhere to hold that herd for over a day once we assemble them," Tommy Jacks said.

"There wasn't lots of grass going to Buffalo Gap either," Billy added between bites.

"We've got to get in on the earliest grass growth to sustain us northward. We get to Colorado late and there hasn't been rain, we'll have fits getting them across there without any water."

"Burt Ramsey had to haul water one year to meet the herd every day," Billy said.

Sam shook his head at the lanky cowboy. "We ain't got the help nor the wagons to do that. Besides, you'd have to haul it from miles away."

"We'll have to beat the summer drought then."

"Right," Sam said. "Six weeks to get to Doane's Store or where we can cross the Red, maybe west of there even. Then we'll take the Canadian to the west and angle into Colorado and then straight north to Ogallala."

He picked up the coffee cup and looked through the vapors. "It'll take six weeks to get across the Nation and Oklahoma, then a month to get across Colorado."

"That's four months," Kathy said.

"That's right. Grass breaks the middle of March. We can head north then. We'll be in Ogallala in mid-July."

"How long to get back?" she asked.

"Six weeks to two months."

"You all won't be back till September then?"

"Close to that."

"Sam, do you recall what you told us up at Buffalo Gap?" Tommy Jacks asked him.

"You boys tell her?" Sam asked.

"No," Tommy Jacks said.

"What's that?" Kathy asked.

"Those cowboys of mine are so fussy about food, they ran off a perfectly bad cook up there. They want to ask you if you'd go to Nebraska and cook for us."

"We'd go, Mom," Darby said.

"Hell — I mean, yes, we would." Hiram ducked down as if expecting to get a rap on the head for cussing.

"Of course, you'd have to drive mules on the chuck wagon. We could put on an extra wagon and get Darby to drive it," Sam said.

Kathy stood holding the tops of the ladder-back chair. She pursed her lips and nodded. "Let me think about it for a while, and I'll give you my answer."

"Think real hard on it, Mom," Hiram piped up and then looked down.

"Kathy, thanks for dinner. I'll get me some sleep now," Sam said.

"You'll be all right in the bunkhouse?" she asked, walking him to the door.

"I'll be fine." Sam waved with his good arm and headed across the dark yard for the barn.

Billy caught up to him halfway there and opened the door. "Sure been different here without you. Good to have you back."

"Guess there wasn't anything out there where I was shot."

"Nothing I saw to pin it on anyone. I can't believe there was a woman there."

"I can't say who she was, but I'd know her voice anywhere."

"I hope we catch them. Here, I'll get a fire

in the stove," Billy said.

Sam sat down on his bunk and forced his boots off with his feet. He knew he'd always ride looking over his shoulder. He had never done anything to the Wagners. But he'd never let them get the drop on him again.

Chapter 27

Late February, peach trees were in bloom and a cold snap swept down and sent everyone for their winter coats. The duration of the cold spell worried Sam more than the loss of the fruit crop. He was busy coordinating everything for the drive from the ranch: bringing cattle in and road-branding, so the crew would be ready to head north when the herd was formed.

His tally book called for two thousand head when all the men were on hand. That was a lot more than he wanted to drive up there. Fifteen hundred would have been plenty on that long of a drive, but he couldn't turn down many of the askers.

Sam had picked up six more riders and a new horse wrangler. He planned to use both Billy and Tommy Jacks as scouts. That way they could find water and the best feed. Most of the cattle he had looked at were thin from the winter's short feed, which would slow them crossing the Indian Nation. Still, if Sam got up to Nebraska too late, the market might be glutted.

Half the herd would be made up of cows, so he'd be hitting calves in the head every day. No way would those newborns keep up, and they'd only make the cows turn back.

"You're sure you want to go?" Sam asked Kathy when she refilled his coffee cup one afternoon.

"I couldn't back out now and live with those kids. Yes, we're ready."

"It won't be pretty out there."

"I know: no hot baths, straining water, buffalo chips for fuel."

"Kathy, I could still find another cook somewhere."

"Sam Ketchem, all your help would quit and you know it."

"I could find a new crew."

Kathy laughed. "No, don't do that. I will have to do one thing."

"What's that?"

"By the time we get to Ogallala, I'll have to decide which one of those big galoots I'm going to marry."

"Billy or Tommy Jacks?" He frowned at her.

"You've not noticed?"

He put down his pencil and laughed at his own lack of observation. "Two good men, that's for sure."

"But I don't want to choose." She shook her head as if troubled.

"I felt the same way about this drive. Good luck. See you at supper." He stopped in the doorway. A breath of cold air swept over him and he buttoned his wool coat. "Oh, the Morayes family is coming over this week to see how to take care of the stock and the crops while we're gone."

An hour later, after Sam had passed Darby driving the kids in a wagon going home after school, he stood at the potbellied stove in the front of the schoolroom. His gloved hands held out to the warmth of the stove, he waited for Etta Faye to finish grading papers.

"When do you leave?" she asked, busy writing on the papers.

"One week."

Etta Faye looked across at the windows on the south side of the room. The deep blue sky was dull, like it wasn't awake. The bare trees and even the cedars looked drab. He felt the heat from the stove on his face and knew his first month on the road would be a bitter one.

"Please don't stop any robbers this time," Etta Faye said.

"I don't think there are many banks out there."

"Knowing you, you'd find one being robbed."

Sam chuckled and shook his head. Then, using his teeth, he pulled off the first glove, then the second one.

"It's not funny."

"This is my last cattle drive."

"Oh."

"I know I said that before, but this one will do it."

"And?" Etta Faye asked.

"If I survive it and get back here, I'm going to ask you a big question."

"And?" She hurried to finish the papers, then glanced at him.

"I'm going to come back and ask you to marry me. I don't want to know the answer now. But when I come back this fall, you be prepared to answer me. You'll have all summer to think about it."

"Where do you plan to live after this drive?"

"Etta Faye, I'm not sure. Probably not here. Those Wagners won't ever get over their feud with me, I'm afraid."

"I thought you would go off with Mrs. McCarty."

"Kathy?"

"Yes."

He shook his head. "You don't understand. Two great cowboys are courting her."

"She's lovely, and a good cook, I understand."

"I hired her to do that."

"I know and I about died over it."

"Now you know her. She's not some low-life. She's a proud woman. Her and her kids were on the edge of starvation when I hired her to cook for us."

"Go. Go drive your cattle north." Etta Faye waved at him with the backs of her hands, as if shooing him away.

"I can bring around your horse. I see they have her hitched."

"No." She pursed her lips and wouldn't look at Sam. "Just leave. Go! Please! I don't want to cry."

Sam wanted to step over to hug her, but some unseen hand held him back. He wanted to comfort her, to swallow the knot big as an apple in his throat. Instead, he slammed on his hat, went out the door into the fresh wind and rode off.

Chapter 28

The slender sprigs of new grass were whipped by the cold March wind. Time to head 'em up and move out! Kathy on the seat of the chuck wagon was sawing on the mules' mouths. Darby with the load of his family's things and his team of horses equally ready. Hiram and Sloan rode ponies. Rowann, behind the tailgate, held up Bob for Sam to see, and they left the ranch, headed north in the purple-orange light. Yates Grossinger, the wrangler, took the cavvy out with them.

Sam gave the command and the herd began to move. Mostly they bawled, knowing that something was a stir, as if they had anticipated the drive.

First-day pains with break-back cattle proved to take lots of effort. The cows were the worst. They wanted nothing to do with the herd. Sam didn't regret the extra hands he'd hired; he could have used more. But by midafternoon, when he could see the new white canvas top of the chuck wagon, and the cattle were full of water, he felt even easier watching the cattle graze in the short grass. He met Billy and Tommy Jacks at the campground.

"We have a good place for tomorrow night. We're going wide of Schade up here. We'll just stay on the road and we won't get in any crops," Billy said.

"Sounds good," Sam said.

"Been so dry, the rivers won't be up," Tommy Jacks said.

"But we don't know what it's doing a thousand miles away either," Sam answered.

"Yeah, I get you."

"Don't take nothing for granted."

"Hey, I'll learn this business."

Sam agreed and went for some fresh coffee. Over by her cooking fire, his cook held up the pot to tell him it was ready.

"How was your day?" he asked.

"I guess all right. Won't no one have to rock me to sleep tonight."

"Sleep will be the last thing we'll get the next few months."

"I have gathered that. Those poor boys don't get six hours a night with riding herd and all," Kathy said.

"They're tough and experienced from the drive to Tom's, except for the new hands, and they did good today."

"It will be a long way up there, won't it?"

"You have any regrets about coming along?"

"No."

"Good 'cause these drovers will be spoiled rotten from your great cooking by the time they get to Nebraska."

"Get out of here." Kathy gave Sam a shove with both hands.

He looked up to see Darby and the others carrying armloads of fresh-cut wood. He nodded in appreciation to them.

"We've got more down there," Darby said to his mother.

"Good. We will need it down the road, if not here."

"Saw down there?" Billy asked, followed by Tommy Jacks. At Darby's nod, he headed for the wood supply.

"I wonder why they never did that for Sancho." Sam blew on his coffee, which was too hot to drink. He smiled at her, and she shook her head at him, then busied herself with food cooking over the fire.

Sam found a place to sit on the ground and watched Sloan hurry after the boys for more wood. Was the boy upset about the ponies Sam had found for the other two boys? Was it a big letdown from the stud horse?

"Rowann, how is the bread?" Kathy called, lifting lids on the Dutch ovens with a hook and replacing them.

"Good."

"She's a big help," Kathy said to Sam.

"I can see that. How's Darby doing?"

"With that pony to ride, why him and Hiram are real cowboys."

"What about Sloan?"

"Oh, he's excited as he gets."

"Good. I figure in a month we'll be at the Red River. That will be our biggest crossing. But we can ferry the wagons, ponies and boys across there. On some of these smaller rivers, we'll have to watch them."

"I will."

"Good. I get busy sometimes. I wouldn't want anything to go wrong."

"We're a pretty tight-knit family."

"You pull hard together."

"Would it have been easier if you'd had Earl and Tom along?"

"No, they'd make me do all the work."

Kathy laughed and mopped her face on a towel. "I bet you've always done it."

"Mostly."

At the two-week mark, the crew had become a team. There had been a fistfight or two between cranky boys, but Sam had swiftly settled. Crossing the Colorado went smooth. The Leon was hardly over knee-deep, and they faced the Brazos in five days. Sam watched clouds develop all day. A spring storm could mean anything, including snow, though by the first of April, such weather was rare south of Fort Worth.

"Boys, we may have to spend the night in the saddle. Keep your horse handy."

"You mean those clouds?" Christian Webber asked, looking at the ominous bank building in the northwest.

"There's a squall in them. You can see it."

"Sam, I've never been in a stampede," Webber said.

"You just ride and try to head them into a circle so they don't run clear out of the country."

Sam halted the drive short of their usual ten- to twelve-mile push. The cattle filled up on the mixture of old and new grass. Many had dropped down to chew their cud. Cows were never as bad as steer to look for an excuse to run. The infusion of the English breeds had also tempered them from the pure Longhorns who'd lived in the Texas brush so long without mankind that they were more like deer than cattle. But sipping on his coffee, with the changing wind in his face, Sam knew that given any excuse at all, this herd would explode.

Billy came by, but didn't dismount. "She's coming, ain't she?"

Sam nodded. "Tell them boys to be careful."

"I will, boss. Guess we better keep trying to hold 'em?"

"Right. I'll be there in a few minutes."

"Fine." Billy left at a short lope.

"Damn," Sam swore to himself, dreading the inevitable and listening hard for the first roll of thunder. At times like that one, he would have traded the job for a sheepherder's position.

"Buckle it down," he said to Kathy as Darby and Hiram took down the fly. "Sorry I don't have any shelter. Best place is in a low spot. We'll huddle up and hope it blows over."

"We'll be all right," she said, above the rising cold wind. "Go help the boys."

Sam nodded. His guts wrenched. Weather like the approaching storm was one reason why he hadn't wanted her and the kids to go along.

Sam rode Rob out to join the men. They had two hours of daylight left, by his calculations. The thunder in the distance sounded like the thump of Indian drums. A low rumble rolled across the open country, and lightning danced on the face of the huge clouds bearing down on the crew.

Cattle began to get up. Sam indicated to the drover that he should keep riding around the perimeter, talking and singing to the cattle. Everyone had slickers on. The severity of the situation was evident from the first great blast of wind out of the mouth of the storm. It threatened hats and flattened the grass.

Then all hell broke loose over them. Lightning came like lances thrown by Comanches, and thunder made the ground tremble. Rain struck in hard drops that felt more solid than liquid. The sky opened up, and it was impossible for the men to see farther than a few feet in front of them. The bawling of the cattle rose to panic. Cowboys shouted loud in the downpour. Sam had to count on his horse to get him around. Then Rob collided with a cow, and she turned back into the herd.

Time and again, Sam ducked as the lightning struck so close he wondered if it had hit anyone. He kept talking to Rob, who danced a jig after each such blast. The cattle were holding so far, but the rain grew even heavier. Near Sam, a cowboy cursed and drove a calf back to the herd, using the chest of his horse as a bumper.

Wind tore at the men, and Sam wondered if there was a tornado rising. Minutes passed like hours. Rob stumbled in a hole and almost went down. Sam lifted his head and the pony, in a scramble, recovered. The moment Sam was on firm ground, his heart stopped beating heavily.

More thunder, more lightning and more heavy rain came on. Then the north wind struck Sam's face in a wet slap, and he could see holes of light. The deluge was going to pass. The curtain of water began to lift, and Sam could soon see the entire wet herd. He began to count faces in the drizzle.

"Everyone's all right here," Tommy Jacks said, coming up at a short lope, riding double behind Harvey Core. "Lightning got my horse. Good thing Harve saw it happen or I'd been afoot."

"You all right?" Sam asked.

"Oh, I'll live, but that old pony's gone."

"Glad that you're all right. We can always get more horses. I'll go check on Kathy and the kids."

"Tell her we're fine."

"I will."

Sam short loped for the camp, which had been deliberately set aside on a point that the scouts thought would not be in the line of any stampede.

Hiram was up on a ladder, tying the canvas fly back up. He had a big grin on his face. "We made her, Mr. Sam."

"Good. Bad as that wind was, I was worried it took you back home."

"Aw, shucks, we never had a moment's trouble, did we, Darby?"

"Nope."

When Sam dismounted and helped Kathy hold up a pole, she asked, "Everyone else fine?"

"Yes. Lightning got Tommy Jacks' horse, but he managed to escape unscathed."

"Good," she said, looking relieved by the news. "We'll have food ready in a little while."

Sam nodded. Providence had been on their side this time, but they certainly would face countless more hardships and dangers before they finished the drive.

Chapter 29

They were a week out from skirting around Fort Worth. Sam was at the chuck wagon busy repairing Thirston Cones' saddle. The youth was riding Sam's rig that afternoon. A horse wreck earlier in the day had torn off the boy's D ring. Thirston came out bruised all over, but all right. The horse — not as lucky — had to be destroyed.

Sam sat on a small log beside the creek and pounded in new copper rivets with a small anvil and hammer. Not a pretty repair, but it would do.

"Here's some coffee." Kathy brought him a tin cup of the steaming brew.

He pushed the hat back on his head and looked up at her. "Thanks. You getting worn-out?"

"No more than I would be at the ranch."

"Good, 'cause we're still a long ways from Ogallala."

"I think I've kind of gotten into the swing of things."

"Oh, I never meant anything was wrong. Mercy sakes, you've spoiled this crew so bad, their mother's cooking won't satisfy them after this drive."

"You are a prize, Sam Ketchem. You can make me feel like a queen at times."

"That poor boy needs a new one." He set the saddle on the ground. "Well, Kathy, you are the queen of this drive, and don't you ever doubt it."

She tried to dismiss his words with a head shake. "You never said and I guess it isn't any of my business, but what about you and Etta Faye?"

He slapped both of his chap-clad legs and quickly nodded. "Now ain't that a deal? I have chased after that girl for ten years. And I told her before we left, she'd need to make up her mind to marry me or not when I got back this fall."

"She will, of course."

"Kathy, you don't know her. She switches sides more than any woman alive."

She took a place on the log beside him, tucking her dress tail underneath her legs to sit down. "Why, Sam, she'd be a damn fool not to marry you."

He glanced over at her. "I'm not any more certain about that than whether one of my horses will or won't buck in the morning."

"Getting late. I better get supper going. Wonder why Billy's not back."

"He should be," Sam said and picked up the saddle. He finished his coffee and gave her the cup. "Thanks."

Suppertime came, and eating his meal, Sam wondered more why Billy had not returned. The scattered dark clouds moving in overhead looked like rain, but no big storm front showed on the horizon.

"Billy say anything to you?" he asked Tommy Jacks on his way to drowning his plate in the washtub.

"No, sir, but I can go look for him."

"Naw," Sam said, turning over his foreman's absence in his mind. "You keep the guard up. We'll get rain in the next few hours. I'll go see if I can find him. It's not like Billy not to be back."

Tommy Jacks rose and brushed off the seat of his pants out of habit. He fell in walking with Sam. "I'll keep the horses saddled and everyone on alert in case the weather gets bad."

"Good. And if we get a chance, we need to find Thirston a different saddle up the road. That one I worked on could fall apart any day."

"Fort Worth?"

"I'll sure be worried about him in that old one."

"We can find him one. Billy mentioned

Lode Eye this morning. Place north of here."

"Never said a word to me. I've never heard of the place."

"Think he lived there once as a kid."

Sam nodded, knowing the sun would be down in an hour.

Thirston had resaddled Sam's horse for him when he came in. Ready to go look for his long overdue foreman, Sam tightened the cinch on his rig and with a wave to Kathy rode Soapy out of camp. He short loped the fresh pony through the rolling grass country, following some wagon tracks headed north.

A few miles out, the dying sun glowed on a handmade sign: LODE 1.5 MILES. He took the tracks and trotted Soapy. In the twilight, he spotted the shadowy building forms in the bottoms. A few lamps showed in windows; he shut Soapy down to a walk and went off the hillside for the village.

At the first drops of rain, he shucked off his slicker and rode on. Light from the saloon's bat-wing doors shone on the small puddles being struck by the drops. He dismounted and tied Soapy at the rack. Not knowing what was in store, he left the girth tight and climbed the steps. On the porch, he unbuttoned the slicker and took the tie down off his Colt. A man never knew what lurked behind some doors.

The coat over his left arm, he entered the smoky den. He could feel some hard looks following him as he went to the half-filled bar and ordered a beer from the bald bar-keep.

"Here you go. New around here, ain't you?" the barkeep asked.

"Yeah, I'm looking for my foreman. About five-nine, brown hair, early twenties. Wears a high-crowned brown hat."

"You must be looking for that guy that got shot up today."

"Shot up?"

"Yeah, got into a gun fight with the Stafford brothers."

"He at the doc's? Where is he?"

The man made a pained face. "We ain't got a doc. They sent for one, but they took him over to Molly's place."

"Where's that?"

"Whorehouse across the street."

"Who're the Stafford boys?"

The bartender leaned forward and said in a low voice, "Don't look now, but the big guy with the beard in the card game. That's Clare. Blair ain't here right now."

"What —"

"Mister" — the bartender gripped Sam's

288

forearm tight and drew closer — "those two are killers, and they'll damn sure kill you, too."

"Thanks," Sam said and paid for his beer.

As he turned to leave, he noticed the big man the bartender had mentioned. First things first. He needed to see what he could do for Billy.

Slinging the coat over his shoulders, he sloshed across the street to the small porch and knocked. Stomping the mud off his boots, he waited, hearing a piano inside tinkling away.

A young woman dressed only in a corset answered the door.

Sam removed his hat. "Ma'am, I understand you have my foreman in here. He was shot today."

"Oh, yes, Billy. Come in. The poor boy's alive, but —"

"But?"

"But Doc Mangam said he didn't even want to try and get the bullets out of him."

Sam let her close the door. "The doc still here?"

With a serious hurt look in her eyes, she shook her head. "No, he had two babies to deliver."

"He coming back?"

"Maybe in the morning. Follow me."

Sam tried not to look at all the exposed flesh ahead of him. The shapely woman in high heels led him through the front room. Some of the doves lounging around waved at him. Then he followed the woman's bare legs up the flight of stairs. She showed Sam to an open door. There was a lamp burning in the room.

"Sam?" came a soft, dry voice.

"It's me, Billy. I'm here."

"I prayed you'd come, boss."

Sam knelt beside the bed and waved away the woman's offer of a chair. Looking at the ashen face of the boy made his heart melt. "I'm here."

"They was kicking this guy. I didn't know his name. Big guys — they'd've sure killed him."

"Joe Graves," the woman said in a soft voice behind Sam.

"Why?" Sam looked back at her. "Why were they beating him?"

"Them two don't need a reason. They hold this whole town in fear."

"Any law here?"

"No, and the sheriff won't even come over here."

"Boss, I know what you're thinking. Go back and get the boys —" Billy held his side and made a face at the pain.

"I'm getting you to a real doctor."

Billy shook his head, as if he needed to hurry and tell Sam something. "Give my wages and things to Kath— tell her — tell her — Tommy Jacks — lucky . . ."

Billy Ford was dead. Sam dropped his face onto the perfume-smelling blanket. His fingers held the cold forearm of the boy he had loved like a son.

"Oh, no —" the woman said behind him. "Those backshooting bastards."

"Get some canvas and wrap him up in it so I can take him back to the herd."

"I can do that —" She waved away his offer of money. "Who's Kathy? He spoke of her a lot today."

"The woman he wanted to marry. She's my camp cook."

"Well, he sure worried a lot about getting word to her, you and the cowboys at the herd."

Sam nodded. From the nightstand, he picked up the small Colt Billy had carried and jammed it in his waistband.

"Mister, you can't go across the street, shoot them Staffords and live to walk out of that place. Been tougher men than you have tried and ended up dead."

"Will anyone help them?"

"No. Everyone fears and hates 'em."

291

"How much does Blair look like the other one?"

"They could be twins."

"Billy have a chance today?"

She shook her head.

"I won't give them one."

She closed her eyes in pain. "How far out is the herd?"

"West and south maybe seven miles. Tommy Jacks Riddle is the man in charge."

"You got any last wishes?"

He shook his head.

"God help you."

"Send someone after his horse. In a half hour, I'll be taking him back."

"Mister, I ain't much on prayers, but I'm going to get on my knees and pray to God that you live through this."

"That won't hurt," he said and hugged the dove.

"Be careful," she whispered when he released her.

He nodded and went out the door. Going down the stairs, he saw four other women standing, watching him with their pale faces. No one said a word, but he knew by their looks that they feared for him.

It occurred to him at the front door that his slicker was upstairs, but he went out on the porch anyway. Light rain still fell. He crossed the muddy street and reset the Colt on his hip as he went. Under the saloon's porch, he let his eyes adjust to the brighter light coming out the bat-wing doors.

He could see the hat Stafford wore. Clare Stafford was still playing cards in the smoke that clouded the room. Sam had to be accurate with his first shot. He dried his gun hand on his vest, then pushed through the doors.

"Clare Stafford?"

"Yeah?" He looked up from his cards like Sam was only a minor inconvenience. The man's back was to the wall, so Sam knew his shots would not endanger any others in the saloon.

"You killed my man this afternoon."

Everyone at the card game, except for Clare Stafford, dove for cover. The Colt in Sam's fist blasted and the bullet struck Clare Stafford in the chest. Hit hard, Stafford fired his own gun through the partially overturned table into the floor. Sam's second shot struck Stafford in the heart.

The wounded man fell with a loud groan. "Ya got me."

"Stay put," Sam ordered and rushed behind the bar. Somewhere under there was a sawed-off shotgun. Every bar had one.

"Here." The bartender delivered it to

Sam, then fled to the back.

Sam laid the shotgun on the bar and re-loaded his Colt. In the barroom, everyone could hear the rumble of bootheels coming that direction on the boardwalk. They backed away.

"What the hell's happened in the saloon?" a loud voice, out of wind, demanded in the distance.

"I heard shots."

"So did I."

The bootheels grew closer. Someone's hard breathing on the porch rasped loud in the still saloon with the crowd huddled down low at the sides of the room. Using both arms to bust through the bat-wing doors, a large man charged like a bull into the room.

"You Blair Stafford?" Sam asked.

"Yeah, who the —"

"Welcome to hell." Sam used both bar-rels on him and blew him out the doors. The boiling black powder smoke filled the room.

Sam handed the shotgun back to the bar-tender. "Thanks. I owe you for two shells."

"Mister, you don't owe me a Gawdamn thing."

"Hey, mister, I want to buy you a drink. Name's Dennis. You done this town the biggest favor it ever could have."

"No, Dennis. The drinks are on me," the bartender said. "What's your name, mister?"

"Sam. Sam Ketchem. Live at Frio Springs. Taking a herd north."

Damn, he didn't want to bury that boy. Those oats Billy planted would be up waving in the wind, with all the rain and good weather. They'd have a barn full of good hay for next winter.

Sam downed a double shot of whiskey and waved aside the townsfolks' offers of more. Once outside, he saw Billy's body draped over the horse at the rack beside Soapy. The dove from across the street stood on the porch, wrapped in a blanket against the night chill.

She handed him his slicker to put on. "Guess praying helps, huh? I ought to do it more often."

"Yes. Do I owe the doc, you, anyone?"

She shook her head to dismiss Sam's concern. "See that bastard in the mud?" Sam nodded at the still form on the ground at the base of the stairs. "Him and his brother ain't ever again going to beat up another woman, an innocent man, or rob anyone of what they have.

"Mister, bend down here. I want to kiss you."

Sam leaned over, and the woman's arms went around his neck. Then she really kissed him. When he stepped back, she closed the blanket over her corset and left him for the house across the muddy street.

At the hitch rail, Sam undid the lead and Soapy's reins. In the saddle, he saluted the crowd on the porch of the saloon, then booted the horse into a trot. The other pony came along. Sam's tears mixed with the light rain and ran down his face.

Chapter 30

No one was ever good at funerals. Sam decided the more times that he ended up in charge of them, the more they hurt, especially with young folks. Webber had carved Billy's name in a board and they used a cedar post to nail it to like a cross.

Red-eyed from crying, Kathy stood surrounded by her wet-faced children and only added to Sam's misery. His crew looked like whipped pups. All of them were sad-eyed.

Wind ruffled the pages of the Bible in his hands. If Reverend Quarry had been there, or even that priest from Saint Ann's to do this job, he would have felt a lot better. But in the end, he was the one who had to deliver that boy to his Maker.

Sam looked up about the time he was ready to start reading. A buggy with six women riding in it drove up.

"Who are they?" Tommy Jacks asked with a frown.

"The angels that stayed with Billy in his last hours. You boys, mind your manners and go bring them over here."

The drovers about fell over themselves to escort the sisters across the space of grass between them and the grave. When Sam looked up again, he saw several other rigs were coming. He closed the Bible. "More of Billy's friends, I guess," he said.

"We brung food and wanted you all to know that we really cared," the man from the saloon said.

"Is there a preacher among you?" Sam asked, looking over the crowd.

"Mr. Ketchem, we all feel you're the man to say words over this boy."

Sam's eyes closed to shut out the bright sun. He shook his bare head. "Lord, we're sending you our best friend and my foreman, Billy Ford. He grew up kinda on his own, Lord. Probably never was inside your house — much. But, Lord, that cowboy loved all your handiwork: the sun, the rain, growing things. He hated having to do away with newborn calves on this drive. It went against his grain. But, Lord, he never asked any of the rest to do his job.

"There wasn't a better man ever rode this grassland. Yesterday, some bullies were beating up on a man in a town nearby here, and Billy went to his rescue. Lord, those heathens shot him — but even as his life slipped away, he worried more about his comrades with the herd than about himself."

A loud amen came from the crowd.

"Take Billy Ford to your ranch in the sky, Lord. We know he'll have a good campsite and plenty of firewood up there for us when we get there. I — we can't wait to see his shining face again. Amen."

"Amen," the others said.

Sam handed Tommy Jacks the Bible. Without another word, he walked away from his sorrows.

"Mr. Sam! Mr. Sam!"

He stopped, turned and looked down at the wet lashes of Rowann. She'd been trying to get him to stop.

"What?" he asked.

"Will we really see Billy up there?"

"Rowann, he'll have the best spot in heaven picked out — why, there will be clear running water and all of it."

She nodded her head and wiped her eyes. "Then I won't cry any more for him."

He squeezed his mouth and agreed. "I won't either then —"

"Now we've got to go and tell Momma so she don't cry anymore."

"Lead the way, my little friend." He took her small hand and went back toward the crowd of strangers and his crew.

"Good, 'cause she needs to know, Mr. Sam," Rowann said.

Chapter 31

Civilization, fences and farms forced Sam far to the west of the Doane's Store crossing in the middle of April. They looked for a good ford for two days. At the spot they found on the Red River, it was a quarter mile wide — and except for a short ways in the main channel, not deep enough to have to swim a horse.

They snaked enough logs out on the river to float the wagons across. Finally they found the place used by other herds in the past. The drovers, with several lariats tied together and secured to the tongue, started across on horseback. They were beyond the deep portion when Sam on the spring seat sent the mules in.

Kathy stood behind him and the rest of the kids were with them in the wagon. He could look aside and see her ashen fingers clutching the backboard. The mules acted spooked by the water. They floundered for a moment when the wagon began to float aside on them. Then they began to swim. Riders were beating their horses to pull, and the attached taut ropes popped in and out of the water.

Sam screamed at the mules, using the lines to encourage them to hurry as the chuck wagon swung farther downstream every second. Then the first team struck the shallow water and they jerked the others after them.

By then, the wagon was at a ninety-degree angle to the course. The riders were still pulling, and the mules with some traction were also hauling on it. Sam began to worry that when the wagon wheels on the right struck the bottom, the whole thing might tip over from the force of the current.

He held the reins to a helpless ending. The cowboys shouted and their horses strained all they could. Mules began jumping forward like they were on fire. The right wheels struck something solid and the wagon tipped toward the right side. Kathy screamed and the kids did, too.

"Get on the upper side!" he shouted.

But there was no way. Then it went back down. The effort of mules and riders began to tell. Soon the wheels were turning. Sam slumped down in the seat.

Smiling, Kathy pounded him on the shoulders. "We've done it!"

Now all he needed was to get the cattle

across. He told Tommy Jacks to take Kathy and the kids over the ridge to set up. She didn't need to hear all the cursing. Besides, most of the boys would get naked to cross.

"We'll bring Darby's wagon over later," Sam shouted and waved her on after the boys cut off the logs that floated hers across.

"We can keep their gear and clothes dry that way." Jammer laughed as he shivered in his wet clothes. "Too damn cold to go swimming — that's for sure."

"You guys did good. Let's get back over and bring that herd across."

"Boss, there ain't no need in you getting wet," Jammer said. "We can bring them."

"Good. Send the horses over first."

"Who — hoo!" Jammer shouted and reined his muddy horse for the Red. "Get them ponies down here, boys!"

Yates and his horses came across in minutes. That left the herd.

The lead steer headed in the water, and his bell ringing, the column followed him. Punchers shouted and waved lariats. Bullwhips cracking, the steer swam across and shook themselves off on the north bank, flinging water all over.

"Keep them coming!" Sam went to help them chouse the first ones up with one eye on the river. Stalled back in the line, they might swim off or go in circles and he'd lose cattle.

A half hour later, the herd was across and they were getting ready to float Darby's wagon over. The youth was there looking anxious at his rig on the far side.

"They'll get it over," Sam said, dropping out of the saddle and squatting down on his boot heels.

"I'd liked to've done it."

"You'll have plenty of chances to prove yourself. You've done right well."

"It ain't like being a drover."

"I think these boys accept you as one of them."

"Yes, sir, they do."

"Keep driving the wagon. I can't spare a hand."

"Thanks." He smiled.

Sam watched Tommy Jacks drive the horses into the water. Sam wondered if the young man needed ropes. The wagon was lots lighter than the chuck wagon, and the horses much larger than its mules. When they reached the deep water, the horse acted calm and began to swim. They soon were on higher ground headed for the bank.

"Better go and get your team from Riddle. He'll be worn-out."

"I doubt it. Tommy Jacks is tough as nails."

Jammer rode by leading his new fore-man's horse to him. "Maybe tougher than that."

"Time will tell." Sam turned Rob toward camp. They were north of the Red River.

Sam rode up the sandy slope. On his own horse, Tommy Jacks caught up with him on the ridge. "Guess from here on we look out for Injuns."

"Anyone comes along begging for food, cut them out a limper."

"I can savvy them."

"It's their grass we're crossing, so we can spare them some."

"I'll do it that way, if you ain't here."

Sam looked off at the low sun. "That's the plan. Be dark soon. We better get them bedded."

"Boys are doing it."

"Good, let's go see about some of Kathy's coffee."

"Hold up. I got a few questions to ask you about women," his foreman asked.

"Land sakes, I'd be the last one to ask." Sam brought Rob down to a walk.

"You knew me and Billy — well, we com-peted for Kathy's favor."

"I knew that."

"Well, she lost her husband six or seven months ago, and now Billy —"

"Give her a little room. I think it'll work out. Six weeks, we should be at the Colorado line, headed north. That means we're ten weeks away from Ogallala."

"Okay, boss. Any of these Injuns dangerous?"

"Only ones I'd worry about are the Comanche or the Kiowa. But hell, there may be others. I haven't heard much else and most of the real renegades are way out on the cap rock. We get up on the Canadian River, we may miss them."

"Suits me. I told the boys they should hold their fire, but be ready."

"It'll do to be careful."

Sam could see the canvas top of the chuck wagon. He set Rob into a trot. He needed some coffee. He didn't want any trouble with Injuns.

Chapter 32

Over the next two weeks, a few thunderstorms had taught the crew that even mixed herds stampeded. Stopped on a rise, Sam hailed the sight of the green cast from cottonwoods in the bottoms. He could see the canvas top and fly stretched out over Kathy's worktable. The Canadian was one of those rivers that was too thick to drink and too thin to plow. The river's water needed to be strained to drink or used in coffee. It also had a fishy taste. But paralleling its course took them northwest without seeking water sources.

The cattle were beginning to pick up weight on the way. If Sam could keep them gaining, he could command a better price for them.

He short loped across the bottoms and saw something from the corner of his eye. A rider? A buck? Someone had been spying on the chuck wagon from the small buttes across the river. Sam decided to send one of the men to check it out.

When Sam dismounted, Darby took

his horse. "Thanks."

The boy gave him a smile.

Sam crossed the distance to the chuck wagon. "Well, how's the boss?" he asked Kathy and pulled up a folding canvas stool.

"So-so."

"Been a buck watching you, until I rode up."

"Oh, where was he?"

"Up on that red butte. He just wanted to know all about you."

"Means I keep the shotgun closer, huh?"

"You better. I'm sending Tommy Jacks up there for a look around."

"What about Jammer? He's supposed to be back from scouting, ain't he?"

Sam took a cup of coffee and blew on the steam. "It's strange he isn't back. Darby, throw that saddle of mine on Sorely. I'll be there in a minute."

"Yes, sir."

Sam hurried toward the herd and waved Tommy Jacks over. The cowboy came on the run and slid his gray up short.

"What's wrong?" Tommy Jacks asked.

"Jammer ain't back from scouting. Be dark in another hour. Want you to go look at the signs on that butte up there. I think I spooked an Injun spying on our camp when I rode in."

"What about Jammer?"

"He may be on his way. I'm going to go look. If I don't get back, you keep them going. Two more days, you'll need to cut over to the North Canadian to hit the Fort Supply Road. I ain't there, you wait ten days at Fort Supply. Then they're yours to take to Ogallala."

"I ain't never been there." Tommy Jacks looked serious.

"You can make it. You'll have to if I don't come back."

"Yeah." Tommy Jacks swallowed hard and looked over at Sam. "God be with you, and come back with that Jammer."

"I aim to come back. You keep your wits about you. Kathy and the kids are lots of responsibility. But you know that. Keep that nighthawk Yates awake at night. They might want our horses."

Tommy Jacks nodded. "I understand. Boy, being a cowhand wasn't near this bad."

Sam hurried back to camp. He had Kathy get him a handful of jerky, and he mounted Sorely. "I'll be back. Don't wait up." He put the jerky in his saddlebags.

"Sam Ketchem, don't be no fool out there."

"Keep that scattergun close."

"I will. Damn, I worry every time you ride out like this."

"Maybe this will turn out better."

"I'll pray it does."

Sam set off short loping the big horse. He had no idea where the boy might be. By sundown, he'd chewed on enough of the hard jerky to take the edge off his appetite. A whiff of smoke floated by on the evening wind, and he wondered if he was about to ride up on an Indian camp. He set Sorely down and headed for high ground for a look.

In the fading sunlight, he saw a shack and some corrals. It was no Indian camp, but there were worse things than Indians out in this land. Some wanted men hid out in the wilderness hundreds of miles from Judge Parker's court and any law. Breeds and mulattos made up roving gangs that robbed and stole for their living. So chances the camp held some law-abiding settlers were less than one out of a hundred.

Sam took Billy's .30 caliber Colt out of the saddlebags. After reloading the pistol, he put it in his waistband and sent Sorely down the hillside. There was no time like the present to see if they knew anything about Jammer.

Sam crossed through the shadow bottoms

and a horse nickered at his. Sorely answered. Sam's heart stopped. A knot grew to boulder size in his stomach. His horse knew the one in the corral.

"Who's out there?"

"A friend."

"What you doing riding up on my camp?" The figure held a rifle, but in the growing darkness, Sam figured he couldn't hit a barn at the distance.

"Just passing through. I been to Fort Supply headed south."

"Well, get your hands up."

"There's been a mistake. I was only riding through. Wanted to buy some grub."

"Got money, huh?"

"Some."

"Get off that horse." The man came around so he was behind Sam. "Hold still."

Sam jerked the .30 caliber out of his belt and smashed the man in the face as he sought to free Sam's other gun. The blow sent the man spinning. He lost the rifle, but like a wounded cat, he came back in leap. Sam drove the muzzle of the barrel into his gut.

The man's fingers sought Sam's face. The small gun fired in a muffled sound. Instantly, the outlaw grabbed for his gut and fell down on his sides, moaning. Sam put his boot in the man's neck and held him down while he threw away knives and an old bulldog pistol into the brush.

"Where's my man?" Sam demanded.

"He's inside the shack."

"Alive?"

"Yeah, yeah."

Sam jerked the man up to his feet and shoved him toward the doorway. "Anyone else here?"

"No."

"He all right?"

"Yeah."

"He better be." Sam propelled him through the doorway. Then he struck a match. He could see the gagged Jammer tied to a chair. He lit a candle on the table and moved cautiously behind his man to release him.

"Who the hell is he?" Sam asked.

"Chicken Charlie," Jammer gasped when the gag came off. "Boss, I figured he'd get you, too."

"Stupid sumbitch. Why did he tie you up?"

"Said when his gang got back, they planned on stealing the herd. They needed to know all about it and said I would tell them when they got through with me."

"What's the name of his gang?" Sam

frowned at the wounded man, who was holding his guts and moaning.

"Chicken Charlie's, I guess."

"I'm dying," the wounded man said.

"Better you than me," Jammer said, strapping on his holster.

"When's his gang due back?"

Jammer shook his head and flipped his hair up to put on his hat. "When's your gang coming back?"

"Couple of days." The man groaned again.

"You want me to step on your neck some more?" Sam made a false start toward Chicken Charlie.

"No, Gawdamn. I'm — I'm dying —"

"Now tell me or I'll stomp you."

"Tomorrow."

"Whew," Jammer said. "That was close."

"How many're coming, Charlie?"

"Four, maybe five. I swear —" Then a deep cough cut off his talking as he balled up on the floor.

"Go get two of the tough hands," Sam said. "All of you get rifles and ammo. Then the three of you get back up here tonight."

Rubbing his wrists, Jammer started out.

"Take Sorely. He's saddled."

"I will, boss. And I'll be back real quick."

"Be careful in the night and don't fall in any holes."

"Oh, yeah. Whew, I figured my goose was cooked." Jammer ran out the doorway.

Sam listened to the boy lope away. Then he tied Charlie's feet and hands. The wounded outlaw cursed and moaned about dying.

"Go ahead — better you than me or Jammer."

Sam found coffee and made some. The beans had been scorched and the coffee was bitter, but he drank it and tried to ignore his prisoner. He found a wanted poster for a Charles Conklin alias Chicken Charlie. One was for robbery of a post office.

"What the hell can you get from robbing a post office?" Sam asked, setting the paper on the table.

"Thirteen dollars, seventeen cents and all the stamps you ever need."

Sam shut his eyes in disbelief over the stupidity of such a thing — to risk a jail sentence for that little gain. Besides, he was willing to bet this guy had never mailed a letter to anyone. Anxious for Jammer and the boys' return, Sam got up and went to the door and listened to the coyotes. Their plaintive howling carried across the bottoms.

Past midnight, Jammer, Webber and one of the new hands named Frank joined him. The men took their horses down to the bottoms and hobbled them so they wouldn't be in sight when Charlie's crew arrived.

Daylight came and Jammer walked in from guard duty. "No sign of them yet."

Frank drew the next round with orders not to shoot or be seen. Sam and Jammer made some biscuits with jerky and they washed them down with more burned coffee.

"They damn sure ain't like Kathy's," Jammer said and shook his head.

"That's why she's the cook." Sam laughed aloud.

"Hey," Webber said scooping up his rifle, "Frank's coming on the double."

"You and Jammer go up in that shed and keep down till we can get them in a cross fire if they try anything. What is it, Frank?"

"They're drunk, from the sounds of their singing. They're coming in from the north, like you said they would."

"Hit the shed," Sam told the other two. "Frank, you and I are going to hide inside here."

"Yes, sir." The boy, who was hardly older than sixteen, swallowed hard.

"It'll be all right. They want to fight, we'll shoot them."

"Sure, Mr. Sam, but I ain't never shot no one."

"Hope we don't need to today." Sam could see the other two hands were concealed in the shed.

From the sounds of the outlaws' singing, at least one of them was sure drunk.

"Charlie, you old sumbitch, where are ya?"

Sam stepped in the doorway with his rifle leveled on them. "Charlie ain't feeling good this morning. Hands high. One move and you're dead," he told the three shocked riders.

Jammer and Webber came out of the shed holding rifles on the outlaws.

"Get their guns and knives," Sam said to Frank.

"Yes, sir."

"You the damn law from Fort Smith?" a bearded man asked.

"No. I'm the drover that Charlie planned to take the herd from."

"Hey, we wasn't in on that. We been to Fort Supply getting us some food and whiskey."

"Keep your hands up. I can't help it. Charlie said you were going to help him."

"Aw, mister, we wasn't going to steal no herd of cattle."

"In Texas, we hang rustlers."

"Not us, please —" The outlaw looked around at his partners. "Speak up. Tell him we ain't rustlers."

"Get off your horses and don't try anything," Sam ordered. "Now shuck your boots."

"Shuck our boots?" the bearded outlaw said.

Jammer made a point with the complainer by jabbing him with the barrel of a rifle. "Do as he says."

"Boys, tie them boots and put them over the saddle horn. Frank, sack up the guns and knives."

"Where's Charlie?" one of the stocking-footed rustlers asked.

"Gut-shot inside. Now back up to that corral. Tie their hands behind their backs to the posts," Sam said. "Frank, go get our horses."

"Mister, what plans you got for us?"

"I really should lynch each one of you. But I'm going to give you a chance you don't deserve. I'm leaving you here tied up, barefooted. I'm taking your horses and saddles and guns as payment for this inconvenience. And if I ever see you again, I'll shoot your ears off."

The bearded outlaw nodded that he understood the terms. "What if we can't get loose?"

"Guess them coyotes and buzzards will have a feast."

"That ain't the Christian way," the youngest of the gang said.

"Should've thought about that before you joined this bunch."

When Sam went inside, Charlie moaned and raised his head off the dirt floor. "Shoot me."

Sam shook his head.

"Then by Gawd, leave me a damn gun, so I can shoot myself. You know this wound's going to kill me."

For a long moment, Sam considered the notion; then he drew out the .30 caliber pistol from his waistband and laid it on the table. Billy Ford didn't need it. Sam walked out into the daylight. The hands had the outlaws' horses on leads and were ready to ride. Sam stepped in the saddle.

"What's your name? I never heard it," the bearded outlaw asked.

"Sam Ketchem. Frio Springs, Texas."

"I'll stay wide of there, Sam Ketchem."

"You do that, 'cause I will shoot you."

They were on the ridge when Jammer

reined up his horse. "I heard a shot back there."

Sam nodded. "Ain't our affair. Tommy Jacks is moving the herd shorthanded. Let's ride, boys."

Chapter 33

Dust boiled up in the sky from the herd. Riding drag meant the hands in the back came in looking like a sand pile. The North Canadian River provided thicker water than downstream, and fewer springs. Daytime temperatures began to climb.

Sam rode in and dismounted. Darby took his horse.

"How was fishing?" Sam asked Hiram, knowing the boys had had some luck downstream.

"Ain't deep enough even for a fish up here."

"I was thinking catfish for dinner again."

Hiram shook his head. "We may have to eat cow chips soon, too."

"Hiram McCarty, what did I tell you?" his mother demanded.

"Quit bitc— I mean, don't complain."

Sam laughed and tousled the boy's hair. "How was your day, Kathy?"

"Fine." She handed him a tin cup full of coffee. "Except that's the reason they aren't off scouting. Three Injuns rode up in camp. I ran them off with the shotgun and told the kids to stay close."

"What did they look like?"

Kathy pushed her hair back, then bent over the fire to tend to her cooking. "They was near naked and had war paint on their faces. I didn't like their looks at all."

"They say anything?"

"I didn't give them a chance. It was kinda scary."

"Were they armed?" Sam blew on the coffee.

"Yeah, two had rifles. One had a long spear."

"Sorry. Another few days and we'll be at Fort Supply. Once we get there, I suspect we'll find less trouble."

"I'll keep the kids closer in."

"Good idea."

Next morning, Sam told Jammer to stay by the camp. "We can find our way. Those renegades might try to raid the wagon."

"I didn't see them. Saw some others on the move — going looking for buffalo, I figured."

"Probably. There were still buffalo in Kansas when I came up the trail the first few times." Sam had never forgotten the big herds. "They wasn't bad eating either.

'Course we just cut the loins out in them days."

"I only seen one or two that they caught. Like to see a herd of them."

"Better hurry. Hunters are killing them fast."

Jammer nodded. "I'll watch out for them."

Fort Supply sat on the creek by the same name; the creek's springs were fresh and clear. A small company of soldiers marched around the parade ground when Sam rode up.

A guard saluted him. "Good day, sir."

Sam returned the greeting. "I guess there's a store around here."

"Beck Wolf's is over there."

"Fine," Sam said. He rode over to the sod-roofed building the soldier indicated.

The man he found inside had a bushy beard streaked with gray. His hoarse, gravelly voice barked at Sam. "Whatcha need?"

"Sugar, raisins, a good barrel of flour, and some hard candy."

"Got a new shipment in this week. Where do you need it?"

"I'll send a wagon in for it."

"No trouble. This cash or credit?" Beck asked.

Sam laughed at the man. "You'd offer me credit?"

The man nodded. His brown eyes shone hard under the bushy brows. "Only had one drover never paid me in my life. I figure he got killed was why he didn't."

"No, I can pay for this."

"Where you headed?"

"Ogallala."

"Keep your eyes and ears open," Beck said.

"Anything in particular?"

"Some Comanche renegades roaming around in small bands. They've killed a few cowboys who worked for the big outfits leasing this country."

"Two days back, three of them showed up at my camp, and my cook ran them off. Two had rifles and one had a lance."

"Lucky for him. That's Glass Eyes, the one with the spear. Only Injun I ever saw had clear blue eyes."

"What's his story?"

"Bullets can't hurt him."

Sam nodded. Then he paid his bill and thanked the storekeeper. He left the store and rode back to the camp. Darby and Jammer hitched up the horses to go after the supplies. Sam found Kathy and Rowann down at the creek, washing clothes. Sloan sat on a rock and his half-grown pup thumped his tail at the sight of Sam, but remained beside the silent boy. Sam nodded to the boy.

"Hi, Kathy. Sent the boys off to get what you ordered from the store," Sam said.

"Good. We should make another five to six weeks on the rest."

"That ought to put us there."

The woman bent back over and doused the dress in her hands. Then she smiled at her daughter. "How we coming?"

"Slow," Rowann said sulkily.

"Aw, Rowann, a woman's work is never done."

"I sure know that. You see Sloan and Bob?" the girl said to Sam.

"Yes. He's trained him to sit there, I guess."

"You're right. Can't see how he does that with no words."

"Sloan could get a chicken to dance." Kathy laughed.

The two females began wringing out the wet clothes. At last, Kathy excused her daughter and began to gather the clothes to dry them on bushes and large rocks.

"That Indian with the lance have blue eyes?" Sam asked, climbing down to where she worked.

Kathy stopped spreading out a shirt on a rock. "That's what was so different about him."

"I found out his name's Glass Eyes. He's Comanche."

"Oh. What else?"

"Seems him and the others have been ambushing lone cowboys."

"They nearly went to Indian heaven or wherever."

"Keep your guard up."

"I will. Any women up there at the fort?"

"Sorry. The trader has a young squaw and I didn't see any officers' ladies."

Kathy nodded and paused to catch her breath. "Just be nice to talk to another woman."

"I bet it would," Sam said and gathered his horse to put him up. The herd would be coming in there in a short while.

They rested a day in the vicinity of Camp Supply and reshod a few horses who needed it the worst or repaired some bridles and saddles. The outlaws' saddles were distributed to those who needed them.

After spending a day or two thinking about the Comanche renegades, Sam came to the conclusion that they weren't a part of the recent killings. He believed that outfits like Chicken Charlie's were letting the blame for their actions ride on the red men.

Late in the day, Tommy Jacks, busy shaving with a straight-edge razor, asked, "How much further to Colorado?"

"Ten days. What is today?" Sam asked.

"Damned if I know. Must be near May first."

"May twenty-seventh," Kathy said, "unless I missed crossing a day or two off."

"There you go," Tommy Jacks said, washing his face with a towel. "Did I get off all the soap?"

"You did fine," she said to him.

"We're close to your schedule, ain't we, Sam?" Tommy Jacks asked.

"Day or so behind, but we'll get there by mid-June. If we can keep this flesh on the cattle going north, we'll really be in good shape."

"Sure ain't many cattle on the trail. We saw signs of two herds of them crossing down at the Red River, but hardly seen any since. Any been by here?"

"Don't know, but you're right," Sam agreed, thinking how they'd seen little trace of other herds.

"They all shipping by train?"

"Must be," Sam said, thankful for another reason he wouldn't have to go up the trail again.

The next day they moved north west across the Strip. They made camp around midafternoon and they strung the herd out along the shallow North Canadian River to water.

Three days later, Sam went out to the herd to check on Lacy Mayberry. The boy had complained of headaches and dizziness, but despite Kathy's concerns over him falling out of the saddle, he went out to scout anyway. At Kathy's insistence, Sam rode out to check on the man.

Lacy said he felt better and Sam thought he had more color in his tanned face. So, after checking with Tommy Jacks, Sam headed back for camp. With Jammer gone to scout the next day's camp and the night hawk trying to get some sleep, Kathy was alone.

Sam came off the long slope and saw Kathy running toward him, holding her dress. Even at a distance, he could tell something was not right. He put spurs to Sorely.

"What is it?" he asked, reining up short of her and jumping out of the saddle. "What's wrong?"

"That" — she gasped for breath — "that blue-eyed bastard got Sloan."

"How?"

"Those three must've been hiding when you left. They rode in, swept up poor Sloan, killed his little dog, then rode out with him."

"Damn."

"Sam, I didn't dare shoot them."

He took Kathy in his arms and hugged her. "I'll find him. Don't worry. Sloan's the toughest one here."

"Oh, Sam, I'm so afraid. He can't hear you call him even."

"I'll have to work that out. I'll get your boy back."

"Did they take him because he was different?" She pushed her hair back and used Sam's handkerchief to wipe her wet eyes.

"Injuns are superstitious. They may have thought that he had powers."

They hurried back to the chuck wagon. He could see Rowann had been crying, too.

"Pack me some jerky and crackers." He went for a box of ammo and put it in his saddlebags. He checked the girth.

"What should I tell Tommy Jacks?" Kathy asked.

"Keep moving. Go around that hellhole town out there on the corner of Colorado and Kansas. I'll catch up after I find Sloan."

"Sam," she cried, "I'm afraid they'll kill him when he can't talk."

He shook his head. "No, they didn't simply want a boy. They wanted a sign and saw something in him."

"I know the boys will want to trail you."

"Tell them all to stay with the herd. If I can't do it, then there isn't a way. Which way did they go?"

"West. Be careful. I don't want you killed."

Sam tied on a blanket with his slicker. Then he mounted. "Take them to Ogallala. I'll be along."

"May God ride with you, Sam Ketchem."

He nodded and rode by red-faced Hiram, who had his hands clutched tight together. "Sam, find Sloan — please."

"I'm going to, Hiram. I'm going to."

Chapter 34

Hours later, Sam found the Indians' old campsite. Cold ashes from a small fire, several hoofprints — two of the horses, no doubt stolen, were shod. The vast rolling country broke into some hills to the west. If that was their destination, then fine. He hoped that they stopped somewhere and gave him a chance to catch up. The iron shoes left good tracks he could follow without getting off his horse — maybe it was a trap.

The wind came up and whipped the short grass and a few flowers hard. Sam paid it little mind. There was a reason for the Indians' madness, he told himself over and over. It wasn't simply to kidnap a small boy.

Sam studied a mesa, wondering if one of the kidnappers was up there peering down at him, but the red rocks looked unscaleable. He rode on. The hills were scattered; the pass between them led upward. A few mesquite bushes dotted the short grass.

The tracks went through a gap with mesas on both sides. Sam reached the top of one of the mesas as the bloody sun began to set. From that vantage point, he tried to see any sign of the kidnappers.

The notion that they might travel after sun down niggled at Sam, but he needed patience to find the Indians and not overrun them. He would choose the place to fight, and not let them. In the morning, he would start across the next basin. He hoped it had a water course in the middle to provide some water for him and Sorely. He ate some peppery jerky, and when the moon rose, he caught his horse and rode down toward the middle of the great basin. He found potholes of water in the streambed that bisected the land.

After a few hours' sleep, he was on the way. The tracks led westward in the peachy light of dawn. He had no idea if the men he sought had camped or ridden all night. But the horse biscuits he found were fresh ones. That and the half-moon depressions of horseshoes kept him going.

By midafternoon, Sam was in some broken country. He was going uphill when Sorely grunted and stumbled. A shot rang out. With barely time to shake his stirrups, he realized they'd shot his horse out from under him. Sprawled on the ground, he could hear the throaty moans of his dying horse. Not daring to move, he knew the shooter could not see him as long as he stayed low.

A few bullets whined over his head. One hit the horse like a hard-thrown rock striking a ripe pumpkin, but Sorely was already dead. The bitter alkali taste of the dirt was on Sam's lips when he wet them. He wondered how he could get to his rifle in the scabbard. When he looked back, he could see it.

Sam began to slither on his belly. Would the shooter see him once he got alongside the dead horse? No shots came, so he crawled over and jerked the .44/40 out of the holster and then rose to look.

He could see someone under an unblocked hat. The man wearing it was jumping bushes. Sam located him in the iron sights and squeezed the trigger. The runner threw his hands up and sprawled facedown.

Sam waited. Where were the other two? He only saw one horse, a quarter mile away. He hoped he had not scared the pony. It was either capture him or walk. But was the sniper dead or only playing possum?

When he reached the body, the man on the ground didn't move and Sam didn't try him. He searched the country to the west for any sign that others might have come back. Nothing. Next he set out to capture the paint. Despite trailing reins, the spotted horse snorted at him several times and spooked away.

"Easy, easy," Sam coaxed and finally set the gun down, thinking the smell of the rifle might have the animal upset.

The paint still evaded him. It went a few yards and then turned back to look and snort softly at Sam. Then the reins tangled around some sagebrush. Sam took two easy steps, and his fingers closed on the leather lines. The whole time he talked softly to the paint and patted him. Relieved, he pressed his forehead against the fork in the western saddle, no doubt stolen from some cowboy.

Where did the other Indians go?

Chapter 35

The Indians were still riding shod horses and must have been herding some spares. Sam squatted beside a pothole in a dry streambed and studied the tracks. Two days since the man had shot Sorely and met his own demise. Sam's supply of jerky was getting low. He had no idea where he was, but suspected the men had cut back south into Texas — maybe they were headed for their band, if they had one.

One thing pleased him. The boy's tracks were in the dust. So he was still alive. Sam's eyes were so burned by the sun and wind, plus the lack of real sleep, they ached in the sockets. His belly felt on fire, and the bad water didn't help him.

The kidnappers knew by this time that their man wasn't returning to them, and if they'd seen Sam in the distance, they must know he'd taken the paint horse. Sam worried about the faraway herd and what Tommy Jacks was doing. He trusted the lanky cowboy, but his foreman was crossing unknown ground for him. They should be close to the line and turning north by this time.

The country began to give way to deep gorges and the tracks went across the crest to it all. There were small playas with bad water, but he and the paint drank it. He even spooked ducks off the surface some. He'd shoot one to eat, but didn't want them warned. Late that evening, he stole some fresh-laid eggs out of a duck's nest and ate them raw.

Sam slept only a few hours that night, then moved on. The next day he saw the two men. They milled around on their mounts across a mesa top as if they might charge him. Something was wrong. They no longer had the herd of horses. Where had they stashed them? Where was Sloan? Was this a trick to get Sam out in the open?

Easing out of the saddle, he wondered if his sea legs would carry him. They did. He slipped rope hobbles on the paint. He needed the horse to carry him out of there if he survived. He checked the chamber of his rifle. It was loaded.

The Indians were waving lances or rifles over their heads and spinning their ponies around beyond the range of anything but a Sharps .50 caliber buffalo gun. They were building their own nerve and hoping to unnerve their enemy.

"Here I am, you sonsabitches. Let's get this over with," Sam said in strange, dry voice he barely recognized as his own.

Kneeling down, he waited, rifle butt to his shoulder. If that blue-eyed Indian wanted to test his immortality he had better get to riding toward Sam. Suddenly the two Indians came at a dead run for him. Their shrill screams shattered the silence. Hooves drummed the ground. The sounds of the straining horses were loud in Sam's ear. Both charging men rode so low set on the backs of their horses, Sam could barely see them.

Sam aimed for the left horse's head. That rider had a rifle — Sam needed him out of commission worse than the one with the lance. He squeezed the trigger, and eye-burning gunsmoke swept across his vision. The horse went nose down and did a cartwheel. Sam couldn't see what happened to the rider. He reloaded the lever-action and swung it to his right. He fired and more smoke flew in his face. The other horse went down, but the rider leaped through the air and landed on his feet.

The blue-eyed Indian never quit his forward charge. Sam could see the red and black stripes across his face. He read the anger, the hatred in the man's features as he ran full-out toward him. Animallike sounds coming out of the Indian's mouth gave Sam goose bumps. The Indian's powerful, brown chest was covered in porcupine quills, which rippled as he ran with deliberate strides. His white shaft was poised above his head; eagle feathers trailed behind the flint point. Sam centered the iron sights and pulled the trigger.

With a thud, the lance stuck in the ground beside Sam. The lance vibrated as the force exerted to throw it was absorbed by the sod. Stopped in midstride, the blue-eyed Indian threw his empty dark hands skyward; a second shot blew him off his feet and onto his back.

Sam reloaded and stood up. Where was the rifle-toting one: dead, injured, or waiting for his chance to strike.

Sam paused, then poked the Comanche with the rifle. Nothing. His blue eyes were already glazed over. He would look at the cloudless sky until the buzzards picked those blue eyes out. Sam Ketchem wasn't going to close them; he walked on.

The sorrel horse was dead, lying on his side. A Rafter H brand was on his hip. Some rancher was missing a good pony. Before Sam reached the bay horse, he swapped his rifle to his left hand and drew his Colt. The animal's pained labored breathing sawed at Sam. A bullet to the brain stopped the misery.

Facedown on the ground lay the last of the three kidnappers. Sam wanted to bring him back and demand to know what the men had done with Sloan. Had the heathen bastards killed him after all? Sam pounded the rifle butt on the ground.

"Rot in hell, you bastards!" he shouted into the wind.

Then the brown shirt at his feet stirred as if awakened by his words. The Comanche rolled over and sprung to his feet, brandishing a huge knife. The Colt in Sam's hand belched fire and smoke again, again and again as the bullets drove the Indian backward. The Colt clicked on an empty chamber, and he threw it aside. Then he used the rifle butt to smash in the Comanche's face.

Shaking from his spent rage, Sam hunched his shoulders to regain his bearings. He closed his burning eyes to shut out the devastation and death on this field of battle. Where was Sloan?

Strong winds swept his face and dried the wetness on his cheeks. How could he go back without the boy? How could he face Kathy and not be able to tell her where her boy was?

Sam located his Colt under a bush and reloaded the weapon. He reset the rig on his hip. Then he found the paint busy grazing; he undid the hobbles. For a long time, he looked at the war lance. If he ever made it back to Texas, he'd like to have that as a reminder of his days in hell. He booted the Winchester in the scabbard, then pulled the lance out of the ground with both hands.

Maybe he could find some tracks to lead him to the horse herd and learn what the Indians had done with Sloan. Once more he shut his eyes and tried to bring some sort of resolution in his own mind to the whole episode. Nothing but the wind answered him. He mounted the paint and set out to follow some tracks that led off into a deep canyon. From the top, he stood in the stirrups and peered down into the depths. He had no idea where the other animals were stashed or if Sloan was even with them. Then he saw some horses coming around the side of the mountain. They walked single file. Sam squinted to see them better. Someone rode the broad-built horse in front. Sam's eyes widened and he let out a shout of joy. Hatless, his fine blond hair tousled by the wind and riding the stud horse with no bridle or saddle was Sloan.

Chapter 36

"The herd, you mean? Ah, they was through here, oh three, four days ago," the trader said, standing on the porch of his outpost. The bearded man wore filthy buckskins, and in his belt, he carried a knife big enough to slay elephants.

"I need a few things —" Sam began.

"That's a Gawdamn stud horse that boy of yours is on?" The man spat tobacco in the dust, looking shocked at what he saw.

"Yeah, that's Sloan McCarty and his horse."

"Why he ain't got a rein or a saddle on him. Boy, how you do that?"

Sam stopped, ready to go inside to get them some food to carry with them. "Sloan can't talk."

The trader scratched his unruly shoulder-length hair. "That beats all. That jack's a buffalo pony, ain't he?"

Sam nodded. "Sloan stole him from a renegade Injun with blue eyes."

"I know that murdering sumbitch. No way that little boy ever stole nothing off him. "Whatcha know about that damn Injun anyway?" the trader asked, following Sam inside the store.

A small hat in his hand for Sloan, Sam turned to the man. "He and two bucks that ran with him are dead."

"You bring his scalp with you?" When Sam shook his head, the trader said, "I don't believe you. That sumbitch has been shot at and never once hit. He's got that medicine —"

"You ever see his lance?"

"Yeah."

"I have it strapped on that paint under my left stirrup. It's all wrapped."

"Holy cow, mister. Then you must have killed him." The man was dazed. "Boys, get over here." He went to waving at the half dozen buckskinners and former enlisted men playing cards around a table. "This guy killed that blue-eyed heathen Injun."

"Mister" — a barrel-chested man, who stood well over six feet tall, stuck out a hand twice as big as Sam's — "that worthless murderer killed my best friend last year."

"Nice to meetcha, laddie," a toothless small man with an Irish accent said.

"That renegade kilt the Hoffman boys last year and got Murray King last winter not three miles from here," the barrel-chested man said.

After a drink of firewater from the trader's stock, Sam found some crackers without worms or weevils, some dry cheese and a sack of candy for Sloan to eat on the way. He also bought six cans of tomato juice and some fruit.

"Put your money away, mister. You ain't going to pay for nothing in here. Got that boy's name, but never did catch yours," the trader said.

"Sam. Sam Ketchem of Frio Springs, Texas. That was my herd came through here a few days ago."

"That your woman with them?" a buckskinner asked, wiping his whiskery mouth on the back of his hand.

"No, that's Sloan's mother."

"No offense intended, but she was a powerfully pretty lady." A row of bearded faces all bobbed in agreement with their man's description of Kathy.

Sam agreed and went outside to share some of the food and candy with the boy. Sloan nodded excitedly at the candy. Sam didn't have the heart to make him eat some of the crackers and cheese first. They'd drink the tomato juice and eat the fruit later. They herded their loose horses and mares ahead and rode north.

Two days later, they topped a rise, and in the valley below, they spied the line of cattle. A dust plume turned up by eight thousand cloven hooves towered sky-high. Sam closed his tired eyes and clasped the saddle horn in his hand on top of the other. "They're on the move. Thank goodness."

Sam pointed to the dust and cattle. "Sloan, we made it to here."

The boy's sharp blue eyes taking it all in, he nodded like he knew what Sam meant.

"Let's go find your mother," Sam said and gave Sloan a wave. He began to chouse the loose horses into a trot and, standing in the stirrups, headed for the head of the line. Somewhere ahead, the chuck wagon would be set up and Sloan's worried mother would be waiting.

"Sloan! Sam! It's both of you!" Kathy shouted at sight of the two. She rushed with her skirts in hands to meet them. Darby tried to pass her, but stumbled. Then he regained his feet, with Hiram and Rowann on his heels.

Sam used the paint to block Kathy. "Easy, easy, everyone. His horse is not used to you all. I'll get Sloan off and put a rope on him. He'll be fine."

"Where did he get that horse?" Hiram asked when Sam had dismounted and gone to uncoil his lariat.

The stud snorted at Sam, so Sloan got a better handhold on his mane, booting him forward with his heels toward Sam. The loop over the horse's head, Sam quickly made a halter. Then he walked beside the stallion and lifted the boy off. On the ground, Sloan rushed to his family. All the hugs and crying and shouting were joyous.

Hiram went over and inspected the horses. "You two got a whole bunch of horses."

"They're Sloan's," Sam said.

"What's he going to do with them?" Hiram asked.

"I guess break and sell them."

"Man, how does he ride that horse, with no saddle or bridle?"

"Trust, I guess."

"I never thought about it as that, but I reckon that's what it is." Hiram nodded, still impressed by the stallion.

"We thought you were dead," Kathy said. "I had the hardest time making Tommy Jacks stay here with the herd. He wanted to go find you — or at least your body."

Sam smiled in her tear-wet face and kissed her on the forehead. "I don't know about that boy, but I am starved for some of your cooking."

With a shake of her head, she patted him on the stomach. "I bet you are."

He put his arm on her shoulders and headed her for the wagon and the cooking fires. "Everyone doing all right?"

"No problems. We must be halfway across Colorado?"

"Yes, we are."

A horse came loping in and slid to a stop. "That you, boss?" Tommy Jacks bailed off his horse, ran over and hugged Sam tight as a bear. "Damn, it is good to see you. I thought you were dead. And Sloan's here?" Sam nodded, and Tommy Jacks asked, "He's fine?"

"Yeah, in good shape for what he's been through. 'Course no one will ever know what did happen?"

"Whose stud horse is that?"

"Sloan's. That's another story."

"My God, you've been through hell, haven't you?"

"Come and eat," Kathy said.

"Man, oh, man, it's sure a relief to see you," Tommy Jacks said.

"Troubles?"

"Well, in the first place, I don't know anything about the sale of these cattle or nothing."

Sam took a heaping plate of food from Kathy. "Thanks. Tommy, it's time you learned all about the sale of cattle."

Tommy Jacks sucked on his tongue and teeth. "Maybe, but I've got lots to learn and never had much schooling."

"Ogallala's going to be your schooling then. Let me eat. What about Sloan?"

"Rowann's going to feed him," Kathy said. "Them boys got a young badger in a cage that Tommy made for them. They're busy looking at it."

"Why badgers're meaner than grizzlies," Sam said. "But, heck, Sloan may make a house cat out of it."

Chapter 37

On July twelfth, Sam rode Soapy into Ogallala. The town was booming. On the street, there were many people dressed in different guises besides ten-gallon hats and chaps imported from Texas. Wagons of furniture and goods, stacked way too high, were pulled by everything from horses and mules to burros and oxen. The railroad had brought them. Soapy about spooked out from under Sam when a steam whistle blew.

Sam paused at the only stone building on the street of false fronts. He dismounted in front of the First National Bank of Nebraska. He brushed at some road flour on his sleeves; then he pulled open the heavy green door and went inside. Hat in hand, he spoke to a young man at a desk behind a low fence. "Is the president in today?"

With a suspicious look on his face, the young man peered at Sam hard. "And the nature of your business?"

"I'm a broker."

"Indeed. Of what?"

Sam scratched the left side of his freshly

shaved face. "Has anyone ever offered to cut your ears off close to your head?"

The young man's eyes widened. "No, sir."

"Good. Tell the president that Sam Ketchem of Frio Springs, Texas, wants ten minutes of his time, and be damn quick about it." Sam looked around at the nice lobby and the clerks in cages.

"But —"

Sam narrowed his look and began to finger his own right earlobe. His actions sent the young man hurrying for the door behind him.

"Sorry, sir, but there's a man out here from Texas to see you."

"Send him in, Barnabas," the bank president said.

He swallowed hard and waved Sam over. "Mr. Capton will see you now."

A man who looked too burly to be a banker stood behind a rosewood desk and extended his hand. "My man did not mention your name?"

"Sam Ketchem." They shook hands and Sam took a chair the man offered him.

Capton tented his fingers and asked what he could do for Sam.

"I felt that you would know the honest from the dishonest in the cattle brokerage business. Since I am new to this market, I came to seek some advice and to open an account."

"Very good. What did you bring — mixed herd?"

"I have some good cattle. They aren't random gathered. Most carry half or more British blood, so they'll bring a good price."

The man looked impressed. "Northern ranges need cattle, but those longhorns from Mexico aren't the ideal meat animal, and to get top prices today, they need to be roan or white-face crosses."

"I know. I have three hundred two year olds that are half or more of those crosses from one ranch."

"You know what they would bring today?" Capton shook his head in disbelief.

Sam shook his head.

"Fifty dollars a head."

Sam closed his eyes. Mr. Mott could sure retire on that much money.

"Could I send a very good customer of the bank out to your herd?" Capton asked.

Settling back in the chair, Sam nodded.

"You're a businessman, aren't you?"

With a wave of his open hands, Sam shrugged. "It's a helluva long ways up here from Texas, and I didn't bring all the trash on my range this far to get nothing for it."

"You'd save lots of men grief explaining that to them down there. They bring everything up here and then get mad 'cause they can't sell it." Capton shook his head.

"My herd's good flesh."

"I can imagine. I'll have the Harbor boys and Sandy Brown go out there and look at them. They're as honest men as I know in this game."

Sam told him where the herd was located west of town and then entered the names and notes in his tally book. "Thanks. I appreciate this."

"No problem. That account you wished to open?"

"Two hundred bucks. I may need to borrow a little, too, for supplies, if we have to stay here very long."

"No problem." Capton counted the paper money Sam put on the desk. "Barnabas will fill out the paperwork." He extended a large hand when Sam rose, and they shook.

Sam felt good walking into the lobby. He liked the banker and was excited about the prices mentioned so far. He planned to go to the saloon next, play some poker and listen for other market news.

After lunch in a café, he went in the Elk

Horn tent whose wooden false front sported an elk rack — a seven by seven that must have come off an elephant-size buck. The floor was a faded red Oriental carpet spread over the grass; it was easy to stumble in. On-stage, a banjo picker and piano player entertained.

"Ruby's coming to sing," the near drunk freighter told him when he found a place in the crowd at the makeshift bar.

"Who's Ruby?"

The man blinked in disbelief at him. "You don't know her. Man, she's the queen of the country. Beautiful girl. She'll steal your heart, mister. Tear it out."

Sam put down the dime for his beer and thanked the man. He realized in an instant that they still had ice in Nebraska in mid-summer when his hand touched the cold glass.

"Where's she from?" Sam asked.

"St. Louis."

"Thanks. I'll watch for her." He took his beer and went where some tall hats gathered around a large table. The men were involved in a five-card stud.

"Want in?" A man with glasses looked up at Sam. "It's a sensible stakes game. Dollar limit on all raises."

"Big boys play over there," a drawling

Texan said. Sam glanced over at the profes-sional-looking men around the other table. He'd played with men like that in Wichita and Dodge.

"Thanks, I may sit in for a hand or so." Sam put down the beer and took a chair. He set part of his money on the table, sat back and watched.

"Never caught your name?" the man shuffling the cards said. He was dressed in trail clothing.

"Ketchem. Sam's what they call me."

The man stopped shuffling for an instant and looked hard at him. The others threw in their names at him when they anted. Caufman, Thomas, Davenport, Latten and the dealer, said, "Sizer."

"Good to meet you."

"You bring in a herd?" Caufman asked from behind a mustache.

Sam nodded. "Parked out west." He picked up his cards and saw two sevens.

"Hope you have more luck than some are having," Latten said. He was an older man with a bad scar on his cheek.

"Will I need it?" Sam asked, watching one man toss in a quarter.

"Yeah, the market ain't worth a damn," Davenport said.

"I understood there was lot of grass

country open north of here." Sam saw Davenport fold.

Then Ruby came onstage in a red velvet dress and her voice filled the place. All talking went down as her rich vocals mesmerized the crowd. Then one drunk stood up and shouted, "I want her!" Someone busted him over the head with a pistol, and he went under the table.

The buxom lady, whom Sam guessed to be in her mid-twenties, never missed a note. He closed his eyes to her music for a moment — she could belt out a song. And when she sang, "Boys, your momma wants you at home —" she stabbed half the crowd in their hearts.

Poker game on hold, everyone watched her as she moved about, directing her lyrics at individuals in the packed bar room. Sam couldn't imagine how many had piled into the tent and even lifted up the sides to get to hear her.

"Why in the hell is she in Ogallala with a voice like that?" Sam asked.

Davenport shook his head. "Beats the fire out of me."

Sam settled back in the chair to enjoy her. "Beats me, too, but her voice sure is nice."

After her session was over, Sam played a few hands more and then went by the post office for the mail. He stood in line for over a half hour with the list Rowann had carefully made for him.

"Man, you must be a drover," the young clerk under the celluloid visor said. "Our policy says we can only take two names at a time."

"My policy says I'm not standing in line again. Now get me the damn mail!"

The youth jumped back and looked with wide eyes at Sam. "I'm only following instructions."

"Get my mail and don't miss a single name on that list."

"Yes, sir."

The clerk began going through the alphabet boxes, checking each one. In a short while he came over and gave letters to Sam. "Here's all I can find. If you leave the list, I will bundle them next time."

"Thanks," Sam said and walked down the line, then outside. He removed one letter for himself and stuffed the rest inside his vest.

Dear Sam,

I know when you receive this you will have successfully arrived in Nebraska. There was never a doubt in anyone's mind down here in Texas that anything else would happen. I have considered your fine offer of matrimony. There was a time I thought you never would ask me and it about broke my heart.

Sam, you have proven yourself time and time again. I can only imagine the adventures you have been involved in while going to Nebraska. But I have considered how different we are and how difficult our lives would be to blend together in a marriage. You could be governor of Texas, but you won't listen.

Sam, that is why I will not be home this fall when you return from Nebraska. I am going to marry a man named Benjamin Hoekstra this July in Austin. My aunt there knows him well. He is a widower with two grown children. He is in banking.

I will always recall the dashing drover who brought me back a gold locket from Kansas ten years ago.

Sincerely yours,
Etta Faye Ralston

Sam's shoulder pressed to the side of the building. He didn't know whether to laugh or cry.

Chapter 38

The other letters Sam passed out that evening at supper. Some were sad: a relative or pet lost. Some got news that their families were moving and wouldn't be around Frio Springs when the men returned, but they could be reached through relatives.

Yates handed his back to Sam. "I can't read. Would you mind?"

Sam agreed and the horse wrangler who never took off his gloves even to eat sat on the ground and kept clasping and reclasping his fingers in the worn-out gloves.

"Something wrong?" Sam asked before he opened the envelope.

Yates shook his head. "Never got a letter in my whole Gawdamn life, and I figure this must be bad news."

"It's from Jennifer Grossinger. Who's she?"

Yates looked all around like he wanted to escape. "My wife."

"We didn't know you were married," Sam said.

"Had to."

"Well," Sam said, "you ain't the first and won't be the last. Where does Jennifer live?"

"At home. Her folks was upset."

"Why?"

"Said she was too young."

"Oh."

"Hell, she turned twelve last month."

Sam just bobbed his head and opened the letter.

Dear Yates darling,

I knows yous be proud. June tenth we done got us a baby boy. He's stout like yous and has big lungs. We names him Yates Barstow Grossinger the second. I can't wait till yous get home.

Your wife,
Jennifer

"Well, ain't that nice," Sam said.

"She's all right?"

"I read the whole thing."

"Don't say nothing's wrong?"

"She's fine and so is Junior."

Yates got up off the ground. "We ain't calling him Junior. We can call him Barstow, or Little Yates, but I hates Junior. Will you write and tell her that boss man?"

Sam agreed. Yates went off, shaking his

head and telling the rest of the crew he was a daddy.

"Reckon that baby was born wearing gloves?" Tommy Jacks asked under his breath.

"Shame on you," Kathy said, handing Sam and Tommy Jacks plates of plum cobbler.

"You get any mail, Sam?"

"One letter."

"What did she say?" Kathy looked anxious to hear.

"Not much."

"Well —"

"You can read it." He dug the folded up letter out and handed it to her.

"I don't want to dig in your personal life." She offered it back.

"No, it's easier for you to read it than me to tell it."

Tommy Jacks looked at him.

"Nothing," he said to dismiss his foreman's concern.

"Nothing my foot," Kathy said, reading away. "How can she do this to you?"

"She's already done it."

"Well, she will in July unless you stop her." She hid behind the page. "This is July."

Sam nodded. "Max Dawson's coming

out from town to look at Mott's heifers in the morning. They aren't hard to spot. The Harbor brothers and Sandy Brown are the cattle buyers coming out to look. You're in charge," he told Tommy Jacks.

"Where are you going?" Kathy asked.

"I'm not certain — just getting some space between me and things."

"She's not the only woman in Texas," Kathy said.

Sam smiled. "You're right, Kathy. But I believed the other way so long, I'll be damned if I can think anything else."

"Stay. Help Tommy Jacks. Lord knows he's concerned about this selling business as anything."

"Get an offer and we'll negotiate the deal and delivery when I get back."

"Where you going?" Kathy stood with her hands on her hips.

"Look at some new country. I won't be gone over a few days."

She hugged him. "Be careful. You worry me."

He left riding Rob with a camping outfit packed on Soapy. He'd promised the boys some time off when he got back in a week and waved to Kathy as he rode out. He paid the toll on the Platte bridge and crossed into the land north. He crossed the first ridge and the waving grass rolled north to Canada. Here and there in a bottom a homestead or two had broken ground for corn or alfalfa.

It looked like a cattleman's paradise as he rode the stage route northward. There were many playas and small streams in mid-summer; the clear running water impressed him. He tried to imagine winter, but the south wind at his back made the task hard. He could imagine other cows raising big calves, those calves growing out to heavy weights as yearlings on this graze.

Sam stopped off at the stage stop and store. He ordered a cup of coffee and the lunch special from a man in a soiled apron.

"I got ham."

"Ham's fine," Sam said.

"Better eat fast. The stage is coming."

"How many on it?"

"Never know. Might be five or six. They're in a hurry."

"I'll give them my seat, if they can't find one."

The man nodded. "You know they could take my franchise."

"That would be bad," Sam agreed.

"Be bad for me. I'll get you a plate."

The coffee tasted bitter. More like burned barley than coffee, and the ham the cook brought out on the plate was rancid.

A woman came inside and shocked Sam. It was the singer Ruby; two men in suits were herding her. Sam didn't like either of them. Something was wrong. Both men acted like long-tailed cats in a roomful of rockers. The tall one kept checking on the gun in his shoulder holster, like it might have fallen out from the last time he touched it. The other dandy must have carried a derringer up each sleeve. They clunked on the table when he put his arms down.

Sam was finished with his sorry meal and tried not to stare at sad-eyed Ruby. She looked like she'd been through hell and needed someone.

"Aren't you the one that sings in the Elk Horn?" he asked.

"Mind your own Gawdamn business," the tall one said and reached inside his coat. "She's my wife."

"Sorry, mister. I was only going to pay her a compliment about her singing."

"I said mind your own business."

Ruby stopped the man with her hand, then spoke to Sam. "Thank you so much. He is only upset. Yes, I was that singer. Have a nice day."

Sam touched his hat to her and started for the doorway.

"You better shut your mouth," the man said.

"He may be the law," Ruby said.

"He'll be dead if he is."

Sam heard that conversation, paid the cook and went outside. The stage driver was sitting on a bench, elbows on his knees, no doubt resting before he had to leave. He was a lanky man in a fringed buckskin shirt.

"You know them two men in there?" Sam asked under his breath, taking a seat on the bench beside him.

"Bob Cole and the tall one's Michael."

"That her husband?"

The stage driver smiled and shook his head. "They're her managers. They collect all the money she makes. Why else would a woman like her" — he lowered his voice — "ever sing in Ogallala for two months? Them two's on the run and she's a slave to them."

"Where they going?"

"Black Hills, I guess. Why?"

"I may call their hand."

The driver shook his head. "Been tried before. That guy came out a loser."

"You stand back when they come out."

"Your funeral, mister, but I'm telling —"

Sam silenced him with a finger to his mouth. The others were coming.

The driver got up and went to open the coach door. He shook his head as if in deep thought.

All three people were past Sam, one man on each side of Ruby, when Sam rose and called out. The six-gun filled his hand. The unmistakable click of the hammer back made them halt.

"Hold it and don't turn around. And don't try for that gun in your coat or those derringers. Both of you step aside from the lady."

"Lady?" the short one said, but both obeyed.

"Now, Ruby, you don't have to go with them one mile farther."

"Who in the hell are you?" Michael asked.

"Sam Ketchem."

"She's my wife."

"Ruby, this is the place where you make the choice. I'm not rich, but I have the money to get you anywhere you want to go from here."

"Who are you, mister?" Her large brown eyes were like those of a frightened doe.

"A damn cowboy, Ruby. You've tried that," Michael said.

Ignoring him, she looked hard at Sam. "You know they'll try to kill you if I go with you."

"Do I look afraid."

"No, you don't."

"Ruby, don't be a fool," Michael threatened with an edge in his voice.

"Stage's leaving," the driver said. "I've got a schedule to keep."

"Ruby, tell this hayseed no and get into that coach!"

There was something in her soft brown eyes when they met Sam's. "I can't do this to you." She started for the coach.

"Smart girl," Michael said.

"Ruby, I'll be in Ogallala a couple of weeks," Sam said.

She paused.

"If I ain't there, my banker, Mr. Capton, will know where I live and stake you to money."

Ruby nodded as if she had heard him and then she went inside the coach.

"You sumbitch," Michael swore at Sam as he climbed in behind Ruby. "I should kill you for this."

Sam grinned big. "Go for your gun."

The driver shook his head in disgust and closed the door after Michael. Then he climbed up on the box and gathered his reins.

"Good to have met you, Sam Ketchem." He saluted and left in the rocking conveyance for parts north.

Chapter 39

Sam made it back to Ogallala in four days. He was still undecided about a move to the north country, after seeing lots of grass and country. He took a room at the Western Hotel, then found a bath and a shave. Afterward, he bought a new pair of canvas pants, a collarless shirt, new socks and underwear. Then he ordered himself a handmade pair of boots from the man in the saddle shop, who promised to have them ready in four days. The next day, Sam rode out to the herd. At the chuck wagon, Kathy came to hug him.

"How's Tommy Jacks getting along?" Sam asked.

Kathy ran and got her pad. "We've been getting offers on lots of the cattle. Mott's heifers are up to sixty dollars a head. We have a cow man coming from Dakota to look at some of the cows. The brokers want the steer."

"Good."

"Some trail boss named Davenport came by a day or so ago looking for you. He said we'd be here till next year trying to sell all our cattle. I knew Tommy Jacks was upset and wanted to tell him no, but he never said a word and thanked him."

"They don't want those Texas cattle up here," Sam said. Then he smiled at her and she laughed.

"You look nice all cleaned up."

"Thanks. We better get busy selling while the iron is hot."

"Tom'll be happy to hear about that. He's busting to get back to Texas."

"Why don't you two have a honeymoon going home?"

Kathy pursed her lips and then laughed as if embarrassed. "We've talked about that."

"How are the kids?"

"Fine. They've gone fishing. We get to eat lots of fish here."

"Sloan all right?"

"Fine. He rides his horse a lot with the men."

"Good. I miss your cooking. I'll be back at sunup. Save me some breakfast."

"You can stay for supper," Kathy called after Sam, but he had already mounted Soapy. He waved and rode for town.

He stabled the horse at the livery with Rob and stopped by the hotel room before he went to find supper. The receptionist handed him a letter with no stamp. The envelope had just his name on it.

Sam,
I heard that you were off looking at some country north of here. I hope to make you a full-time customer. I have some connections in this town. They offer me some information from time to time on a fee basis. A man named George Sizer sent a telegram to Frio Springs, Texas, telling that you were here. The reply was to kill you. Be careful. This Sizer is a known hired killer.
Winston Capton

"Anything wrong, Mr. Ketchem?" the receptionist asked.

"No, just a message about a cattle sale," Sam said and started up the stairs.

Sizer was the last name of the dealer in the card game who had paused when Sam had said his name. Now Sam knew why. He was on the man's death list.

The next morning, before daylight, Sam went out the back of the hotel to the livery and short loped Rob out to the herd. His enemies wouldn't catch him napping.

"That Mike Harbor says we can get fifty

for the big steer," Tommy Jacks said as Sam, some others, and he sat on the ground eating breakfast.

"How many head and how tough a cut does he want?"

Tommy Jacks shook his head. "Some English outfit needs them, he says."

"Tell him we'll take it, but no cut."

"Aw, you know them buyers. They'll want a cut."

"We didn't bring a lot of junk up here. Right now we have some good cattle to sell and you wouldn't believe the grass north of here." Sam picked up his coffee to sip on it.

"Lots of it, huh?"

"Belly deep on my horses."

"You thinking about moving up here?"

Sam shook his head and looked off at the dawn breaking on the horizon. "I can't get away from them up here."

"What's that mean?"

"There's a hired gun out to kill me in Ogallala."

"Who's that?" Tommy Jacks made a sour face.

"George Sizer."

"Know him?"

"Met him in a card game."

"How in the hell is he hooked up to those damn Wagners?"

"He telegrammed them that I was here and the reply was to kill me."

Tommy Jacks shook his head in disbelief. "What's the matter with those people?"

"It's a Texas feud. The Wagners can't tell you why. They want to kill my family. They just want all the Ketchems dead."

"What can I do?"

"Keep the cattle on grass and water. Let's sell all we can and see what's left."

"Your banker's friend wants the Mott heifers at sixty?" Tommy Jacks asked.

"Good place to start."

"Fine. We'll cut them out today and bunch them. Then we'll cut out and tally the three-year-old steer. Harbor can decide on them. I bet he takes them all."

"The outfit wants the cows?"

"He's been by and looked. I think he'll take most of them at fifty. He said those heifers at sixty-five were too rich for him."

As Darby brought the coffeepot, Sam held out his cup for a refill. "We get the herd size cut down, some of the boys can take some time off. I'll advance them some money."

"They're sure itching to go."

"We all know how that is." Sam shook his head, recalling his youthful days in Abilene, Newton and Wichita.

"What about Sizer?" Tommy Jacks asked.

"Guess I'll cross that bridge when I get there."

"Don't cross it alone." Tommy Jacks looked hard at Sam.

"All right, not alone."

"Good. Kathy said that Texas schoolmarm turned you down."

"I kinda got that behind me. Funny thing, you think about someone for so long, and then one day, it goes up in smoke like it never was to be in the first place."

"Billy Ford said that you'd never marry that girl."

Sam pushed off his knees to stand. "Kind of profound, him saying that, huh?"

"Yeah." Tommy Jacks dropped his head and went off.

A knot in Sam's throat was too big to swallow. He missed that boy, too.

That day, Sam stayed close to the herd. He sat on Rob and helped Tommy Jacks tally heifers. Bringing a heifer out of the herd was never easy. But the cowboys had plenty of practice. They also knew the best cutting horses in the cavvy, and they used them.

Webber rode a little dish-faced horse called Lightning. Nothing got by the horse. He could get down and face off cow brutes and switch ends from side to side until they gave up and went where Lightning wanted them to go.

Sam helped Jammer McCay keep the cows in a bunch apart from the main herd. In a few hours, the number grew. Pacho Morayes' bullwhip cracked as he drove some more heifers into the bunch. Finally, at noontime, they lacked only five head. Tommy Jacks left two boys with the heifers, and they rode in for lunch.

"Five damn head," Jammer swore. "Boy, they'll be a bitch to get out."

"Beats picking corn," Webber said and they all laughed.

"A cowboy's got to bitch," Sam said.

"Why's that, boss?" Webber asked.

"Why, if they didn't, folks would think cowboying was the best job in the world and all get a job punching. Then real cowboys couldn't get a job."

"Where you hear that?"

"The colonel used to tell us that every drive."

"Kinda sums it up," Tommy Jacks said.

Sam agreed. Sitting in the saddle all day, he had enjoyed watching the boys and horses work, and he'd made up his mind. After lunch, he was riding back to town and calling out this Sizer. *Never put off what needs to be done.* His mama said that a lot. If he could only figure out what he needed to do with his life after the cattle were sold, he'd be happy. Always before, he'd had a purpose in life. His folks usually needed help or his brothers needed ranches. And he always had the hope of marrying Etta Faye. All that gone with the wind.

"Stay for supper," Kathy pleaded when Sam dropped by the wagon and didn't dismount.

"Thanks. I'll ride on into town."

"Sam." Kathy's eyes narrowed and she grew serious. "Don't take those men on by yourself."

"You mean that little hired killer Sizer?" Sam smiled.

"Tommy Jacks said the Wagners hired someone to kill you."

"Ah, Kathy, if I backed down from every would-be gunman, I'd need to stay home and hide under the bed."

"Sam, be serious. The boys want to back you."

He shook his head. "Those boys ain't gunfighters. They're cowboys. I saw two of them like that get shot down in a ruckus in Dodge. I ain't riding back to Texas with that on my conscience."

Kathy slapped his leg to get his attention. "Listen to me."

"I am."

"Wait."

"Kathy darling, you and Tommy Jacks can handle this deal. I trust you two will see it through — if anything happens."

"If I was a man I'd hog-tie you."

"Damn, girl, Tommy Jacks is lucky." Sam winked at Kathy and turned Rob away from her. "I'll be back in the morning."

"Sam! Don't —"

He waved and short loped Rob toward Ogallala. Maybe he'd get one thing cleared up that evening anyway.

Chapter 40

Sam dismounted in front of Hannigan's Stables. In the open doorway, he adjusted his pants and chaps, then reset his Colt. Nothing looked out of place. There was the usual confusion of heavy traffic and freighters on Main Street. An old hustler named Smoky came out of the office and looked upset.

"What's wrong?" Sam asked.

"Been three guys here today asking questions about you."

"Who were they?"

"Don't have handles for 'em. The guy doing the talking was short and chisel-faced."

"George Sizer?"

"Could be. I knowed they wasn't here looking for no cattle. The big guy's got on a red-checked shirt. Looks like a boxer. The third one was fancy dressed. He had on cuffs with stones mounted on them. Wasn't nothing precious."

"Tillman Wagner," Sam said aloud in dismay.

"Sam, they went off toward the Elk Horn. Ain't seen them in a couple hours, so they may be liquored up by now."

"Thanks, Smoky. Let me know if you learn anything else." He gave the man a dollar.

"Oh, I will." Smokey licked the lips behind his bushy gray-black beard. "That's sure generous of you." He took Rob, assuring Sam he'd rub the horse down, then feed and water him right.

"You may spoil him to death." Sam chuckled at the notion and set out for the boardwalk. "See you."

Sam chose the east side of Main Street and kept under the porches with a wary eye on the Elk Horn across the way. Too many people were in the street. If a gunfight broke out, someone innocent would get hurt. He wondered about the town law. They wouldn't choose sides. Maybe he had better go and talk to Winston Capton at the bank.

When Sam left the porch, he managed to mingle with the street traffic. So far he had not seen anyone come in or out of the Elk Horn Saloon who looked like Sizer or his men. Sam ducked inside the bank.

"Mr. Ketchem," Barnabas said from his desk, then quickly finished the paper he was working on and rose. "You wish to see Mr. Capton?"

"Yes, if he's not too busy."

"Good to see you," the banker said when the boy showed Sam in. "How are the cattle?"

"Fine. Things are shaping up on sales. Your client is taking the heifers we talked about. Make him a super set of mother cows."

"Good. Have a chair. What can I do for you?"

Sam went to the barred window and looked out at the backyard. "Who's the law?"

"Beck Stevens is the chief of police. Why?"

"That hired gun and two men are in the Elk Horn. I guess waiting for me."

"That's why I wrote the note you obviously received."

"Yes. Thanks."

"You ain't thinking about taking on that gunman by yourself are you?" Capton frowned. "What's the commotion going on in the lobby?"

Barnabas broke in. "Sorry, sir, but some boy is out here screaming for Mr. Ketchem."

"What's he want?" Capton asked.

"I'll handle it," Sam said and swept out the door. He looked at a dirty-faced boy of twelve.

"You Sam Ketchem?"

"Yes."

"Tillman Wagner said be in the street in ten minutes, or he'd come in here and drag you out there."

"You tell him fine, but one more thing." His words halted the boy, who was about to run for the front door. "Be sure and tell him to wear his best clothes."

"Huh?"

"I don't want the folks in hell seeing him any other way."

The boy made a face, swept his un-combed hair back and nodded. "Yeah, I'll tell him." He fled.

"You can't go out there alone," Capton said, sounding shocked Sam would even consider doing so.

"They gunned down my brother and ambushed me once. It's time we settled this feud." Sam looked at the clock on the wall. It would soon be six p.m.

Several shocked people rushed out of the bank. Soon there were shouts in the street outside.

Sam removed his Colt and loaded the chamber under the hammer, then carefully eased the hammer down. It was dangerous to have a live cartridge under the firing pin.

"You have a shotgun in here?" Sam asked Capton.

"We do." He motioned for Barnabas to fetch it. "I can still send word to the law."

"Doubt it would help."

When Capton's assistant returned and handed Sam the weapon, Sam broke open the well oiled Greener. Both chambers were loaded.

"Get him some shells," Capton said.

Sam viewed the scene outside the front windows. Word must have reached the people in the street, for the traffic had rapidly dissipated. Five minutes were left on the clock. Sam might be giving his enemies time to set up an ambush. Somehow he felt that Sizer would never try a head-on gunfight. Tillman would because of his own stupidity, but he might be a decoy.

"I've got some whiskey in my desk drawer," Capton said.

Sam shook his head and undid his gun belt. He decided to shed the chaps. The stiff leather would only hinder his movements if he needed to move fast. He handed Capton the shotgun and his holster rig. In seconds he had removed the chaps and taken back the holster to strap it on. Then he filled his vest with brass casings for the weapon Barnabas had brought him.

"Have you been in many gunfights?" the youth asked in a soft voice.

Sam shook his head and took the Greener. "No. I don't want to be in any more, either. Thanks." He saluted them and turned for the thick door.

"God be with you," Capton said after Sam as Barnabas swung back the door.

Sam let his eyes adjust to the bright light, then stepped on the porch. Three riders were coming up the empty street from the south. He recognized the gray in the lead and the rider standing in the stirrups: Tommy Jacks.

The rider reined up at the rack and nodded to Sam. "Where are they?"

"They've been in the Elk Horn up the street for some time, but I figure they've moved. They sent word for me to meet them in the street. I can handle them." He looked hard at Tommy Jacks, Jammer and Webber, who all dismounted.

"We're here now," Tommy Jacks said and stepped down, jerking a Winchester out of the scabbard. "Jammer, you get up on the boardwalk. "Webber, you take this one. I'll be in the street with you."

"I can handle them," Sam said.

"We can handle them better together."

Sam nodded. "I didn't —"

"We know you didn't ask for any help. But we're here. Where are they?"

"Coming out of the Elk Horn right now."

Tommy Jacks nodded. "Watch 'em, boys."

Both of the other drovers nodded and advanced with Sam and Tommy Jacks.

The silence impressed Sam — only the wind in his ears and the clink of spur rowels sounded as they walked up the street. Sizer, Wagner and a big guy waited two hundred feet away.

"Four against three, huh?" Sizer said.

"We didn't come to fight fair," Sam said. "We came to kill you. Now it's time to cut or shoot. This is your party."

"All right," Sizer said. "I made a mistake." He held his hands wide of his body. "Deal me out."

"Getting too hot for you?" Tommy Jacks asked. "Been different three on one, wouldn't it?"

"Well, I ain't out of it! I want that sumbitch who killed my brothers dead." Tillman Wagner's hand went for his gun.

A blast from the bank's shotgun threw Wagner five feet backward, and his own gun exploded in his holster as he slumped to the ground. Hit by rifle and pistol shots, the other two men wilted in the dust of the street without firing a shot. Sam thought Sizer had tried to turn and run, but too late. The big man's expression never changed. Wind swept the gunsmoke away as three law officers rushed on the scene, shouting, "Hold your fire."

"We have," Sam said, then walked to the bank to return the weapon.

"Stage is coming!" someone shouted, and others started dragging the bodies out of the way.

For a moment, Sam paused as the dust cleared from the four horses pulling the stage. The driver climbed down and opened the coach door.

"Ogallala," he shouted and stepped back.

An attractive woman stuck her head out and then stepped down. "Sam Ketchem?" she asked in her smoky voice.

Absently he handed the shotgun to Barnabas and started across the street.

"Yes, ma'am, I'm Sam Ketchem, and I live at Frio Springs, Texas." He swept off his hat. "Be my pleasure to show you that Texas Hill country. They don't have a singer down there who would hold a candle to you."

Her sleepy brown eyes sparkled. "Have

you been in another altercation here today?"

"Yes, ma'am, Miss Ruby, I have. But we didn't shoot anyone who didn't need it."

"I understand. I didn't expect to find you — but you said —"

Sam couldn't take his eyes off her. His guts roiled. "Ma'am, I'd like to introduce my crew, and then I'd like to find the finest meal in Nebraska."

"Good. I thought a lot about you drawing your gun on my managers." She took his arm. "I figured a man with that much gall might treat me like a lady."

"By dang, I can sure do that, Miss Ruby."

She kissed him on the cheek, and they went on toward the hotel.

Epilogue

Sam Ketchem married Ruby Zacowski a week later in the Methodist church in Ogallala, Nebraska Territory. Kathy McCarty married Tommy Jacks Riddle the same day.

Over the next decade the Bar K grew. Riddle became Sam's ranch foreman, then his overseer. Sam added more land to his spread and became active in politics. After being elected to the legislature, he soon became a force in the state senate.

Miss Ruby met Etta Faye at the governor's ball and the two had a long discussion about Sam. Later that evening, Miss Ruby confided in Sam that Etta Faye had told her how she was the one who pushed him into seeking office. He only shrugged away the answer.

In 1892, Texas state senator Samuel Ketchem, while en route to a political party gathering, was riding on a lonely stretch of road between Kerrville and Frio Springs when he was ambushed by parties unknown. Despite the efforts of the Texas

Rangers and other law enforcement agencies, the crime was never solved. An unknown woman driving a buggy on that same road on the eve of the murder was never identified.

When Miss Ruby passed on, ten years later, with no children, the Bar K was divided among Tommy Jacks and Kathy Riddle's children. Darby took the old home place and kept the brand. Darby's son, Samuel, inherited the place upon his death. A lawyer and politician, Samuel McCarty kept the home ranch and added to the holdings. His oldest son, S. K. McCarty, became the rancher in the family. He still burns the Bar K brand on his cattle in the Texas Hill Country.